TALES FROM
THE ARABIAN
NIGHTS

TALES FROM
THE ARABIAN
NIGHTS

Translated by Andrew Lang

Illustrations by Edmund Dulac and Others

Afterword by Pete Hamill

THE WORLD'S BEST READING

The Reader's Digest Association, Inc.

Pleasantville, N.Y. · Montreal · Sydney · Auckland

Tales From the Arabian Nights

This Reader's Digest edition contains selected stories from Andrew Lang's *The Arabian Nights Entertainments,* first published in 1898.

Illustrations by Edmund Dulac appear on pages 11, 39, 51, 101, 133, 159, 175, and 199.
Illustrations by René Bull appear on pages 17, 31, 69, 93, 215, and 227.
Illustrations by H. J. Ford appear on pages 20, 46, 117, 145, 149, 169, 184, 245, 256, 267, 275, 281, and 291.
Illustrations by W. H. Lister appear on pages 57 and 263.
Illustrations by Monro S. Orr appear on pages 79 and 239.

Library of Congress Catalog Card Number 90-62641
ISBN 0-89577-374-0

Printed in the United States of America

Reader's Digest Fund for the Blind is publisher of the Large-Type Edition of *Reader's Digest.* For subscription information about this magazine, please contact Reader's Digest Fund for the Blind, Inc., Dept. 250, Pleasantville, N.Y. 10570.

CONTENTS

ILLUSTRATIONS

Color Plates

ILLUSTRATIONS

Black-and-white Plates

SCHEHERAZADE

In the chronicles of the ancient dynasty of the Sassanidae, who reigned for about four hundred years from Persia to the borders of China beyond the great river Ganges itself, we read the praises of one of the kings of the race, who was said to be the best monarch of his time. His subjects loved him and his neighbors feared him, and when he died he left his kingdom in a more prosperous and powerful condition than any king had done before him.

The two sons who survived him loved each other tenderly, and it was a real grief to the elder, Schahriar, that the laws of the empire forbade him to share his dominions with his brother Schahzaman. Indeed, after ten years, during which this state of things had not ceased to trouble him, Schahriar cut off the country of Great Tartary from the Persian Empire and made his brother king.

Now the Sultan Schahriar had a wife whom he loved more than all the world, and his greatest happiness was to surround her with splendor and give her the finest dresses and the most beautiful jewels. It was, therefore, with the deepest shame and sorrow that he accidentally discovered, after several years, that she had deceived him completely, and her whole conduct turned out to have been so bad he felt himself obliged to carry out the law of the land, and order the grand vizir to put her to death.

The blow was so heavy that his mind almost gave way, and he declared he was quite sure all women were as wicked as the sultana, if you could only find them out, and that the fewer the world contained the better. So every evening he married a fresh wife and had her strangled the following morning before the grand vizir, whose duty it was to provide these unhappy brides for the sultan. The poor man fulfilled his task with reluctance, but there was no escape, and every day saw a girl married and a wife dead.

This behavior caused the greatest horror in the town, where nothing was heard but cries and lamentations. In one house was a father weeping for the loss of his daughter, in another perhaps a mother trembling for the fate of her child; and instead of the blessings that had formerly been heaped on the sultan's head, the air was now full of curses.

The grand vizir himself was the father of two daughters, of whom the elder was called Scheherazade and the younger Dinarzade. Dinarzade had no particular gifts to distinguish her from other girls but her sister was clever and courageous in the highest degree. Her father had given her the best masters in philosophy, medicine, history and the fine arts and, besides all this, her beauty excelled that of any girl in the kingdom of Persia.

One day, when the grand vizir was talking to his elder daughter, who was his delight and pride, Scheherazade said to him, "Father, I have a favor to ask of you. Will you grant it to me?"

"I can refuse you nothing," replied he, "that is just and reasonable."

"Then listen," said Scheherazade. "I am determined to stop this barbarous practice of the sultan's and to deliver the girls and mothers from the truly awful fate that hangs over them."

"It would be an excellent thing to do," returned the grand vizir, "but how do you propose to accomplish it?"

13

"My father," answered Scheherazade, "it is you who have to provide the sultan daily with a fresh wife, and I implore you, by all the affection you bear me, to allow the honor to fall upon me."

"Have you lost your senses?" cried the grand vizir, starting back in horror. "What has put such an idea into your head? You ought to know by this time what it means to be the sultan's bride!"

"Yes, my father, I know it well, and I am not afraid to think of it. If I fail, my death will be a glorious one, and if I succeed I shall have done a great service to my country."

"It is of no use," said the grand vizir, "I shall never consent. If the sultan were to order me to plunge a dagger in your heart, I should have to obey. What a task for a father! Ah, if you do not fear death, fear at any rate the anguish you would cause me."

"Once again, my father," said Scheherazade, "will you grant me what I ask?"

"Are you still so obstinate?" exclaimed the grand vizir. "Why are you so resolved upon your own ruin?"

But the maiden absolutely refused to heed her father's words. At length, in despair, the grand vizir was obliged to give way, and went sadly to the palace to tell the sultan that the following evening he would bring him Scheherazade.

The sultan received this news with the greatest astonishment. "How have you made up your mind," he asked, "to sacrifice your own daughter to me?"

"Sire," answered the grand vizir, "it is her own wish. Even the sad fate that awaits her could not hold her back."

"Let there be no mistake, vizir," said the sultan. "Remember you will have to take her life yourself. If you refuse, your head shall pay forfeit."

"Sire," returned the vizir, "whatever the cost, I will obey you. Though a father, I am also your subject." So the sultan told the grand vizir he might bring his daughter as soon as he liked.

The vizir took back this news to Scheherazade, who received it as if it had been the most pleasant thing in the world. She thanked her father warmly for yielding to her wishes and, seeing him still bowed down with grief, told him that she hoped he would never repent having allowed her to marry the sultan. Then she went to prepare herself for the marriage and begged that her sister Dinarzade should be sent for to speak to her.

When they were alone, Scheherazade addressed her thus. "My dear sister, I want your help in a very important affair. My father is going to take me to the palace to celebrate my marriage with the sultan. When His Highness receives me, I shall beg him, as a last favor, to let you sleep in our chamber, that I may have your company during the last night I am alive. If, as I hope, he grants me my wish, be sure that you wake me an hour before dawn and speak to me in these words, 'My sister, if you are not asleep, I beg you, before the sun rises, to tell me one of your charming stories.' Then I shall begin, and I hope by this means to deliver the people from the terror that reigns over them."

Dinarzade replied that she would do with pleasure what her sister wished.

When the usual hour arrived the grand vizir conducted Scheherazade to the palace and left her alone with the sultan, who bade her raise her veil and was amazed at her beauty. But seeing her eyes full of tears, he asked what was the matter.

"Sire," replied Scheherazade, "I have a sister who loves me as tenderly as I love her. Grant me the favor of allowing her to sleep this night in the same room, as it is the last we shall be together." Schahriar consented to Scheherazade's petition, and Dinarzade was sent for.

An hour before daybreak Dinarzade awoke and exclaimed, as she had promised, "My dear sister, if you are not asleep, tell me, I pray you, before the sun rises, one of your charming stories. It is the last time I shall have the pleasure of hearing you."

Scheherazade did not answer her sister but turned to the sultan. "Will Your Highness permit me to do as my sister asks?"

"Willingly," he answered. So Scheherazade began:

THE
MERCHANT
AND THE GENIE

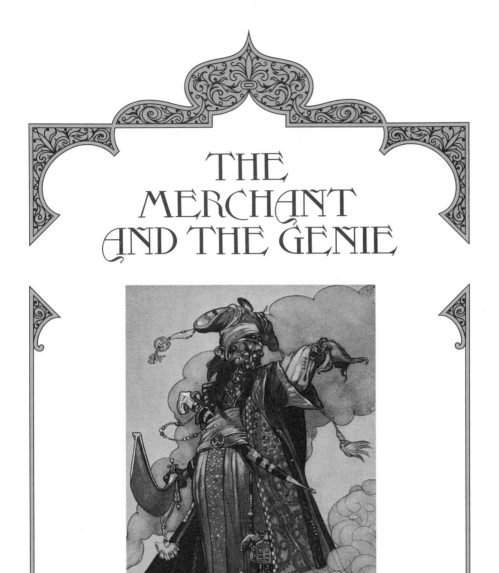

ire, there was once upon a time a merchant who possessed great wealth, in land and merchandise as well as in ready money. He was obliged from time to time to take journeys to arrange his affairs. One day, having to go a long way from home, he mounted his horse, taking with him a small wallet in which he had put a few biscuits and dates, because he had to pass through a desert where no food was to be had. He arrived without any mishap and, having finished his business, set out on his return. On the fourth day of his journey, the heat of the sun being very great, he turned out of his road to rest under some trees. He found at the foot of a large walnut tree a fountain of clear and running water. He dismounted, fastened his horse to a branch of the tree, and sat down by the fountain, after having taken from his wallet some of his dates and biscuits. While eating the dates he threw the stones right and left. When he had finished this frugal meal he washed his face and hands in the fountain.

While he was thus employed he saw an enormous genie, white with rage, coming toward him with a scimitar in his hand.

"Arise," he cried in a terrible voice, "and let me kill you as you have killed my son!" As he uttered these words, the genie gave a frightful yell.

The merchant, quite as much terrified at the hideous face of the monster as at his words, answered him tremblingly. "Alas, good sir, what can I have done to you to deserve death?"

"I shall kill you," repeated the genie, "as you have killed my son."

"But," said the merchant, "how can I have killed your son? I do not know him; I have never even seen him."

"When you arrived here did you not sit down on the ground?" asked the genie. "Did you not take some dates from your wallet and, while eating them, throw the stones about?"

"Yes," said the merchant, "I certainly did so."

"Then," said the genie, "you have killed my son, for while you were throwing the stones my son passed by and one of them struck him in the eye and killed him. So I shall kill you."

"Ah, sir, forgive me!" cried the merchant.

"I will have no mercy on you," answered the genie.

"But I killed your son quite unintentionally, so I implore you to spare my life."

"No, I shall kill you as you killed my son." And so saying the genie seized the merchant by the arm, threw him on the ground, and lifted his saber to cut off his head.

The merchant, protesting his innocence, bewailed his wife and children and tried pitifully to avert his fate. The genie, his scimitar raised, waited till he had finished but was not in the least touched.

Scheherazade, at this point, seeing that it was day and knowing that the sultan always rose very early to attend the council, stopped speaking.

"Indeed, Sister," said Dinarzade, "this is a wonderful story."

"The rest is still more wonderful," replied Scheherazade, "and you would say so, if the sultan would allow me to live another day and would give me leave to tell it to you the next night."

Schahriar, who had been listening to Scheherazade with pleasure, said to himself, "I will wait till tomorrow. I can always have her killed when I have heard the end of her story."

All this time the grand vizir was in a terrible state of anxiety. But he was much delighted when he saw the sultan enter the council chamber without giving him the terrible command he was expecting.

The next morning, before the day broke, Dinarzade said to her sister, "Dear sister, if you are awake I pray you to go on with your story."

The sultan did not wait for Scheherazade to ask his leave. "Finish the story of the genie and the merchant," said he. "I am curious to hear the end."

So Scheherazade went on with the story. This happened every morning. The sultana told a story and the sultan let her live to finish it.

Scheherazade continued telling her story.

When the merchant saw that the genie was determined to cut off his head, he said, "One word more, I entreat you. Grant me a little delay, just a short time to go home to bid my wife and children farewell and to make my will. When I have done this I will come back here, and you shall kill me."

"But," said the genie, "if I grant you the delay you ask, I am afraid you will not come back."

"I give you my word of honor," answered the merchant, "that I will come back without fail."

"How long do you require?" asked the genie.

"I ask you for a year's grace," replied the merchant. "I promise you that tomorrow twelvemonth, I shall be waiting under these trees to give myself up to you."

On this the genie left him near the fountain and disappeared. The merchant, having recovered from his fright, mounted his horse, and went on his road.

When he arrived home his wife and children received him with the greatest joy. But instead of embracing them he began to weep so bitterly that they soon guessed something terrible was the matter.

"Tell us, I pray you," said his wife, "what has happened."

"Alas!" answered her husband. "I have only a year to live."

Then he told them what had passed between him and the genie, and how he had given his word to return at the end of a year to be killed. When they heard this sad news they were in despair and wept much.

The next day the merchant began to settle his affairs and, first of all, to pay his debts. He gave presents to his friends and large alms to the poor. He set his slaves at liberty and provided for his wife and children.

The year soon passed away and he was obliged to depart. When he tried to say good-bye he was quite overcome with grief and with difficulty tore himself away. At length he reached the place where he had first seen the genie, on the very day he had appointed. He dismounted and sat down at the edge of the fountain, where he awaited the genie in terrible suspense.

21

While he was thus waiting, an old man leading a hind came toward him. They greeted one another, and then the old man said to him, "May I ask, Brother, what brought you to this desert place, where there are so many evil genii about? To see these beautiful trees one would imagine it was inhabited, but it is a dangerous place in which to stop long."

The merchant told the old man why he was there. He listened in astonishment.

"This is a most marvelous affair. I should like to be a witness of your interview with the genie." So saying, he sat down by the merchant.

While they were talking another old man came up, followed by two black dogs. He greeted them and asked what they were doing in this place. The old man who was leading the hind told him the adventure of the merchant and the genie. The second old man had no sooner heard the story than he, too, decided to stay there to see what would happen. He sat down by the others and was talking when a third old man arrived. He asked why the merchant who was with them looked so sad. They told him the story and he also resolved to see what would pass between the genie and the merchant, so he waited with the rest.

They soon saw in the distance a thick smoke like a cloud of dust. This smoke came nearer and nearer and then, all at once, it vanished and they saw the genie who, without speaking to them, approached the merchant, sword in hand, and taking him by the arm, said, "Get up, and let me kill you as you killed my son."

The merchant and the three old men began to weep and groan.

Then the old man leading the hind threw himself at the monster's feet and said, "O Prince of the Genii, I beg of you to stay your fury and listen to me. I am going to tell you my story and that of the hind I have with me, and if you find it more marvelous than that of the merchant whom you are about to kill, I hope you will do away with a third part of his punishment."

The genie considered some time, and then he said, "Very well, I agree to this."

22

THE FIRST OLD MAN

I am now going to begin my story, said the old man, so please attend. This hind that you see with me is my wife. We have no children of our own, therefore I adopted the son of a favorite slave and determined to make him my heir. My wife, however, took a great dislike to both mother and child, which she concealed from me till too late. When my adopted son was about ten years old I was obliged to go on a journey. Before I went I entrusted to my wife's keeping both the mother and child, and begged her to take care of them during my absence, which lasted a whole year.

During this time she studied magic in order to carry out her wicked scheme. When she had learnt enough she took my son into a distant place and changed him into a calf. Then she gave him to my steward and told him to look after a calf she had bought. She also changed the slave into a cow, which she sent to my steward.

When I returned I inquired after my slave and the child. "Your slave is dead," she said, "and as for your son, I have not seen him for two months and I do not know where he is."

I was grieved to hear of my slave's death, but as my son had only disappeared, I thought I should soon find him. Eight months, however, passed and still no tidings of him; then the feast of Bairam came.

To celebrate it I ordered my steward to bring me a very fat cow to sacrifice. He did so. I did not know that the cow he brought was my unfortunate slave. I bound her, but just as I was about to kill her she began to low piteously, and I saw that her eyes were streaming with tears. It seemed to me most extraordinary and, feeling pity, I ordered the steward to lead her away and bring another.

My wife, who was present, scoffed at my compassion which made her malice of no avail. "What are you doing?" she cried. "Kill this cow. It is the best we have to sacrifice."

To please her I tried once more, but again the animal's lows and tears disarmed me. "Take her away," I said to the steward, "and kill her; I cannot."

The steward killed the cow, but on skinning her found that she was nothing but bones although she appeared so fat. I was vexed.

"Keep her for yourself," I said to the steward, "and if you have a fat calf bring that in her stead."

In a short time he brought a very fat calf which, although I did not know it, was my son. It tried hard to break its cord and come to me. It threw itself at my feet with its head on the ground, as if it wished to excite my pity and beg me not to take away its life. I was even more surprised and touched at this action than I had been at the tears of the cow.

"Go," I said to the steward, "take back this calf, take great care of it and bring me another in its place instantly."

When my wife heard me say this she at once cried out, "What are you doing, Husband? Do not sacrifice any calf but this."

"Wife," I answered, "I will not sacrifice this calf." And in spite of all her remonstrances, I remained firm.

I had another calf killed; this one was led away. The next day the steward asked to speak to me in private.

"I have come," he said, "to tell you some news which I think you will like to hear. I have a daughter who knows magic. Yesterday, when I was leading back the calf which you refused to sacrifice, I noticed that she smiled and then directly afterward began to cry. I asked her why she did so.

" 'Father,' she answered, 'this calf is the son of our master. I smile with joy at seeing him still alive, and I weep to think of his mother who was sacrificed yesterday as a cow. These changes have been wrought by our master's wife, who hated the mother and son.' "

At these words, O Genie, continued the old man, I leave you to imagine my astonishment. I went immediately with the steward to speak with his daughter myself. First of all I went to the stable to see my son and he replied in his dumb way to all my caresses. When the steward's daughter came I asked her if she could change my son back to his proper shape.

"Yes, I can," she replied, "on two conditions. One is that you will give him to me for my husband, and the other that you will let me punish the woman who changed him into a calf."

"To the first condition," I answered, "I agree with all my heart and I will give you an ample dowry. To the second I also agree, only I beg you to spare her life."

"That will I do," she replied; "I will treat her as she treated your son."

She took a vessel of water and pronounced over it some words I did not understand. Then, on throwing the water over the calf, he became immediately a young man once more.

"My son, my dear son!" I exclaimed, kissing him in a transport of joy. "This kind maiden has rescued you from a terrible enchantment, and I am sure that out of gratitude you will marry her."

He consented joyfully, but before they were married the young girl changed my wife into a hind and it is she you see before you. I wished her to have this form rather than a stranger one, so we could see her in the family without repugnance.

Since then my son has become a widower and has gone traveling. I am now going in search of him and, not wishing to confide my wife to the care of other people, I am taking her with me. Is not this a most marvelous tale?

"It is indeed," said the genie, "and because of it I grant to you the third part of the punishment of this merchant."

When the first old man had finished his story, the second, who was leading the two black dogs, said to the genie, "I am going to tell you what happened to me and I am sure you will find my story even more astonishing than the one to which you have just been listening. But when I have related it, will you grant me also the third part of the merchant's punishment?"

"Yes," replied the genie, "provided your story surpasses that of the hind."

With this agreement, the second old man began in this way:

THE SECOND OLD MAN

Great Prince of the Genii, you must know that we are three brothers—these two black dogs and myself. Our father died, leaving us each a thousand sequins. With this sum we all three took up the same profession and became merchants. A short time after we had opened our shops, my eldest brother, one of these two dogs, resolved to travel in foreign countries for the sake of merchandise. With this intention he sold all he had and bought merchandise suitable to the voyages he was about to make. He set out and was away a whole year.

At the end of this time a beggar came to my shop. "Good day," I said. "Good day," he answered, "is it possible that you do not recognize me?" Then I looked at him closely and saw he was my brother. I made him come into my house and asked him how he had fared in his enterprise.

"Do not question me," he replied, "seeing me, you see all I have. It would but renew my trouble to tell of all the misfortunes that have befallen me in a year and have brought me to this state."

I shut up my shop and paid him every attention, taking him to the bath and giving him my most beautiful robes. I examined my accounts and found that I had doubled my capital—that is, I now possessed two thousand sequins. I gave my brother half, saying, "Now, Brother, you can forget your losses." He accepted the money with joy and we lived together as we had before.

Some time afterward my second brother wished also to sell his business and travel. My eldest brother and I did all we could to dissuade him but it was of no use. He joined a caravan and set out. He came back at the end of a year in the same state as his elder brother. I took care of him, and as I had a thousand sequins to spare I gave them to him and he reopened his shop.

One day, my two brothers came to me to propose that we should make a journey and trade. At first I refused to go. "You traveled," I said, "and what did you gain?" But they came to me repeatedly and, after having held out for five years, I at last gave way. But when they had made their preparations and began to buy the merchandise we needed, they found they had spent every piece of the thousand sequins I had given each of them. I did not reproach them. I divided my six thousand sequins, giving a thousand to each and keeping one for myself, and the other three I buried in a corner of my house. We bought merchandise, loaded a vessel with it, and set forth with a favorable wind.

After two months' sailing we arrived at a seaport, where we disembarked and did a great trade. Then we bought the merchandise of the country and were just going to set sail once more when I was stopped on the shore by a beautiful though very poorly dressed woman. She came up to me, kissed my hand, and implored me to marry her and take her on board.

At first I refused, but she begged so hard and promised to be such a good wife to me that at last I consented. I got her some beautiful dresses and, having married her, we embarked and set sail.

During the voyage, I discovered so many good qualities in my wife that I began to love her more and more. But my brothers began to be jealous of my prosperity and to plot against my life. One night when

27

we were sleeping, they threw my wife and myself into the sea. My wife, however, was a fairy, and so she did not let me drown but transported me to an island.

When the day dawned she said to me, "When I saw you on the seashore I took a great fancy to you and wished to try your good nature, so I presented myself in the disguise you saw. Now I have rewarded you by saving your life. But I am very angry with your brothers and shall not rest till I have taken their lives."

I thanked the fairy for all she had done for me but begged her not to kill my brothers. I appeased her wrath, and in a moment she transported me from the island where we were to the roof of my house and disappeared a moment afterward. I went down, opened the doors, and dug up the three thousand sequins which I had buried. I went to the place where my shop was, opened it, and received from my fellow merchants congratulations on my return.

When I went home I saw two black dogs who came to meet me with sorrowful faces. I was much astonished, but the fairy, who reappeared, said to me, "Do not be surprised to see these dogs; they are your two brothers. I have condemned them to remain for ten years in these shapes." Then, having told me where I could hear news of her, she vanished.

The ten years are nearly passed, and I am on the road to find her. As in passing I met this merchant and the old man with the hind, I stayed with them.

This is my history, O Prince of Genii! Do you not think it a most marvelous one?

"Yes, indeed," replied the genie, "and I will give up to you the third of the merchant's punishment."

Then the third old man made the same request the other two had, and the genie promised him the last third of the merchant's punishment if his story surpassed both the others. So he told his history to the genie, but I cannot tell you what it was as I do not know.

28

But I do know it was even more marvelous than either of the others, for the genie was astonished and said to the third old man, "I will give up to you the third part of the merchant's punishment. He ought to thank all three of you for having interested yourselves in his favor. But for you, he would be here no longer."

So saying, he disappeared, to the great joy of the company. The merchant did not fail to thank his friends, and then each went on his way. The merchant returned to his wife and children and passed the rest of his days happily with them.

"But, sire," added Scheherazade, "however beautiful are the stories I have just told you, they cannot compare with the story of the fisherman."

THE FISHERMAN

ire, there was once upon a time a fisherman so old and so poor that he could scarcely manage to support his wife and three children. He went every day to fish very early, and each day he made a rule not to throw his nets more than four times. He started out one morning by moonlight and came to the seashore. He undressed and threw his nets, and as he was drawing them toward the bank he felt a great weight. He thought he had caught a large fish and felt very pleased. But a moment afterward, seeing that instead of a fish he had in his nets only the carcass of an ass, he was much disappointed.

Vexed with having such a bad haul, when he had mended his nets which had been broken in several places, he threw them a second time. In drawing them in he again felt a great weight, so he thought they were full of fish. But he found only a large basketful of rubbish. He was much annoyed.

"O Fortune," he cried, "do not trifle thus with me, a poor fisherman, who can hardly support his family!"

So saying, he threw away the rubbish and, after having washed his nets clean of the dirt, he threw them for the third time. But he drew in only stones, shells and mud. He was almost in despair.

Then he threw his nets for the fourth time. When he thought he had a fish he drew them in with a great deal of trouble. There was no fish, however, but he found a yellow pot, which by its weight seemed full of something, and he noticed that it was fastened and sealed with lead, impressed with a seal. He was delighted. "I will sell it to the founder," he said. "With the money I get for it I shall buy a measure of wheat."

He examined the jar on all sides; he shook it to see if it would rattle. But he heard nothing and, judging from the impression of the seal and the lid, he thought there must be something precious inside. To find out, he took his knife and, with a little trouble, opened it. He turned the jar upside down but nothing came out, which surprised him very much. He set it in front of him and while he was looking at it attentively such thick smoke came out that he had to step back a pace or two.

This smoke rose up to the clouds and, stretching over the sea and the shore, formed a thick mist, which caused the fisherman much astonishment. When all the smoke was out of the jar it gathered itself together and became a thick mass in which appeared a genie, twice as large as the largest giant. When he saw such a terrible-looking monster, the fisherman would have run away, but he trembled so with fright he could not move a step.

"Great King of the Genii," cried the monster, "I will never again disobey you!"

At these words the fisherman took courage. "What is this you are saying, great Genie? Tell me your history and how you came to be shut up in that vase."

At this, the genie looked at the fisherman haughtily. "Speak to me more civilly," he said, "before I kill you."

"Alas! Why should you kill me?" cried the fisherman. "I have just freed you; have you already forgotten that?"

"No," answered the genie; "but that will not prevent me from

33

killing you, and I am only going to grant you one favor, to choose the manner of your death."

"But what have I done to you?" asked the fisherman.

"I cannot treat you in any other way," said the genie, "and if you would know why, listen to my story.

"I rebelled against the King of the Genii. To punish me, he shut me up in this vase of copper and put on its leaden cover his seal, which is enchantment enough to prevent my coming out. Then he had the vase thrown into the sea. During the first period of my captivity I vowed that if anyone should free me before a hundred years passed, I would make him rich even after his death. But that century passed and no one freed me. In the second century I vowed I would give all the treasures in the world to my deliverer; but he never came.

"In the third, I promised to make him a king, to be always near him and to grant him three wishes every day; but that century passed away as the other two had and I remained in the same plight. At last I grew angry at being a captive for so long and vowed that if anyone would release me I would kill him and would only allow him to choose in what manner he should die. As you have freed me today, choose in what way you will die."

The fisherman was very unhappy. "What an unlucky man I am to have freed you! I implore you to spare my life."

"I have told you," said the genie, "that is impossible. Choose quickly; you are wasting time."

The fisherman began to devise a plot. "Since I must die," he said, "before I choose the manner of my death, I conjure you on your honor to tell me if you really were in that vase?"

"Yes, I was," answered the genie.

"I really cannot believe it," said the fisherman. "That vase could not contain one of your feet even, and how could it hold your whole body? I cannot believe it unless I see you go into the vase."

Then the genie began to change himself into smoke which, as before, spread over the sea and the shore and then, collecting itself together, began to go back into the vase slowly and evenly till there was nothing left outside. Then a voice came from the vase, which said to the fisherman, "Well, unbelieving fisherman, here I am in the vase. Do you believe me now?"

The fisherman, instead of answering, took the lid of lead and shut it down quickly on the vase.

"Now, O Genie," he cried, "ask pardon of *me*, and choose by what death you will die! But no, it will be better if I throw you into the sea whence I drew you out, and I will build a house on the shore to warn fishermen, who come to cast their nets here, against fishing up such a wicked genie as you are, who vows to kill the man who frees you."

At these words the genie did all he could to get out, but he could not because of the enchantment on the lid. Then he tried to get out by cunning.

"If you will take off the cover," he said, "I will repay you."

"No," answered the fisherman, "if I trust myself to you I am afraid you will treat me as a certain Greek king treated the physician, Douban. Listen, and I will tell you":

THE GREEK KING AND THE PHYSICIAN

In the country of Zouman, in Persia, there lived a Greek king. This king was a leper and all his doctors had been unable to cure him, when a very clever physician named Douban came to his court.

The physician was very learned in all languages and knew a great deal about herbs and medicines. As soon as he was told the king's illness he put on his best robe and presented himself before the king.

"Sire," said he, "I know that no physician has been able yet to cure

Your Majesty, but if you will follow my instructions, I promise to cure you without any medicines or outward application."

The king listened to this proposal. "If you are clever enough to do this," he said, "I promise to make you and your descendants rich forever."

The physician went to his house and made a polo club, the handle of which he hollowed out and put in it the drug he wished to use. Then he made a ball, and with these things he went next day to the king.

He told him that he wished him to play at polo. Accordingly the king mounted his horse and went to the place where he played.

There the physician approached him with the club he had made, saying, "Take this, sire, and strike the ball till you feel your hand and whole body in a glow. When the remedy that is in the handle of the club is warmed by your hand it will penetrate throughout your body. Then you must return to your palace, bathe and go to sleep, and when you awake tomorrow morning you will be cured."

The king took the club and urged his horse after the ball which he had thrown. He struck it and then it was hit back by the courtiers who were playing with him. When the king felt very hot he stopped playing and returned to the palace, went into the bath and did all that the physician had said.

The next day when he arose he found, to his great joy and astonishment, that he was completely cured. When he entered his audience chamber all his courtiers, who were eager to see if the wonderful cure had been effected, were overwhelmed with joy.

The physician, Douban, entered the hall and bowed low to the ground. The king, seeing him, called him, made him sit by his side and showed him every mark of honor.

That evening the king gave him a long, rich robe of state and presented him with two thousand sequins. The following days he continued to load him with favors.

Now the king had a grand vizir who was avaricious and envious and a very bad man. He grew extremely jealous of the physician and determined to bring about his ruin. In order to do this he asked to speak in private with the king, saying that he had a most important communication to make.

"What is it?" asked the king.

"Sire," answered the grand vizir, "it is most dangerous for a monarch to confide in a man whose faithfulness is not proved. You do not know that this physician is not a traitor come here to assassinate you."

"I am sure," said the king, "that this physician is the most faithful and virtuous of men. If he wished to take my life, why did he cure me? Cease to speak against him. I see what it is, you are jealous of him, but do not think that I can be turned against him. I remember well what a vizir said to King Sinbad, his master, to prevent him from putting the prince, his son, to death."

What the Greek king said excited the vizir's curiosity and he said to him, "Sire, I beg Your Majesty to have the condescension to tell me what the vizir said to King Sinbad."

"This vizir," he replied, "told King Sinbad that one ought not to believe everything that a mother-in-law says and told him this story."

THE HUSBAND AND THE PARROT

A good man had a beautiful wife, whom he loved passionately and never left if he could avoid it. One day, when he was obliged by important business to go away from her, he went to a place where all kinds of birds are sold and bought a parrot. This parrot not only spoke well but it had the gift of telling all that had been done before it. The man brought it home in a cage, asking his wife to put it in her room and to take great care of it while he was away. Then he departed. On his return he asked the parrot what had happened during his absence, and the parrot told him some things which made him scold his wife.

She thought that one of her slaves must have been telling tales of her, but they told her it was the parrot and she resolved to revenge herself on it.

When her husband next went away for a day she told one slave to turn a hand mill under the parrot's cage, another to throw water down from above the cage and a third to take a mirror and turn it in front of its eyes from left to right by the light of a candle. The slaves did this for part of the night and did it very well.

The next day when the husband came back he asked the parrot what he had seen. The bird replied, "My good master, the lightning, thunder and rain disturbed me so much all night long that I cannot tell you what I have suffered."

The husband, who knew that it had neither rained nor thundered in the night, was convinced that the parrot was not speaking the truth, so he took it out of the cage and threw it so roughly on the ground that he killed it. Nevertheless he was sorry afterward, for he found that the parrot had spoken the truth.

When the Greek king had finished the story of the parrot, he added to the vizir, "And so, vizir, I shall not listen to you, and I shall take care of the physician, in case I repent as the husband did when he had killed the parrot."

But the vizir was determined. "Sire," he replied, "the death of the parrot was nothing. But when it is a question of the life of a king it is better to sacrifice the innocent than save the guilty. It is no uncertain thing, however. The physician, Douban, wishes to assassinate you. My zeal prompts me to disclose this to Your Majesty. If I am wrong I deserve to be punished as a vizir was once punished."

"What had the vizir done," asked the Greek king, "to merit the punishment?"

"I will tell Your Majesty, if you will do me the honor to listen," answered the vizir.

THE
VIZIR WHO
WAS PUNISHED

There was once upon a time a king who had a son who was very fond of hunting. He often allowed him to indulge in this pastime, but he had ordered his grand vizir always to go with him and never to lose sight of him. One day the huntsman roused a stag, and the prince, thinking the vizir was behind, gave chase and rode so hard that he found himself alone.

He stopped and, having lost sight of the stag, turned to rejoin the vizir who had not been careful enough to follow him. But he lost his way. While he was trying to find it, he saw on the side of the road a beautiful lady, who was crying bitterly. He drew his horse's rein and asked her who she was and what she was doing in this place and if she needed help.

"I am the daughter of an Indian king," she answered, "and while riding in the country I fell asleep and tumbled off. My horse has run away and I do not know what has become of him."

The young prince had pity on her and offered to take her behind him, which he did. As they passed by a ruined building the lady dismounted and went in. The prince also dismounted and followed her. To his great surprise, he heard her saying to someone inside, "Rejoice, my children; I am bringing you a very nice fat youth." And other voices replied, "Where is he, Mamma, that we may eat him at once; we are very hungry."

The prince at once saw the danger he was in. He now knew that the lady, who had said she was the daughter of an Indian king, was an ogress who lived in desolate places and, by a thousand wiles, surprised passersby. He was terrified and threw himself on his horse. The pretended princess appeared at this moment and, seeing that she had lost her prey, said to him, "Do not be afraid. What do you want?"

"I am lost," he answered, "and I am looking for the road."

"Keep straight on," said the ogress, "and you will find it."

The prince could hardly believe his ears and rode off as hard as he could. He found his way and arrived safe and sound at his father's house, where he told him of the danger he had run because of the grand vizir's carelessness. The king was very angry and had the vizir strangled immediately.

"Sire," went on the vizir to the Greek king, "to return to the physician, Douban. If you do not take care, you will repent of having trusted him. Who knows that this remedy with which he has cured you may not in time have a bad effect on you?"

The Greek king was naturally very weak and did not perceive the wicked intention of his vizir, nor was he firm enough to keep to his first resolution.

"Well, vizir," he said, "you are right. Perhaps he did come to take my life. He might do it by the mere smell of one of his drugs. I must see what can be done."

"The best means, sire, to put your life in security is to send for him at once and to cut off his head directly he comes," said the vizir.

"I really think," replied the king, "that will be the best way."

He then ordered one of his ministers to fetch the physician, who came at once. "I have had you sent for," said the king, "in order to free myself from you by taking your life."

The physician was astonished beyond measure when he heard he was to die. "What crime have I committed, Your Majesty?"

"I have learnt," replied the king, "that you are a spy and intend to kill me. But I will be first and kill you. Strike," he added to the executioner who was nearby, "and rid me of this assassin."

At this cruel order the physician threw himself on his knees. "Spare my life," he cried, "and yours will be spared."

The Greek king, however, had no mercy on him, and the executioner bound his eyes. All those present begged for his life, but in vain.

The physician on his knees, and bound, said to the king, "At least let me put my affairs in order and leave my books to persons who will make good use of them. There is one which I should like to present to Your Majesty. It is very precious and ought to be kept carefully in your treasury. It contains many curious things, the chief being that when you cut off my head, if Your Majesty will turn to the sixth leaf and read the third line of the left-hand page, my head will answer all the questions you ask it."

The king, eager to see such a wonderful thing, put off the execution to the next day and sent Douban under a strong guard to his house. There the physician put his affairs in order, and the next day there was a great crowd assembled in the hall to see his death and the doings after it.

The physician went up to the foot of the throne with a large book in his hand. He carried a basin, on which he spread the coverings of the book and, presenting it to the king, said, "Sire, take this book, and when my head is cut off let it be placed in the basin on the covering of this book; as soon as it is there the blood will cease to flow. Then open the book and my head will answer all your questions. But, sire, I implore your mercy, for I am innocent."

"Your prayers are useless, and if it were only to hear your head speak when you are dead, you should die."

So saying, the king took the book from the physician's hands and ordered the executioner to do his duty.

The head was so cleverly cut off that it fell into the basin and directly the blood ceased to flow. Then, to the great astonishment of the king, the eyes opened and the head said, "Your Majesty, open the book." The king did so, and finding that the first leaf stuck against the second, he put his finger in his mouth, to turn it more easily. He did the same thing till he reached the sixth page and, not seeing any writing on it, said, "Physician, there is no writing."

"Turn over a few more pages," answered the head. The king went on turning, still putting his finger in his mouth, till the poison in which each page was dipped took effect. His sight failed him, and he fell at the foot of his throne.

When the physician's head saw that the poison had taken effect and that the king had only a few more minutes to live, it cried, "Tyrant, see how cruelty and injustice are punished." Scarcely had it uttered these words than the king died, and the head also lost the little life that had remained in it.

That is the end of the story of the Greek king, and now let us return to the fisherman and the genie.

"If the Greek king," said the fisherman, "had spared the physician, he would not have thus died. The same thing applies to you. Now I am going to throw you into the sea."

"My friend," said the genie, "do not do such a cruel thing. Do not treat me as Imma treated Ateca."

"What did Imma do to Ateca?" asked the fisherman, who was filled with curiosity.

"Do you think I can tell you while I am shut up here?" replied the genie. "Let me out and I will make you rich."

The hope of no longer being poor made the fisherman give way. "If you will give me your promise to do this, I will open the lid. I do not think you will dare to break your word."

The genie promised and the fisherman lifted the lid. He came out at once in smoke, and then, having resumed his proper form, the first thing he did was to kick the vase into the sea. This frightened the fisherman, but the genie laughed and said, "Do not be afraid; I only did it to frighten you; and to show you that I intend to keep my word take your nets and follow me."

He began to walk in front of the fisherman, who followed him with some misgivings. They passed by the town and went up a mountain and then down into a great plain, where there was a large lake lying between four hills.

When they reached the lake the genie said to the fisherman, "Throw your nets and catch fish."

The fisherman did as he was told, hoping for a good catch, as he saw plenty of fish. What was his astonishment at seeing there were four quite different kinds, some white, some red, some blue, and some yellow. He caught four, one of each color. As he had never seen any like them he admired them very much, and he was very pleased to think how much money he would get for them.

"Take these fish and carry them to the sultan, who will give you more money for them than you have ever had in your life. You can come every day to fish in this lake, but be careful not to throw your nets more than once every day, otherwise some harm will happen to you. If you follow my advice carefully you will find it good."

Saying these words, the genie struck his foot against the ground, which opened, and when he had disappeared it closed immediately. The fisherman resolved to obey the genie exactly, so he did not cast his nets a second time but walked into the town to sell his fish at the palace.

When the sultan saw the fish he was much astonished. He looked at them one after the other, and when he had admired them long enough, he said to his first vizir, "Take these fish and give them to the clever cook the Emperor of the Greeks sent me. I think they must be as good as they are beautiful."

The vizir took them himself to the cook, saying, "Here are four fish that have been brought to the sultan. He wants you to cook them."

Then he went back to the sultan who told him to give the fisherman four hundred gold pieces. The fisherman, who had never before possessed such a large sum of money, could hardly believe his good fortune. He at once relieved the needs of his family and made good use of it.

But now we must return to the kitchen which we shall find in great confusion. The cook, when she had cleaned the fish, put them in a pan with some oil to fry them. When she thought them cooked enough on one side she turned them on the other. But scarcely had she done so when the walls of the kitchen opened, and a young and beautiful damsel came out. She was dressed in an Egyptian dress of flowered satin, and she wore earrings and a necklace of huge pearls, bracelets of gold set with rubies, and she held a wand of myrtle in her hand.

She went up to the pan, to the great astonishment of the cook who stood motionless at the sight of her. She struck one of the fish with her rod. "Fish, fish," said she, "are you doing your duty?"

The fish answered nothing, and then she repeated her question, whereupon they all raised their heads together and answered very distinctly, "Yes, yes. If you reckon, we reckon. If you pay your debts, we pay ours. If you fly, we conquer, and we are content."

When they had spoken the girl upset the pan and entered the opening in the wall, which at once closed and appeared the same as before.

When the cook had recovered from her fright she lifted up the fish which had fallen into the ashes, but she found them as black as cinders and not fit to serve up to the sultan. She began to cry.

"Alas! What shall I say to the sultan? He will be so angry with me and I know he will not believe me!"

While she was crying the grand vizir came in and asked if the fish were ready. She told him all that had happened and he was much surprised. He sent at once for the fisherman, and when he came said to him, "Fisherman, bring me four more fish like those you have brought already, for an accident has happened to them and they cannot be served up to the sultan."

A mysterious damsel overturned the frying pan.

The fisherman did not say what the genie had told him but excused himself from bringing them that day on account of the length of the way. He promised to bring them next day.

In the night he went to the lake, cast his nets and, on drawing them in, found four fish which were like the others, each of a different color. He went back at once and carried them to the grand vizir as he had promised.

The grand vizir then took them to the kitchen and shut himself up with the cook, who began to fry them as she had the four others on the previous day. When she was about to turn them on the other side, the wall opened, the damsel appeared, addressed the same words to the fish, received the same answer, and then overturned the pan and disappeared.

The grand vizir was filled with astonishment. "I shall tell the sultan all that has happened," said he. And he did so.

The sultan was very much astounded and wished to see this marvel for himself. So he sent for the fisherman and asked him to procure four more fish. The fisherman asked for three days, which was granted. He then cast his nets in the lake and again caught four different colored fish. The sultan was delighted to see he had got them and gave him again four hundred gold pieces.

As soon as the sultan had the fish he had them carried to his room with all that was needed to cook them. Then he shut himself up with the grand vizir, who began to prepare them and to cook them. When they were done on one side he turned them over on the other.

Then the wall of the room opened, but instead of the maiden a black slave came out. He was enormously tall and carried a large green stick with which he touched the fish, saying in a terrible voice, "Fish, fish, are you doing your duty?"

To these words the fish, lifting up their heads, replied, "Yes, yes. If you reckon, we reckon. If you pay your debts, we pay ours. If you fly, we conquer, and are content."

The black slave overturned the pan in the middle of the room and the fish were turned to cinders. Then he stepped proudly back into the wall, which closed round him.

"After having seen this," said the sultan, "I cannot rest. These fish signify some mystery I must clear up."

He sent for the fisherman. "Fisherman," he said, "the fish you have brought us have caused me some anxiety. Where did you get them?"

"Sire," the fisherman answered, "I got them from a lake lying in the middle of four hills beyond yonder mountains."

"Do you know this lake?" asked the sultan of the grand vizir.

"No, though I have hunted many times round that mountain, I have never even heard of it," said the vizir.

As the fisherman said it was only three hours' journey away, the sultan ordered his whole court to mount and ride thither, and the fishermen led them. They climbed the mountain and then, on the other side, saw the lake as the fisherman had described. The water was so clear that they could see the four kinds of fish swimming about in it. They looked at them for some time, and then the sultan ordered them to make a camp by the edge of the water.

When night came the sultan called his vizir and said to him, "I have resolved to clear up this mystery. I am going out alone, do you stay here in my tent and, when my ministers come tomorrow, say I am not well and cannot see them. Do this each day till I return."

The grand vizir tried to persuade him not to go, but in vain. The sultan took off his state robes and put on his sword, and when all was quiet in the camp he set forth alone.

He climbed one of the hills and then crossed the great plain till, just as the sun rose, he beheld far in front of him a large building. When he came near to it he saw it was a splendid palace of beautiful black polished marble, covered with steel as smooth as a mirror.

The sultan went to the gate, which stood half-open, and went in, as nobody came when he knocked. He passed through a magnificent courtyard and still saw no one, though he called aloud several times.

He entered large halls where the carpets were of silk, the lounges and sofas covered with tapestry from Mecca, and the hangings of the most beautiful Indian stuffs of gold and silver. Then he found himself in a splendid room, with a fountain supported by golden lions. The water out of the lions' mouths turned into diamonds and pearls, and the leaping water almost touched a most beautifully painted dome. The palace was surrounded on three sides by magnificent gardens, lakes and woods. Birds sang in the trees, which were netted over to keep them always there.

Still the sultan saw no one, but he heard a plaintive cry and a voice which said, "Oh, that I could die, for I am too unhappy to wish to live any longer!"

The sultan looked round to discover who it was who thus bemoaned his fate and at last saw a handsome young man, richly clothed, sitting on a throne raised slightly from the ground. His face was very sad.

The sultan approached him and bowed to him. The young man bent his head very low but did not rise.

"Sire," he said to the sultan, "I cannot rise and do you the reverence that I am sure should be paid to your rank."

"Sir," answered the sultan, "I am sure you have a good reason for not doing so. Having heard your cry of distress, I am come to offer you my help. Whose is this palace, and why is it thus empty?"

Instead of answering, the young man lifted up his robe and showed the sultan that, from the waist downward, he was a block of black marble.

The sultan was horrified and begged the young man to tell him his story.

"Willingly I will tell you my sad history," said the young man.

THE
YOUNG KING OF
THE BLACK ISLES

ou must know, sire, that my father was Mahmoud, the king of this country, the Black Isles, so called from the four little mountains which were once islands, while the capital was the place where now the great lake lies. My story will tell you how these changes came about.

My father died when he was sixty-six, and I succeeded him. I married my cousin, whom I loved tenderly, and thought she loved me too.

But one afternoon, when I was half-asleep and was being fanned by two of her maids, I heard one say to the other, "What a pity it is that our mistress no longer loves our master! I believe she would like to kill him if she could, for she is an enchantress."

I soon found by watching that they were right, for when I mortally wounded a favorite slave of hers for a great crime, she begged that she might build a palace in the garden, where she wept and bewailed him for two years. At last I begged her to cease grieving for him, for although he could not speak or move, by her enchantments she just kept him alive. She turned upon me in a rage and said over me some magic words, and I instantly became as you see me now, half man and half marble.

Then this wicked enchantress changed the capital, which was a populous and flourishing city, into the lake and desert plain you saw. The fish of four colors which are in it are the different races who lived in the town; the four hills are the four islands which gave the name to my kingdom. All this the enchantress told me to add to my troubles. And this is not all. Every day she comes and beats me with a whip of buffalo hide.

When the young king had finished his sad story he burst once more into tears, and the sultan was much moved. "Tell me," he cried, "where is this wicked woman, and where is the miserable object of her affection, whom she just manages to keep alive?"

"Where she lives I do not know," answered the unhappy prince, "but she goes every day at sunrise to see if the slave can yet speak to her, after she has beaten me."

"Unfortunate king," said the sultan, "I will do what I can to avenge you."

So he consulted with the young king over the best way to bring this about, and they agreed their plan should be put in effect the next day. The sultan then rested, and the young king gave himself up to happy hopes of release. The next day the sultan arose and went to the palace in the garden where the slave was. He drew his sword and destroyed the little life that remained in him and then threw the body down a well. He then lay down on the couch where the slave had been and waited for the enchantress.

She went first to the young king, whom she beat with a hundred blows. Then she came to the room where she thought her wounded slave was, but where the sultan really lay.

She came near his couch and said, "Are you better today, my dear slave? Speak but one word to me."

"How can I be better," answered the sultan, imitating the language of the Ethiopians, "when I can never sleep for the cries and groans of your husband?"

"What joy to hear you speak!" answered the queen. "Do you wish him to regain his proper shape?"

53

"Yes," said the sultan; "hasten to set him at liberty that I may no longer hear his cries."

The queen at once went out, took a cup of water, and said over it some words that made it boil as if it were on the fire. Then she threw it over the prince, who at once regained his own form. He was filled with joy, but the enchantress said, "Hasten away from this place and never come back, lest I kill you."

So he hid himself to see the end of the sultan's plan.

The enchantress went back to the Palace of Tears and said, "Now I have done what you wished."

"What you have done," said the sultan, "is not enough to cure me. Every day at midnight all the people whom you have changed into fish lift their heads out of the lake and cry for vengeance. Go quickly and give them their proper shape."

The enchantress hurried away and said some words over the lake. The fish then became men, women, and children, and the houses and shops were once more filled. The sultan's suite, who had encamped by the lake, were not a little astonished to see themselves in the middle of a large and beautiful town.

As soon as she had disenchanted it the queen went back to the palace. "Are you quite well now?" she asked.

"Come near," said the sultan. "Nearer still."

She obeyed. Then he sprang up, and with one blow of his sword he cut her in two.

Then he went to the prince. "Rejoice," he said, "your cruel enemy is dead."

The prince thanked him again and again.

"And now," said the sultan, "I will go back to my capital, which I am glad to find is so near yours."

"So near mine!" said the King of the Black Isles. "Do you know it is a whole year's journey from here? You came here in a few hours because it was enchanted. But I will accompany you on your journey."

"It will give me much pleasure if you will escort me," said the sultan, "and as I have no children, I will make you my heir."

The sultan and the prince set out together, the sultan laden with rich presents from the King of the Black Isles.

The day after he reached his capital the sultan assembled his court and told them all that had befallen him and how he intended to adopt the young king as his heir. Then he gave each man presents in proportion to his rank.

As for the fisherman, as he was the first cause of the deliverance of the young prince, the sultan gave him much money and made him and his family happy for the rest of their days.

ALI BABA AND THE FORTY THIEVES

In a town in Persia there dwelt two brothers, one named Cassim, the other Ali Baba. Cassim was married to a rich wife and lived in plenty, while Ali Baba had to maintain his wife and children by cutting wood in a neighboring forest and selling it in the town. One day, when Ali Baba was in the forest, he saw a troop of men on horseback coming toward him in a cloud of dust. He was afraid they were robbers and climbed into a tree for safety. When they came up to him and dismounted, he counted forty of them. They unbridled their horses and tied them to trees.

The finest man among them, whom Ali Baba took to be their captain, went a little way among some bushes and said, "Open, Sesame!" so plainly that Ali Baba heard him. A door opened in the rocks and, having made the troop go in, he followed them and the door shut again of itself.

They stayed some time inside and Ali Baba, fearing they might come out and catch him, was forced to sit patiently in the tree. At last the door opened again and the forty thieves came out. As the captain went in last he came out first, and made them all pass by him; he then closed the door, saying, "Shut, Sesame!" Every man bridled his horse and mounted, the captain put himself at their head, and they returned as they came.

Then Ali Baba climbed down and went to the door concealed among the bushes and said, "Open, Sesame!" and it flew open. Ali Baba, who expected a dull, dismal place, was greatly surprised to find it large and well lighted, and hollowed by the hand of man in the form of a vault, which received the light from an opening in the ceiling. He saw rich bales of merchandise—silk stuffs, brocades, all piled together, gold and silver in heaps, and money in leather purses. He went in and the door shut behind him. He did not look at the silver but brought out as many bags of gold as he thought his asses, which were browsing outside, could carry, loaded them with the bags, and hid it all with fagots. Using the words, "Shut, Sesame!" he closed the door and went home.

Then he drove his asses into the yard, shut the gates, carried the moneybags to his wife and emptied them out before her. He bade her keep the secret and he would bury the gold.

"Let me first measure it," said his wife. "I will borrow a measure of someone while you dig the hole."

So she ran to the wife of Cassim and borrowed a measure. Knowing Ali Baba's poverty, the sister was curious to find out what sort of grain his wife wished to measure and artfully put some suet at the bottom of the measure. Ali Baba's wife went home and set the measure on the heap of gold and filled it and emptied it often, to her great content. She then carried it back to her sister, without noticing that a piece of gold was sticking to it.

Cassim's wife perceived it directly her back was turned. She grew very curious and said to Cassim when he came home, "Cassim, your brother is richer than you. He does not count his money, he measures it."

He begged her to explain this riddle, which she did by showing him the piece of money and telling him where she had found it. Then Cassim grew so envious that he could not sleep and went to his brother in the morning before sunrise.

"Ali Baba," he said, showing him the gold piece, "you pretend to be poor and yet you measure gold."

By this Ali Baba perceived that through his wife's folly Cassim and his wife knew his secret, so he confessed all and offered Cassim a share.

"That I expect," said Cassim, "but I must know where to find the treasure, otherwise I will discover all and you will lose all."

Ali Baba, more out of kindness than fear, told him of the cave and the very words to use. Cassim left Ali Baba, meaning to be beforehand with him and get the treasure for himself. He rose early next morning and set out with ten mules loaded with great chests. He soon found the place and the door in the rock. He said, "Open, Sesame!" and the door opened and shut behind him.

He could have feasted his eyes all day on the treasures, but he now hastened to gather together as much of it as possible; but when he was ready to go he could not remember what to say for thinking of his great riches. Instead of "Sesame," he said, "Open, Barley!" and the door remained fast. He named several other sorts of grain, all but the right one, and the door still stuck fast. He was so frightened at the danger he was in that he had as much forgotten the word as if he had never heard it.

About noon the robbers returned to their cave and saw Cassim's mules roving about with great chests on their backs. This gave them the alarm. They drew their sabers, and went to the door, which opened on their captain's saying, "Open, Sesame!" Cassim, who had heard the trampling of their horses' feet, resolved to sell his life dearly, so when the door opened he leaped out and threw the captain down. In vain, however, for the robbers with their sabers soon killed him. On entering the cave they saw all the bags laid ready, and could not imagine how anyone had got in without knowing their secret. They cut Cassim's body into four quarters and nailed them up inside the cave, in order to frighten anyone who should venture in, and went away in search of more treasure.

As night drew on Cassim's wife grew very uneasy, ran to her

60

brother-in-law and told him where her husband had gone. Ali Baba did his best to comfort her and set out to the forest in search of Cassim. The first thing he saw on entering the cave was his dead brother. Full of horror, he put the body on one of his asses and bags of gold on the other two and, covering all with fagots, returned home. He drove the two asses laden with gold into his own yard and led the other to Cassim's house. The door was opened by the slave Morgiana, whom he knew to be both brave and cunning.

Unloading the ass, he said to her, "This is the body of your master, who has been murdered, but whom we must bury as though he had died in his bed. I will speak with you again, but now tell your mistress I am come."

The wife of Cassim, on learning the fate of her husband, broke out into cries and tears, but Ali Baba offered to take her to live with him and his wife if she would promise to keep his counsel and leave everything to Morgiana; whereupon she agreed, and dried her eyes.

Morgiana, meanwhile, sought an apothecary and asked him for some lozenges. "My poor master," she said, "can neither eat nor speak and no one knows what his distemper is." She carried home the lozenges and returned next day weeping, and asked for an essence only given to those just about to die. Thus, in the evening, no one was surprised to hear the shrieks and cries of Cassim's wife and Morgiana, telling everyone that Cassim was dead.

The next day Morgiana went to an old cobbler near the gates of the town, who opened his stall early, put a piece of gold in his hand and bade him follow her with his needle and thread. Having bound his eyes with a handkerchief, she took him to the room where the body lay, pulled off the bandage and bade him sew the quarters together, after which she covered his eyes again and led him home.

Then they buried Cassim, and Morgiana, his slave, followed him to the grave, weeping and tearing her hair, while Cassim's wife stayed at home uttering lamentable cries. Next day she went to live with Ali Baba, who gave Cassim's shop to his eldest son.

61

The forty thieves, on their return to the cave, were much astonished to find Cassim's body gone as well as some of their moneybags.

"We are certainly discovered," said the captain, "and shall be undone if we cannot find out who it is that knows our secret. Two men must have known it; we have killed one, we must now find the other. To this end one of you who is bold and artful must go into the city, dressed as a traveler, and discover whom we have killed and whether men talk of the strange manner of his death. If the messenger fails he must lose his life, lest we be betrayed."

One of the thieves started up and offered to do this and, after the rest had highly commended him for his bravery, he disguised himself and happened to enter the town at daybreak, just by Baba Mustapha's stall. The thief bade him good day, saying, "Honest man, how can you possibly see to stitch at your age?"

"Old as I am," replied the cobbler, "I have very good eyes, and you will believe me when I tell you that I sewed a dead body together in a place where I had less light than I have now."

The robber was overjoyed at his good fortune and, giving the cobbler a piece of gold, desired to be shown the house where he had stitched up the dead body. At first Mustapha refused, saying that he had been blindfolded. But when the robber gave him another piece of gold he began to think he might remember the turnings if blindfolded as before. This means succeeded. The robber partly led him and was partly guided by him right in front of Cassim's house, the door of which the robber marked with a piece of chalk.

Then, well pleased, he bade farewell to Baba Mustapha and returned to the forest. By and by Morgiana, going out, saw the mark the robber had made, quickly guessed that some mischief was brewing and, fetching a piece of white chalk, marked two or three doors on each side, without saying anything to her master or mistress.

The thief, meanwhile, told his comrades of his discovery. The captain thanked him and bade him show him the house he had marked. But when they came to it they saw that five or six of the houses were chalked in the same manner. The guide was so confounded that he knew not what answer to make, and when they returned to the cave he was at once beheaded for having failed. Another robber was dispatched and, having won over Baba Mustapha, marked the house in red chalk; but Morgiana being again too clever for them, the second messenger was put to death also.

The captain now resolved to go himself but, wiser than the others, he did not mark the house but looked at it so closely he could not fail to remember it. He returned and ordered his men to go into the neighboring villages and buy nineteen mules and thirty-eight leather jars, all empty, except one which was full of oil. The captain put one of his men, fully armed, into each, rubbing the outside of the jars with oil from the full vessel. Then the nineteen mules were loaded with thirty-seven robbers in jars and the jar of oil, and reached the town by dusk.

The captain stopped his mules in front of the house and said to Ali Baba, who was sitting outside for coolness, "I have brought some oil from a distance to sell at tomorrow's market, but it is now so late that I know not where to pass the night, unless you will do me the favor to take me in."

Though Ali Baba had seen the captain of the robbers in the forest, he did not recognize him in the disguise of an oil merchant. He bade him welcome, opened his gates for the mules to enter, and went to Morgiana to bid her prepare a bed and supper for his guest. He brought the stranger into his hall, and after they had supped went again to speak to Morgiana in the kitchen, while the captain went into the yard under pretence of seeing after his mules but really to tell his men what to do.

Beginning at the first jar and ending at the last, he said to each man, "As soon as I throw some stones from the window of the chamber where I lie, cut the jars open with your knives and come out, and I will be with you in a trice."

He returned to the house and Morgiana led him to his chamber. She then told Abdallah, her fellow slave, to set on the pot to make some broth for her master, who had gone to bed. Meanwhile her lamp went out and she had no more oil in the house.

"Do not be uneasy," said Abdallah, "go into the yard and take some out of one of those jars."

Morgiana thanked him for his advice, took the oil pot, and went into the yard. When she came to the first jar the robber inside said softly, "Is it time?"

Any other slave but Morgiana, on finding a man in the jar instead of the oil she wanted, would have screamed and made a noise. But she, knowing the danger her master was in, bethought herself of a plan and answered quietly, "Not yet, but presently."

She went to all the jars, giving the same answer, till she came to the jar of oil. She now saw that her master, thinking to entertain an oil merchant, had let thirty-eight robbers into his house. She filled her oil pot, went back to the kitchen and, having lit her lamp, went again to the oil jar and filled a large kettle full of oil. When it boiled she went and poured enough oil into every jar to stifle and kill the robber inside. When this brave deed was done she went back to the kitchen, put out the fire and the lamp, and waited to see what would happen.

In a quarter of an hour the captain of the robbers awoke, got up and opened the window. As all seemed quiet he threw down some little pebbles which hit the jars. He listened and as none of his men seemed to stir, he grew uneasy and went down into the yard. On going to the first jar and saying, "Are you asleep?" he smelt the hot boiled oil and knew at once that his plot to murder Ali Baba and his household had been discovered. He found all the gang were dead and, missing the oil out of the last jar, became aware of the manner of their death. He then forced the lock of a door leading into a garden and, climbing over several walls, made his escape. Morgiana heard and saw all this and, rejoicing at her success, went to bed and fell asleep.

At daybreak Ali Baba arose and, seeing the oil jars there still, asked why the merchant had not gone with his mules. Morgiana bade him look in the first jar and see if there was any oil. Seeing a man, he started back in terror.

"Have no fear," said Morgiana, "the man cannot harm you; he is dead."

Ali Baba, when he had recovered somewhat from his astonishment, asked what had become of the merchant.

"Merchant!" said she. "He is no more a merchant than I am!" and she told him the whole story, assuring him that it was a plot of the robbers of the forest, of whom only three were left, and that the white and red chalk marks had something to do with it. Ali Baba at once gave Morgiana her freedom, saying that he owed her his life. They then buried the bodies in Ali Baba's garden, while the mules were sold in the market by his slaves.

The captain returned to his lonely cave, which seemed frightful to him without his lost companions, and firmly resolved to avenge them by killing Ali Baba. He dressed himself carefully and went into the town, where he took lodgings at an inn. In the course of a great many journeys to the forest he carried away many rich stuffs and much fine linen, and set up a shop opposite that of Ali Baba's son. He called himself Cogia Hassan, and as he was both civil and well dressed he soon made friends with Ali Baba's son and through him with Ali Baba, whom he was continually asking to sup with him.

Ali Baba, wishing to return his kindness, invited him into his house and received him smiling, thanking him for his kindness to his son. When the merchant was about to take his leave Ali Baba stopped him, saying, "Where are you going, sir, in such haste? Will you not stay and sup with me?"

The merchant refused, saying that he had a reason and, on Ali Baba's asking him what that was, he replied, "It is, sir, that I can eat no victuals that have any salt in them."

"If that is all," said Ali Baba, "let me tell you there shall be no salt in either the meat or the bread that we eat tonight."

He went to give this order to Morgiana, who was much surprised. "Who is this man," she said, "who eats no salt with his meat?"

"He is an honest man, Morgiana," returned Ali Baba, "therefore do as I bid you."

But she could not withstand a desire to see this strange man, so she helped Abdallah carry up the dishes and saw in a moment that Cogia Hassan was the robber captain and carried a dagger under his garment. "I am not surprised," she said to herself, "that this wicked man who intends to kill my master will eat no salt with him, but I will hinder his plans."

She sent up the supper by Abdallah, while she made ready for one of the boldest acts that could be thought on. When the dessert had been served, Cogia Hassan was left alone with Ali Baba and his son, whom he thought to make drunk and then murder them.

Morgiana, meanwhile, put on a headdress like a dancing-girl's and clasped a girdle round her waist, from which hung a dagger with a silver hilt, and said to Abdallah, "Take your tabor, and let us go and divert our master and his guest."

Abdallah took his tabor and played before Morgiana until they came to the door, where Abdallah stopped playing and Morgiana made a low curtsy.

"Come in, Morgiana," said Ali Baba, "let Cogia Hassan see what you can do," and turning to his guest, he said, "She is my housekeeper."

Cogia Hassan was by no means pleased, for he feared that his chance of killing Ali Baba was gone for the present, but he pretended great eagerness to see Morgiana, and Abdallah began to play and Morgiana to dance. After she had performed several dances she drew her dagger and made passes with it, sometimes pointing it at her own breast, sometimes at her master's, as if it were part of the dance. Suddenly, out of breath, she snatched the tabor from Abdallah with her left hand and holding the dagger in her right, held out the tabor to her master. Ali Baba and his son put a piece of gold into it and Cogia Hassan, seeing that she was coming to him, pulled out his purse to make her a present, but while he was putting his hand into it Morgiana plunged the dagger into his heart.

"Unhappy girl!" cried Ali Baba and his son. "What have you done to ruin us?"

"It was to preserve you, master, not to ruin you," answered Morgiana. "See here," opening the false merchant's garment and showing the dagger, "see what an enemy you have entertained! Remember, he would eat no salt with you; what more would you have? Look at him! He is both the false oil merchant and the captain of the forty thieves."

Ali Baba was so grateful to Morgiana for thus saving his life that he offered her to his son in marriage, who readily consented; and a few days after, the wedding was celebrated with great splendor. At the end of a year Ali Baba, hearing nothing of the two remaining robbers, judged they were dead, and set out to the cave. The door opened on his saying, "Open, Sesame!" He went in and saw that nobody had been there since the captain left it. He brought away as much gold as he could carry and returned to town. He told his son the secret of the cave, which his son handed down in his turn, so the children and grandchildren of Ali Baba were rich to the end of their lives.

PRINCE AHMED
AND
THE FAIRY

here was a sultan who had three sons and a niece. The eldest of the princes was called Houssain, the second Ali, the youngest Ahmed, and the princess, his niece, Nouronnihar.

The Princess Nouronnihar was the daughter of the younger brother of the sultan, who had died when the princess was very young. The sultan took upon himself the care of his niece's education and brought her up in his palace with the three princes, proposing to marry her when she arrived at a proper age and to contract an alliance with some neighboring prince by that means. But when he perceived that the three princes, his sons, loved her passionately, he thought more seriously on that affair. He was very much concerned; the difficulty he foresaw was to make them agree, and that the two youngest should consent to yield her up to their elder brother.

As he found them positively obstinate, he sent for them all together, and said to them, "Children, since for your good and quiet I have not been able to persuade you no longer to aspire to the princess, your cousin, I think it would not be amiss if each of you traveled separately into different countries. And, as you know I am very curious and delight in everything that's singular, I promise my niece in marriage to him who shall bring me the most extraordinary rarity. For the purchase of the rarity you shall go in search of and the expense of traveling I will give you each a sum of money."

As the three princes were always submissive and obedient to the sultan's will and each flattered himself fortune might prove favorable to him, they all consented to it. The sultan paid them the money he had promised them; and that very day they gave orders for the preparations for their travels and took their leaves of their father that they might be the more ready to go the next morning. Accordingly they all set out at the same gate of the city, each dressed like a merchant, attended by an officer of confidence dressed like a slave, and all well mounted and equipped.

They went the first day's journey together and lay at an inn, where the road divided into three different directions. At night when they were at supper together, they all agreed to travel for a year and to meet at that inn; the first who came should wait for the rest that, as they had all three taken leave together of the sultan, they might all return together. The next morning by break of day, after they had embraced and wished each other good success, they mounted their horses and took each a different road.

Prince Houssain, the eldest brother, arrived at Bisnagar, the capital of the kingdom of that name, and the residence of its king. He lodged at a khan appointed for foreign merchants. Having learnt that there were four principal sections where merchants of all sorts sold their commodities and kept shops and in the midst of which stood the king's palace, he went to one of these sections the next day.

Prince Houssain could not view this section without admiration. It was large and divided into several streets, all vaulted and shaded from the sun, and yet very light too. The shops were all of a size, and all who dealt in the same sort of goods lived in one street; as did the handicrafts men, who kept their shops in the smaller streets.

The multitude of shops, stocked with all sorts of merchandise, such as the finest linens from several parts of India, some painted in the most lively colors and representing beasts, trees, and flowers; silks and brocades from Persia, China, and other places; porcelain both from Japan and China; and tapestries, surprised him so much that he knew not how to believe his own eyes; but when he came to the goldsmiths and jewelers he was in a kind of ecstasy to behold such prodigious quantities of wrought gold and silver and was dazzled by the luster of the pearls, diamonds, rubies, emeralds, and other jewels exposed for sale.

Another thing Prince Houssain particularly admired was the great number of rose sellers who crowded the streets, for the Indians are such great lovers of that flower not one will stir without a nosegay in his hand or a garland on his head, and the merchants keep them in pots in their shops so the air is perfectly perfumed.

After Prince Houssain had gone through that section, street by street, his thoughts fully employed on the riches he had seen, he was very tired, and a merchant perceiving this civilly invited him to sit down in his shop. He accepted but had not been there long before he saw a crier pass by with a piece of tapestry on his arm, about six feet square, cried at thirty purses. The prince called to the crier and asked to see the tapestry, which seemed to him to be valued at an exorbitant price not only for the size of it but the meanness of the stuff. When he had examined it well he told the crier that he could not comprehend how so small a piece of tapestry of so indifferent appearance could be set at so high a price.

The crier, who took him for a merchant, replied, "If this price seems so extravagant to you, your amazement will be greater when I tell you I have orders to raise it to forty purses and not to part with it under that figure."

"Certainly," answered Prince Houssain, "it must have something very extraordinary in it, which I know nothing of."

"You have guessed it, sir," replied the crier, "and will own it when you come to know that whoever sits on this piece of tapestry may be transported in an instant wherever he desires to be, without being stopped by any obstacle."

At this discourse of the crier the Prince of the Indies, considering that the principal motive of his travel was to bring to the sultan, his father, some singular rarity, thought he could not meet with any which could give him more satisfaction.

"If the tapestry," said he to the crier, "has the virtue you assign it, I shall not think forty purses too much but shall make you a present besides."

"Sir," replied the crier, "I have told you the truth, and it is an easy matter to convince you of it, as soon as you have closed the bargain for forty purses on condition I show you the experiment. But as I suppose you have not so much about you, and to receive the money I must go with you to the khan where you lodge, with the leave of the master of the shop we will go into the back and I will spread the tapestry. When we have both sat down and you have formed the wish to be transported into your apartment of the khan; if we are not transported thither it shall be no bargain, and you shall be at your liberty. As to your present, though I am paid for my trouble by the seller, I shall receive it as a favor and be very much obliged to you and thankful."

On the credit of the crier the prince accepted the conditions and concluded the bargain, and having the master's leave, they went into his back shop. They both sat down on the tapestry, and as soon as the prince formed his wish to be transported into his apartment at the khan he presently found himself and the crier there. As he wanted no more sufficient proof of the virtue of the tapestry, he counted the crier out forty purses of gold and gave him twenty pieces for himself.

In this manner Prince Houssain became the possessor of the tapestry and was overjoyed that on his arrival at Bisnagar he had found so rare a piece, which he never doubted would gain him the hand of Nouron-nihar. In short, he looked upon it as an impossible thing for the princes, his younger brothers, to find anything to be compared with it. It was in his power, by sitting on his tapestry, to be at the place of meeting that very day, but as he was obliged to wait there for his brothers, as agreed, and as he was curious to see the King of Bisnagar and his court and to inform himself of the strength, laws, customs, and religion of the kingdom, he chose to make a longer abode there and to spend some months in satisfying his curiosity. After which he transported himself and the officer he had brought with him to the inn where he and his brothers were to meet and where he passed for a merchant till they came.

Prince Ali, the second brother, who decided to travel into Persia, joined a caravan three days after he parted with his brothers, and after four days' travel arrived at Schiraz which was the capital of the Kingdom of Persia. Here he passed for a jeweler.

The next morning Prince Ali, who traveled only for his pleasure and had brought nothing but necessaries along with him, took a walk into that part of the town which they at Schiraz called the bezestein.

Among all the criers who passed backward and forward with several sorts of goods, offering them for sale, he was not a little surprised to see one who held in his hand an ivory telescope of about a foot in length and the thickness of a man's thumb, and cried it at thirty purses.

At first he thought the crier mad and to inform himself went to a shop and said to the merchant, who stood at the door, "Pray, sir, is not that man mad who cried the ivory perspective glass at thirty purses? If he is not, I am very much deceived."

"Indeed, sir," answered the merchant, "he was in his right senses yesterday. I can assure you he is one of the ablest criers we have and the most often employed when anything valuable is to be sold. If he cries the ivory perspective glass at thirty purses it must be worth as much or more, on some account or other. He will come by presently and we will call him and you shall be satisfied; in the meantime sit down on my sofa and rest yourself."

Prince Ali accepted the merchant's obliging offer, and presently afterward the crier passed by. The merchant called him by his name and, pointing to the prince, said to him, "Tell that gentleman, who asked me if you were in your right senses, what you mean by crying an ivory perspective glass, which seems not to be worth much, at thirty purses. I should be very much amazed myself if I did not know you."

The crier, addressing himself to Prince Ali, said, "Sir, you are not the only person that takes me for a madman on the account of this glass. You shall judge yourself whether I am or no. When I have told you its property I hope you will value it at as high a price as those I have showed it to already, who had as bad an opinion of me as you. First, sir," pursued the crier, presenting it to the prince, "observe that this pipe is furnished with a glass at both ends and consider that by looking through one of them you see whatever object you wish to behold."

"I am," said the prince, "ready to make you all imaginable reparation for the scandal I have thrown on you if you will make the truth of what you advance appear." As he had the ivory pipe in his hand, after he had looked at the two glasses he said, "Show me through which of these ends I must look that I may be satisfied."

The crier presently showed him, and he looked, wishing at the same time to see the sultan, his father, whom he immediately beheld in perfect health on his throne in the midst of his council. Afterward, as there was nothing in the world so dear to him after his father as the Princess Nouronnihar, he wished to see her, and saw her at her toilet, laughing and in a pleasant humor, with her women about her.

Prince Ali wanted no other proof to be persuaded that this perspective glass was the most valuable thing in the world and believed that, if he should neglect to purchase it, he should never meet again with such another rarity. He therefore took the crier with him to the khan where he lodged, told him out the money and received the perspective glass.

Prince Ali was overjoyed at his bargain and persuaded himself that, as his brothers would not be able to meet with anything so rare and admirable, the Princess Nouronnihar would be the recompense of his fatigue and trouble. So he thought of nothing but visiting the Court of Persia incognito, and seeing whatever was curious in Schiraz and thereabouts till the caravan with which he came returned to the Indies. As soon as the caravan was ready to set out the prince joined them and arrived happily without any accident or trouble, other than the length of the journey and fatigue of traveling, at the place of rendezvous where he found Prince Houssain, and both waited for Prince Ahmed.

Prince Ahmed who took the road to Samarkand, the day after his arrival there went, as his brothers had done, into the bezestein, where he had not walked long before he heard a crier, who had an artificial apple in his hand, cry it at five and thirty purses.

Upon hearing this Ahmed stopped the crier and said to him, "Let me see that apple and tell me what virtue and extraordinary properties it has to be valued at so high a rate."

"Sir," said the crier, giving it into his hand, "if you look at the outside of this apple it is worthless, but if you consider its properties, virtues, and the great use and benefit it is to mankind, you will say it is no price for it and that he who possesses it is master of a great treasure. In short, it cures all sick persons of the most mortal diseases; if the patient is dying it will recover him immediately and restore him to perfect health; and this is done in the easiest manner in the world, through the patient's smelling the apple."

"If I may believe you," replied Prince Ahmed, "the virtues of this apple are wonderful and it is invaluable, but what ground have I, for all you tell me, to be persuaded of the truth of this matter?"

"Sir," replied the crier, "the thing is known and averred by the whole city of Samarkand. Without going any farther, ask all these merchants you see here and hear what they say. You will find several of them who will tell you they had not been alive this day if they had not made use of this excellent remedy. And, that you may the better comprehend what it is, I must tell you it is the fruit of the experiments of a celebrated philosopher of this city, who applied himself all his lifetime to the study and knowledge of the virtues of plants and minerals and at last attained this composition, by which he performed such surprising cures in this town as will never be forgotten. But he died suddenly himself before he could apply his sovereign remedy and left his wife and young children behind him in very indifferent circumstances. She, to support her family and provide for her children, is resolved to sell the apple."

While the crier informed Prince Ahmed of the virtues of the artificial apple, a great many persons came about them and confirmed what he said. One among the rest said he had a friend, dangerously ill, whose life was despaired of; and that was a favorable opportunity to show Prince Ahmed the experiment. Upon which the prince told the crier he would give him forty purses if he cured the sick person.

The crier, who had orders to sell it at that price, said to Prince Ahmed, "Come, sir, let us go and make the experiment, and the apple shall be yours; I can assure you that it will always have the desired effect." In short, the experiment succeeded and the prince, after he had counted out to the crier forty purses and had received the apple, waited patiently for the first caravan that should return to the Indies, and arrived in perfect health at the inn where the Princes Houssain and Ali waited for him.

When the princes met they showed each other their treasures and immediately saw through the glass that the princess was dying. They then sat down on the carpet, wished themselves with her, and were there in a moment.

Prince Ahmed no sooner perceived himself in Nouronnihar's chamber than he rose off the tapestry, as his brothers did also, went to the bedside and put the apple under her nose. Some moments afterward the princess opened her eyes and turned her head from one side to another, looking at the persons who stood about her, and then rose up in the bed and asked to be dressed, just as if she had waked out of a sound sleep. Her women having presently informed her, in a manner that showed their joy, that she was obliged to the three princes for the sudden recovery of her health and particularly to Prince Ahmed, she immediately expressed her joy at seeing them and thanked them all together, and afterward Prince Ahmed in particular.

While the princess was dressing, the princes went to throw themselves at the feet of the sultan, their father, and to pay their respects to him. But when they came before him they found he had been informed of their arrival by the chief of the princess' eunuchs and by what means the princess had been perfectly cured. The sultan received and embraced them with the greatest joy, both for their return and the recovery of his niece, whom he loved as well as if she had been his own daughter, and who had been given up by the physicians.

After the usual ceremonies and compliments each of the princes presented his rarity: Prince Houssain his tapestry which he had taken care not to leave behind him in the princess' chamber, Prince Ali his ivory perspective glass, and Prince Ahmed his artificial apple. And after each had commended his present when he put it into the sultan's hands, they begged of him to pronounce their fate and declare to which of them he would give the Princess Nouronnihar for a wife, according to his promise.

The Sultan of the Indies, having heard without interrupting all that the princes could represent further about their rarities and being well informed of what had happened in relation to the Princess Nouronnihar's cure, remained for some time silent as if he were thinking on what answer he should make.

At last he broke the silence and said to them, "I would declare for one of you children with a great deal of pleasure if I could do it with justice, but consider whether I can do it or not. 'Tis true, Prince Ahmed, the princess is obliged to your artificial apple for her cure, but I must ask you whether or not you could have been so serviceable to her if you had not known by Prince Ali's perspective glass the danger she was in and if Prince Houssain's tapestry had not brought you so soon. Your perspective glass, Prince Ali, informed you and your brothers that you were like to lose the princess, your cousin, and there you must own a great obligation.

"You must also grant that the knowledge would have been of no service without the artificial apple and the tapestry. And lastly, Prince

The carpet whisked them to the chamber of the princess.

Houssain, the princess would be very ungrateful if she should not show her acknowledgment of the service of your tapestry, which was so necessary a means toward her cure. But consider, it would have been of little use if you had not been acquainted with her illness by Prince Ali's glass and Prince Ahmed had not applied his artificial apple. Therefore, as neither tapestry, ivory perspective glass, nor artificial apple has the least preference one before the other, but on the contrary there's a perfect equality, I cannot grant the princess to any one of you. The only fruit you have reaped from your travels is the glory of having equally contributed to restore her health.

"If all this be true," added the sultan, "you see that I must have recourse to other means to determine rightly in the choice I ought to make among you. As there is time enough before nightfall, I'll do it today. Go and get each of you a bow and arrow and repair to the great plain where they exercise horses. I'll soon come to you and I will give the Princess Nouronnihar to him who shoots the farthest."

The three princes had nothing to say against the decision of the sultan. When they were out of his presence they each provided themselves with a bow and arrow, which they delivered to one of their officers, and went to the appointed plain, followed by a great concourse of people.

The sultan did not make them wait long for him, and as soon as he arrived Prince Houssain, as the eldest, took his bow and arrow and shot first; Prince Ali shot next, and much beyond him; and Prince Ahmed last of all. It so happened that nobody could see where Prince Ahmed's arrow fell; notwithstanding all the diligence used by himself and everybody else, it was not to be found far or near. And though it was believed that he shot the farthest and that he therefore deserved the Princess Nouronnihar it was, however, necessary that his arrow should be found to make the matter more evident and certain. Notwithstanding his remonstrance, the sultan judged in favor of Prince Ali and gave orders for preparations to be made for the wedding, which was celebrated a few days later with great magnificence.

Prince Houssain would not honor the feast with his presence. In short, his grief was so violent and insupportable that he left the court and, renouncing all right of succession to the crown, became a hermit.

Prince Ahmed, also, did not come to the wedding of Prince Ali and the Princess Nouronnihar but did not renounce the world as Prince Houssain had done. But as he could not imagine what had become of his arrow, he stole away from his attendants and resolved to search for it, that he might not have anything to reproach himself with. With this intent he went to the place where his brothers' arrows were gathered up and, going straight forward from there looking carefully on both sides of him, he went so far that at last he began to think his labor was all in vain. But yet he could not help going forward till he came to some steep craggy rocks, which were bounds to his journey and were situated in a barren country about four leagues distant from where he set out.

When Prince Ahmed came nigh to these rocks he perceived an arrow, which he gathered up, looked earnestly at, and was greatly astonished to find it was the same he shot away.

"Certainly," said he to himself, "neither I nor any man living could shoot an arrow so far." Finding it lay flat, not sticking into the ground, he judged that it rebounded against the rock. "There must be some mystery in this," said he to himself again, "and it may be advantageous to me. Perhaps fortune, to make me amends for depriving me of what I thought the greatest happiness, may have reserved a greater blessing for my comfort."

As these rocks were full of caves, some of them deep, the prince entered into one and, looking about, cast his eyes on an iron door which seemed to have no lock, but he feared it was fastened. However, thrusting against it, the door opened and revealed an easy descent along an incline, down which he walked, carrying his arrow in his hand. At first he thought he was going into a dark, obscure place, but presently a quite different light succeeded that out of which he came and, entering into a large, spacious place about fifty or sixty paces distant, he perceived a magnificent palace, which he had not then time enough to look at. At the same moment a lady of majestic bearing advanced as far as the porch, attended by a large troop of ladies, so finely dressed and beautiful that it was difficult to distinguish which was the mistress.

As soon as Prince Ahmed perceived the lady, he made all imaginable haste to go and pay his respects. The lady, on her part, seeing him coming, prevented him from addressing his discourse to her first but said to him, "Come nearer, Prince Ahmed, you are welcome."

It was no small surprise to the prince to hear himself named in a place he had never heard of, though so nigh to his father's capital, and he could not comprehend how he should be known to a lady who was a stranger to him.

At last he returned the lady's compliment by throwing himself at her feet and, rising up again, said to her, "Madam, I return you a thousand thanks for the assurance you give me of a welcome to a place where I believed my imprudent curiosity had made me penetrate too far. But, madam, may I without being guilty of ill manners dare ask you by what adventure you know me? And how you, who live in the same neighborhood with me, should be so great a stranger to me?"

"Prince," said the lady, "let us go into the hall; there I will gratify you in your request."

After these words the lady led Prince Ahmed into the hall. Then she sat down on a sofa and when the prince by her entreaty had done the same, she said, "You are surprised, you say, that I should know you and not be known by you but you will be no longer surprised when I inform you who I am. You are undoubtedly sensible that your religion teaches you to believe that the world is inhabited by genii as well as men. I am the daughter of one of the most powerful and distinguished of genii; my name is Paribanou. The only thing I have to add is that you seemed to me worthy of a happier fate than that of marrying the Princess Nouronnihar. In order that you might attain to it I was present when you drew your arrow and foresaw it would not go beyond Prince Houssain's. I took it in the air and gave it the necessary motion to strike against the rocks near which you found it, and it lies in your power to make use of the favorable opportunity which presents itself to make you happy."

As the Fairy Paribanou pronounced these last words with a different tone and looked, at the same time, tenderly upon Prince Ahmed, with a modest blush on her cheeks, it was no hard matter for the prince to comprehend what happiness she meant. He presently considered that the Princess Nouronnihar could never be his, and the Fairy Paribanou excelled her infinitely in beauty, agreeableness, wit and, as much as he could conjecture by the magnificence of the palace, in immense riches. He blessed the moment that he thought of seeking after his arrow a second time and yielded to his love.

"Madam," replied he, "should I all my life have the happiness of being your slave and the admirer of the many charms which ravish my soul, I should think myself the most blest of men. Pardon in me the boldness which inspires me to ask this favor and don't refuse to admit into your court a prince who is entirely devoted to you."

"Prince," answered the fairy, "will you not pledge your faith to me as I give mine to you?"

"Yes, madam," replied the prince, in an ecstasy of joy, "what can I do better and with greater pleasure? Yes, my queen, I'll give you my heart without the least reserve."

"Then," answered the fairy, "you are my husband and I am your wife. But I suppose you have eaten nothing today; a slight repast shall be served up for you while preparations are being made for our wedding feast at night, and then I will show you the apartments of my palace and you shall judge if this hall is not the meanest part of it."

Some of the fairy's women who came into the hall with them guessed her intentions, and went out immediately, returning presently with some excellent meats and wines.

When Prince Ahmed had eaten and drunk as much as he cared for, the Fairy Paribanou took him through all the apartments, where he saw diamonds, rubies, emeralds, and all sorts of fine jewels, intermixed with pearls, agate, jasper, porphyry together with the most precious marbles. But not to mention the richness of the furniture, which was inestimable, there was such profuseness throughout that the prince, instead of ever having seen anything like it, owned he could not have imagined there was anything in the world that could come up to it.

"Prince," said the fairy, "if you admire my palace so much, which, indeed, is very beautiful, what would you say to the palaces of the chief of our genii, which are much more beautiful, spacious and magnificent? I could also charm you with my gardens, but we will let that alone till another time. Night draws near, and it will be time to go to supper."

The next hall into which the fairy led the prince, and where the cloth was laid for the feast, was the last apartment the prince had not seen and not in the least inferior to the others. He admired the infinite number of sconces of wax candles perfumed with amber, the multitude of which were placed with a symmetry that formed an agreeable and pleasant sight. A large side table was set out with all sorts of gold plate so finely wrought that the workmanship was much more valuable than the weight of the gold. Several choruses of beautiful women, whose voices were ravishing, began a concert, accompanied with all sorts of the most harmonious instruments. When they were at table the Fairy Paribanou took care to serve Prince Ahmed with the most delicate meats, which she named as she invited him to eat of them, and which the Prince found to be so delicious he commended them with exaggeration and said that the entertainment far surpassed those of men. He found also the same excellence in the wines which neither he nor the fairy tasted till the dessert was served, which consisted of the choicest sweetmeats and fruits.

The wedding feast was continued the next day, rather, the days following the celebration were a continual feast.

At the end of six months Prince Ahmed, who always loved and honored his father, conceived a great desire to know how he was and that desire could not be satisfied without his going to see. He told the fairy of it and desired she would give him leave.

"Prince," said she, "go when you please. But first, don't take it amiss that I give you some advice how you shall behave yourself where you are going. First, I don't think it proper for you to tell the sultan, your father, of our marriage, nor of my quality, nor the place where you have been. Beg of him to be satisfied in knowing you are happy and desire no more, and let him know that the sole end of your visit is to make him easy and inform him of your fate."

She appointed twenty gentlemen, well mounted and equipped, to attend him. When all was ready Prince Ahmed took his leave of the fairy, embraced her and renewed his promise to return soon. Then his horse, which was finely caparisoned and was as beautiful a creature as any in the Sultan of the Indies' stables, was led to him, and he mounted it with an extraordinary grace. After bidding the fairy a last adieu he set forth on his journey.

As it was not a great way to his father's capital Prince Ahmed soon arrived there. The people, glad to see him again, received him with acclamations of joy and followed him in crowds to the sultan's apartment. The sultan received and embraced him with great joy, complaining at the same time with a fatherly tenderness of the affliction his long absence had been to him, which he said was the more grievous for fortune having decided in favor of Prince Ali, his brother, he was afraid he might have committed some rash action.

The prince told a story of his adventures without speaking of the fairy, whom he said he must not mention, and added, "The only favor I ask of Your Majesty is to give me leave to come often and pay you my respects and to know how you are."

"Son," answered the Sultan of the Indies, "I cannot refuse you the leave you ask me, but I should much rather you would resolve to stay with me. At least tell me where I may send to you if you should fail to come or when I may think your presence necessary."

"Sir," replied Prince Ahmed, "what Your Majesty asks of me is part of the mystery I spoke of. I beg of you to give me leave to remain silent on this point, for I shall come so frequently that I am afraid I shall sooner be thought troublesome than be accused of negligence in my duty."

The Sultan of the Indies pressed Prince Ahmed no more but said to him, "Son, I penetrate no further into your secrets but leave you at your liberty. However, I can tell you that you could not do me a greater pleasure than to come and by your presence restore to me the joy I have not felt this long time. You shall always be welcome when you come, without interrupting your business or pleasure."

Prince Ahmed stayed but three days at his father's court, and on the fourth returned to the Fairy Paribanou, who did not expect him so soon.

A month after Prince Ahmed's return from his visit to his father, the Fairy Paribanou observed that the prince, since the time that he gave her an account of his journey, his discourse with his father, and the leave he asked to go and see him often, never talked of the sultan as if there were no such person in the world, whereas before he was always speaking of him. She thought he forbore on her account; therefore she took an opportunity to say to him one day:

"Prince, don't you remember the promise you made to go and see the sultan, your father, often? For my part, I have not forgotten what you told me at your return and so put you in mind of it that it may not be long before you acquit yourself of your promise."

So Prince Ahmed went the next morning with the same attendance as before, but much finer and himself more magnificently mounted and dressed, and was received by the sultan with the same joy and satisfaction. For several months he constantly paid his visits, each time in a richer and finer equipage.

At last some viziers, the sultan's favorites, who judged Prince Ahmed's grandeur and power by the figure he cut, made the sultan jealous of his son, saying it was to be feared he might inveigle himself into the people's favor and dethrone him.

The Sultan of the Indies was so far from thinking Prince Ahmed capable of so pernicious a design as his favorites would make him believe that he said to them, "You are mistaken; my son loves me, and I am certain of his tenderness and fidelity as I have given him no reason to be otherwise."

But the favorites went on abusing Prince Ahmed till the sultan said, "Be it as it will, I don't believe my son Ahmed is so wicked as you would persuade me he is. However, I am obliged to you for your good advice and don't dispute but that it proceeds from your good intentions."

The Sultan of the Indies said this that his favorites might not know the impressions their discourse had made on his mind. It had so alarmed him that he resolved to have Prince Ahmed watched, unknown to his grand vizir. So he sent for a noted sorceress.

"Go immediately," he said, "follow my son and watch him so well that you find out where he retires, then return and bring me word."

The magician left the sultan and, knowing the place where Prince Ahmed found his arrow, went immediately thither and hid herself near the rocks so nobody could see her.

The next morning Prince Ahmed set out by daybreak, without taking leave either of the sultan or any of his court, according to custom. The magician, seeing him coming, followed him with her eyes till on a sudden she lost sight of him and his attendants. As the rocks were very steep and craggy they were an insurmountable barrier, so the magician judged either that the prince retired into some cavern or an abode of genii or fairies.

Thereupon she came out of the place where she was hid and went directly to the hollow way, which she traced till she came to the farther end, looking carefully about on all sides. But, notwithstanding all her diligence, she could perceive no opening, not so much as the iron gate Prince Ahmed had discovered, which was to be seen and opened to none but men and only to such whose presence was agreeable to the Fairy Paribanou.

The magician, who saw it was in vain for her to search any farther, was obliged to be satisfied with the discovery she had made and returned to give the sultan an account.

The sultan was well pleased with the magician's conduct and said to her, "Do you as you think fit; I'll wait patiently the event of your promises," and to encourage her made her a present of a diamond of great value.

As Prince Ahmed had obtained the Fairy Paribanou's leave to visit the Sultan of the Indies once a month he never failed, and the magician, knowing the time, went a day or two before to the foot of the rock where she had lost sight of the prince and his attendants and waited there.

The next morning Prince Ahmed went out, as usual, at the iron gate with the same attendants as before, and passed by the magician. Seeing her lie with her head against the rock, complaining as if she were in great pain, he pitied her, turned his horse about, went to her and asked what was the matter with her, and what he could do to ease her.

The artful sorceress looked at the prince in a pitiful manner, without ever lifting up her head, and answered in broken words and sighs, as if she could hardly fetch her breath, that she was going to the capital city, but on the way thither she was taken by so violent a fever that her strength failed her, and she was forced to lie down where he saw her, far from any habitation, and without any hopes of assistance.

"Good woman," replied Prince Ahmed, "you are not so far from help as you imagine. I am ready to assist you and convey you where you will meet with a speedy cure; only get up and let one of my people take you behind him."

At these words the magician, who pretended sickness only to know where the prince lived and what he did, accepted the charitable offer he made her and, that her actions might correspond with her words, she made many pretended vain endeavors to get up. At the same time two of the prince's attendants, alighting off their horses, helped her up, set her behind another, and mounted their horses again, following

88

the prince, who turned back to the iron gate, which was opened by one of his retinue who rode before. And when he came into the fairy's outer court, without dismounting himself, he sent to tell her he wanted to speak with her.

The Fairy Paribanou came with all imaginable haste, not knowing what made Prince Ahmed return so soon.

He not giving her time to ask him the reason, said, "Princess, I desire you would have compassion on this good woman," pointing to the magician, who was held up by two of his retinue. "I found her in the condition you see her in and promised her the assistance she stands in need of, and am persuaded that you, out of your own goodness as well as upon my entreaty, will not abandon her."

The Fairy Paribanou, who had her eyes fixed upon the pretended sick woman all the time the Prince was talking to her, ordered two of her women to take her from the two men who held her and carry her into an apartment of the palace and take as much care of her as of herself.

While the two women executed the fairy's commands she went up to Prince Ahmed and, whispering in his ear, said, "Prince, this woman is not so sick as she pretends to be; I am very much mistaken if she is not an impostor who will be the cause of great trouble to you. But don't be concerned, let what will be devised against you; be persuaded that I will deliver you out of all the snares that shall be laid for you. Go and pursue your journey."

This discourse of the fairy's did not in the least frighten Prince Ahmed. "My princess," said he, "as I do not remember I ever did or designed anybody an injury I cannot believe anybody can have a thought of doing me harm, but if they have I shall not, nevertheless, forbear doing good whenever I have an opportunity." Then he went on to his father's palace.

In the meantime the two women carried the magician into a very fine apartment, richly furnished. First they sat her down upon a sofa with her back supported by a cushion of gold brocade, while they made a bed for her; the quilt was finely embroidered with silk, the sheets of the finest linen, and the coverlet cloth-of-gold. When they had put her into bed (for the old sorceress pretended that her fever was so violent she could not help herself in the least) one of the women went out and returned soon again with a china dish in her hand, full of a certain liquor, which she presented to the magician while the other helped her to sit up.

"Drink this," said she. "It is the Water of the Fountain of Lions, and a sovereign remedy against all fevers whatsoever. You will feel the effect of it in less than an hour's time."

The magician, to dissemble the better, took it after a great deal of entreaty, but at last, holding back her head, swallowed down the liquor. When she was laid down again the two women covered her up. "Lie quiet and get a little sleep if you can. We'll leave you and hope to find you perfectly cured when we come again an hour hence."

The two women came again at the time they said they would, and found the magician up and dressed, sitting upon the sofa. "O admirable potion!" she said. "It has wrought its cure much sooner than you told me it would; I shall be able to continue my journey."

The two women who were fairies as well as their mistress, after they had told the magician how glad they were that she was cured so soon, walked before her and conducted her through several apartments, all more noble than that wherein she had rested, into a large hall, the most richly and magnificently furnished of all the palace.

Paribanou sat in this hall on a throne of massive gold, enriched with diamonds, rubies, and pearls of an extraordinary size, attended on each hand by a great number of beautiful fairies, all richly clothed. At the sight of so much majesty, the magician was not only dazzled but was so amazed that after she had prostrated herself before the throne she could not open her lips to thank the fairy as she proposed.

However, Paribanou saved her the trouble, and said to her, "Good woman, I am glad I had an opportunity to oblige you and to see you are able to pursue your journey. I won't detain you, but perhaps you may not be displeased to see my palace; follow my women and they will show it to you."

Then the magician went back and related to the Sultan of the Indies all that had happened, and how very rich Prince Ahmed was since his marriage with the fairy, richer than all the kings in the world, and how there was danger that he should come and take the throne from his father.

Though the Sultan of the Indies was very well persuaded that Prince Ahmed's natural disposition was good, yet he could not help being concerned at the discourse of the old sorceress to whom, when she was for taking her leave, he said, "I thank you for the pains you have taken and your wholesome advice. I am so sensible of the great importance it is to me that I shall deliberate upon it in council."

Now the favorites advised that the prince should be killed, but the magician advised differently.

"Make him give you all kinds of wonderful things, by the fairy's help, till she tires of him and sends him away. For example, every time Your Majesty goes into the field you are obliged to be at great expense, not only in pavilions and tents for your army but likewise in mules and camels to carry their baggage. Now, engage him to use his interest with the fairy to procure you a tent which might be carried in a man's hand and which should be so large as to shelter your whole army against bad weather."

When the magician had finished her speech the sultan asked his favorites if they had anything better to propose. Finding them all silent, he determined to follow the magician's advice, as the most reasonable and most agreeable to his mild government.

Next day the sultan did as the magician advised him and asked for the pavilion. Prince Ahmed never expected that his father would ask for something which at first appeared so difficult, not to say impossible. Though he knew not how great the power of genii and fairies was, he doubted whether it extended so far as to compass such a tent as his father desired.

At last he replied, "Though it is with the greatest reluctance imaginable, I will not fail to ask of my wife the favor Your Majesty desires but will not promise you to obtain it, and if I should not have the honor to come again to pay you my respects that shall be the sign I have not had success. But, beforehand, I desire you to forgive me and consider that you yourself have reduced me to this extremity."

"Son," replied the Sultan of the Indies, "I should be very sorry if what I ask of you should cause me the displeasure of never seeing you more. I find you don't know the power a husband has over a wife; and yours should show her love for you was very indifferent if she, with the power she has of a fairy, should refuse you so trifling a request as this I desire you to ask of her for my sake."

The prince went back and was very sad for fear of offending the fairy. She kept pressing him to tell her what was the matter, and at last he said, "Madam, you may have observed that hitherto I have been content with your love and have never asked you any favor. Consider then, I conjure you, that it is not I but the sultan, my father, who indiscreetly, or at least I think so, begs of you a pavilion large enough to shelter him, his court and army from the violence of the weather, but which a man may carry in his hand. Remember it is my father who asks this favor."

"Prince," replied the fairy, smiling, "I am sorry that so small a matter should disturb you and make you so uneasy as you appeared to be."

Then the fairy sent for her treasurer to whom she said, "Nourgihan, bring me the largest pavilion in my treasury." Nourgihan returned presently with the pavilion which she could not only hold in her hand but in the palm of her hand when she shut her fingers and presented it to her mistress, who gave it to Prince Ahmed to look at.

When Prince Ahmed saw the pavilion which the fairy called the largest in her treasury, he fancied she had a mind to jest with him and thereupon the marks of his surprise appeared presently in his countenance, which Paribanou perceiving burst out laughing.

"What, Prince," cried she, "do you think I jest with you? You'll see presently that I am in earnest. Nourgihan," said she to her treasurer, taking the tent out of Prince Ahmed's hands, "go and set it up, that the prince may judge whether it may be large enough for the sultan, his father."

The treasurer went immediately with it out of the palace and carried

The small object was handed to Prince Ahmed.

93

it a great way off. When she had set it up, one end reached to the very palace: at which time the prince found it large enough to shelter two armies greater than his father's, and then said to Paribanou:

"I ask my princess a thousand pardons for my incredulity; after what I have seen I believe there is nothing impossible to you."

"You see," said the fairy, "that the pavilion is larger than your father may have occasion for, but you must know that it has one property—it is larger or smaller according to the army it is to cover."

The treasurer took down the tent again and brought it to the prince, who took it and, without staying any longer than the next day, mounted his horse and went with the same attendants to his father.

The sultan, who was persuaded there could not be any such tent as he had asked for, was greatly surprised at the prince's diligence. He took the tent and, after he had admired its smallness, his amazement was so great that he could not recover himself. When the tent was set up in the great plain he found it large enough to shelter an army twice as large as he could bring into the field. But the sultan was not yet satisfied.

"Son," said he, "I have already expressed to you how much I am obliged for the present of the tent you have procured me; I look upon it as the most valuable thing in all my treasury. But you must do one thing more for me which will be every whit as agreeable to me. I am informed that the fairy your spouse makes use of a certain water called the Water of the Fountain of Lions, which cures all sorts of fevers, even the most dangerous, and as I am perfectly well persuaded my health is dear to you I don't doubt that you will ask her for a bottle of that water for me and bring it me as a sovereign medicine, which I may make use of when I have occasion. Do me this other important service and thereby complete the duty of a good son toward a tender father."

The prince returned and told the fairy what his father had said.

"There's a great deal of wickedness in this demand," she answered, "as you will understand by what I am going to tell you. The Fountain of Lions is situated in the middle of a court of a great castle, the entrance into which is guarded by four fierce lions, two of which sleep alternately while the other two are awake. But don't let that frighten you; I'll give you means to pass by them without any danger."

The Fairy Paribanou was at that time hard at work and as she had several clews of thread by her she took up one and, presenting it to Prince Ahmed, said, "First take this clew of thread. I'll tell you presently the use of it. In the second place, you must have two horses; one you must ride yourself and the other you must lead, which last must be loaded with a sheep cut into four quarters, that must be killed today. In the third place, you must be provided with a bottle, which I will give you, to bring back the water. Set out early tomorrow morning and, when you have passed the iron gate, throw the clew of thread before you; it will roll till it comes to the gates of the castle. Follow it and when it stops, as the gates will be open, you will see the four lions; the two that are awake will by their roaring wake the other two, but don't be frightened. Throw each of them a quarter of mutton and then clap spurs to your horse and ride to the fountain; fill your bottle without alighting and then return with the same expedition. The lions will be so busy eating they will let you pass by them."

Prince Ahmed set out the next morning at the time appointed by the fairy and followed her directions punctually. When he arrived at the gates of the castle, he distributed the quarters of mutton among the four lions and, passing through the midst of them bravely, got to the fountain, filled his bottle, and returned as safe and sound as he went.

When he had gone a little distance from the castle gates he turned about and, perceiving two of the lions coming after him, he drew his saber and prepared himself for defence. But as he went forward he saw that one of them turned out of the road at some distance and showed that he did not come to do him any harm but only to go before him and that the other stayed behind to follow. Therefore, he put his sword back again in its scabbard. Guarded in this manner, he arrived at the capital of the Indies, but the lions never left him till they had conducted him to the gates of the sultan's palace. After which they returned the same way they came, though not without frightening all who saw them for all they went in a very gentle manner and showed no fierceness.

A great many officers came to attend the prince while he dismounted his horse, and afterward conducted him into the sultan's apartment, who was at that time surrounded with his favorites. He approached the throne, laid the bottle at the sultan's feet, and kissed the rich tapestry which covered his footstool, and then said:

"I have brought you the healthful water which Your Majesty desired so much to keep among your other rarities in your treasury but at the same time wish you such extraordinary health as never to have occasion to make use of it."

After the prince had made an end of his compliment the sultan placed him on his right hand and then said to him, "Son, I am very much obliged to you for this valuable present, also because of the great danger you have exposed yourself to upon my account, which I have been informed of by a magician who knows the Fountain of Lions. But do me the pleasure," continued he, "to inform me by what address, or rather, by what incredible power you have been secured."

"Sir," replied Prince Ahmed, "I have no share in the compliment Your Majesty is pleased to make me; all the honor is due to my wife, whose good advice I followed." Then he informed the sultan what those directions were and, by the relation of this, let him know how well he had behaved himself. When he had done, the sultan, who showed outwardly all the demonstrations of great joy but secretly became more jealous, retired into an inward apartment, where he sent for the magician.

The magician, at her arrival, saved the sultan the trouble of telling her of the success of Prince Ahmed's journey, which she had heard of before she came and therefore was prepared with an infallible means to destroy him as she pretended. This she communicated to the sultan, who declared it the next day to the prince in the midst of all his courtiers in these words:

"Son," said he, "I have one thing more to ask of you, after which I shall expect nothing more from your obedience nor your interest with your wife. This request is, to bring me a man not above a foot and a half high whose beard is thirty feet long, who carries a bar of iron upon his shoulders of five hundredweight, which he uses as a quarterstaff."

Prince Ahmed, who did not believe there was such a man in the world as his father described, would gladly have excused himself. But the sultan persisted in his demand and told him the fairy could do more incredible things.

The next day the prince returned to his dear Paribanou to whom he told his father's new demand which, he said, he looked upon to be more impossible than the two first requests. "For," added he, "I cannot imagine there can be such a man in the world; without doubt, he has a mind to try whether or not I am so silly as to go about it, or he has a design for my ruin. In short, how can he suppose that I should lay hold on a man so well armed, though he is but little? What arms can I make use of to reduce him to my will? If there are any means I beg you will tell me them and let me come off with honor this time."

"Don't affright yourself, Prince," replied the fairy. "You ran a risk in fetching the Water of the Fountain of Lions for your father. There's no danger in finding out this man, who is my brother Schaibar, but is far from being like me though we both had the same father. He is of so violent a nature that nothing can prevent his giving cruel marks of his resentment for a slight offence; yet, on the other hand, is so good as to oblige everyone in whatever they desire. He is made exactly as the sultan your father has described him and has no other weapon than a bar of iron of five hundred pounds' weight, without which he never stirs and which makes him respected. I'll send for him, and you shall judge of the truth of what I tell you; but be sure to prepare yourself against being frightened at his extraordinary figure when you see him."

"What! my Queen," replied Prince Ahmed, "do you say Schaibar is your brother? Let him be never so ugly or deformed, I shall be so far from being frightened at the sight of him that as our brother I shall honor and love him."

The fairy ordered a gold chafing dish to be set with a fire in it under the porch of her palace, with a box of the same metal which was a present to her, out of which she took a perfume and, throwing it into the fire, there arose a thick cloud of smoke.

Some moments afterward the fairy said to Prince Ahmed, "See, there comes my brother." The prince immediately perceived Schaibar coming gravely, with his heavy bar on his shoulder, his long beard which he held up before him and a pair of thick moustachios which were tucked behind his ears and almost covered his face. His eyes were very small and deep-set in his head, which was far from being of the smallest size, and on his head he wore a grenadier's cap; besides all this he was very much humpbacked.

If Prince Ahmed had not known that Schaibar was Paribanou's brother, he would not have been able to look at him without fear but, knowing first who he was, he stood by the fairy without the least concern.

Schaibar, as he came forward, looked at the prince earnestly enough to have chilled his blood in his veins and asked Paribanou, when he first accosted her, who that man was.

To which she replied, "He is my husband, Brother. His name is Ahmed; he is son to the Sultan of the Indies. The reason I did not invite you to my wedding was because I was unwilling to divert you from an expedition you were engaged in and from which, I heard with pleasure, you returned victorious; so I took the liberty now to call for you."

At these words Schaibar, looking on Prince Ahmed favorably, said, "Is there anything, Sister, wherein I can serve him? It is enough for me that he is your husband to engage me to do for him whatever he desires."

"The sultan, his father," replied Paribanou, "has a curiosity to see you, and I desire he may be your guide to the sultan's court."

"He needs but lead the way, I'll follow him."

"Brother," replied Paribanou, "it is too late to go today, therefore stay till tomorrow morning. In the meantime I'll inform you of all that has passed between the Sultan of the Indies and Prince Ahmed since our marriage."

The next morning, after Schaibar had been informed of the affair, he and Prince Ahmed set out for the sultan's court. When they arrived at the gates of the capital the people no sooner saw Schaibar than they ran and hid themselves; some shut up their shops and locked themselves in their houses while others, flying, communicated their fear to all they met, who stayed not to look behind them but ran too. Insomuch that Schaibar and Prince Ahmed as they went along found the streets all desolate till they came to the palace, where the porters, instead of keeping the gates, ran away too, so that Prince Ahmed and Schaibar advanced without any obstacle to the council hall where the sultan was seated on his throne, giving audience. Here likewise the ushers, at the approach of Schaibar, abandoned their posts and gave them free admittance.

Schaibar went boldly and fiercely up to the throne, without waiting to be presented by Prince Ahmed, and accosted the Sultan of the Indies in these words: "Thou hast asked for me; see, here I am. What wouldst thou have with me?"

The sultan, instead of answering him, clapped his hands before his eyes to avoid the sight of so terrible an object. At this uncivil and rude reception Schaibar was so much provoked, after he had given him the trouble to come so far, that he instantly lifted up his iron bar and killed the sultan before Prince Ahmed could intercede in his behalf. All that he could do was to prevent his killing the grand vizir, who sat not far from him, representing to him that he had always given the sultan his father good advice.

"These are the ones, then," said Schaibar, "who gave him bad," and as he pronounced these words he killed all the other vizirs and flattering favorites of the sultan who were Prince Ahmed's enemies. Every time he struck he killed someone or other, and none escaped but they who were not so frightened as to stand staring and gaping and saved themselves by flight.

When this terrible execution was over Schaibar came out of the council hall into the midst of the courtyard with the iron bar upon his shoulder and, looking hard at the grand vizir who owed his life to Prince Ahmed, he said, "I know there is a certain magician who is a greater enemy of my brother-in-law's than all these base favorites I have chastised. Let the magician be brought to me presently."

The grand vizir immediately sent for her, and as soon as she was brought, Schaibar said, as he struck her with his iron bar, "Take the reward of thy pernicious counsel and learn not to feign sickness again."

After this he said, "This is not yet enough; I will use the whole town after the same manner if they do not immediately acknowledge Prince Ahmed, my brother-in-law, for their sultan and the Sultan of the Indies." Then all that were present made the air echo again with the repeated acclamations of "Long life to Sultan Ahmed"; and immediately after, he was proclaimed through the whole town. Schaibar had him clothed in the royal vestments, installed him on the throne, and after he had caused all to swear homage and fidelity to him went and fetched his sister, Paribanou, whom he brought with all the pomp and grandeur imaginable, and made her be owned Sultana of the Indies.

As for Prince Ali and Princess Nouronnihar, as they had no hand in the conspiracy against Prince Ahmed and knew nothing of it, Prince Ahmed assigned them a considerable province with its capital, where they spent the rest of their lives. Afterward he sent an officer to Prince Houssain to acquaint him with the change and make him an offer of which province he liked best, but that prince thought himself so happy in his solitude that he bade the officer return the sultan his brother thanks for the kindness he designed him, assuring him of his submission and that the only favor he desired of him was to give him leave to live retired in the place he had chosen for his retreat.

SINBAD
THE SAILOR

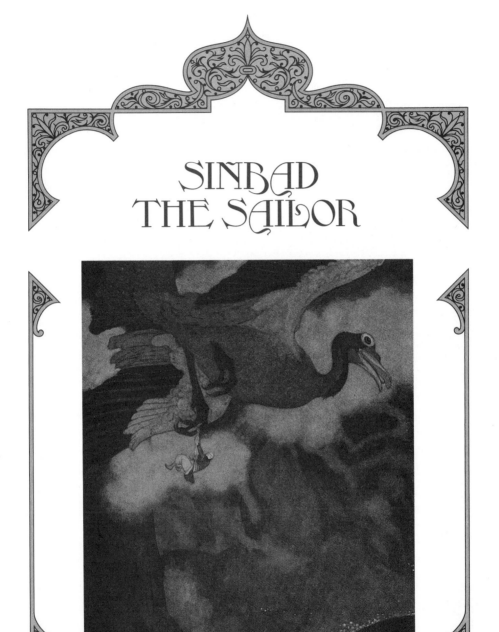

n the times of Caliph Harun al-Rashid there lived in Baghdad a poor porter named Hinbad who, on a very hot day, was sent to carry a heavy load from one end of the city to the other. Before he had accomplished half the distance he was so tired that, finding himself in a quiet street where the pavement was sprinkled with rosewater and a cool breeze was blowing, he set his burden upon the ground and sat down to rest in the shade of a grand house.

Very soon he decided he could not have chosen a pleasanter place; a delicious perfume of aloes wood and pastilles came from the open windows and mingled with the scent of the rosewater which steamed up from the hot pavement. Within the palace he heard some music, as of many instruments cunningly played, and the melodious warble of nightingales and other birds; and by this, and the appetizing smell of many dainty dishes of which he presently became aware, he judged that feasting and merrymaking were going on.

He wondered who lived in this magnificent house which he had never seen before, the street in which it stood being one which he seldom had occasion to pass. To satisfy his curiosity he went up to some splendidly dressed servants, who stood at the door, and asked one of them the name of the master of the mansion.

"What," replied he, "do you live in Baghdad and not know that here lives the noble Sinbad the Sailor, that famous traveler who sailed over every sea upon which the sun shines?"

The porter, who had often heard people speak of the immense wealth of Sinbad, could not help feeling envious of one whose lot seemed to be as happy as his own was miserable. Casting his eyes up to the sky he exclaimed aloud:

"Consider, Mighty Creator of all things, the difference between Sinbad's life and mine. Every day I suffer a thousand hardships and misfortunes and have hard work to get even enough barley bread to keep myself and my family alive, while the lucky Sinbad spends money right and left and lives upon the fat of the land! What has he done that you should give him his pleasant life—what have I done to deserve so hard a fate?"

So saying he stamped upon the ground like one beside himself with misery and despair. Just at this moment a servant came out of the palace and, taking him by the arm, said, "Come with me, the noble Sinbad, my master, wishes to speak to you."

Hinbad was not a little surprised at this summons and feared that his unguarded words might have drawn upon him the displeasure of Sinbad, so he tried to excuse himself upon the pretext that he could not leave the burden which had been entrusted to him in the street. However, the lackey promised him it should be taken care of and urged him to obey the call so pressingly that, at last, the porter was obliged to yield.

He followed the servant into a vast room, where a great company was seated round a table covered with all sorts of delicacies. In the place of honor sat a tall, grave man whose long white beard gave him a venerable air. Behind his chair stood a crowd of attendants eager to minister to his wants. This was the famous Sinbad himself. The porter, more than ever alarmed at the sight of so much magnificence, tremblingly saluted the noble company.

Sinbad, making a sign to him to approach, caused him to be seated at his right hand and himself heaped choice morsels upon his plate, and poured out for him a draught of excellent wine and presently, when the banquet drew to a close, spoke to him familiarly, asking his name and occupation.

"My lord," replied the porter, "I am called Hinbad."

"I am glad to see you here," said Sinbad. "And I will answer for the rest of the company that they are equally pleased, but I wish you to tell me what it was that you said just now in the street." For Sinbad, passing by the open window before the feast began, had heard the porter's complaint and therefore had sent for him.

At this question Hinbad was covered with confusion and, hanging down his head, replied, "My lord, I confess that, overcome by weariness and ill humor, I uttered indiscreet words, which I pray you to pardon me."

"Oh," replied Sinbad, "do not imagine that I am so unjust as to blame you. On the contrary, I understand your situation and can pity you. Only you appear to be mistaken about me, and I wish to set you right. You doubtless imagine that I have acquired all the wealth and luxury that you see me enjoy without difficulty or danger, but this is indeed far from being the case. I have only reached this happy state after having for years suffered every possible kind of toil and danger.

"Yes, my noble friends," he continued, addressing the company, "I assure you that my adventures have been strange enough to deter even the most avaricious men from seeking wealth by traversing the seas. Since you have, perhaps, heard but confused accounts of my seven voyages, and the dangers and wonders that I have met with by sea and land, I will now give you a full and true account of them, which I think you will be well pleased to hear."

As Sinbad was relating his adventures chiefly on account of the porter, he ordered, before beginning his tale, that the burden which had been left in the street should be carried by some of his own servants to the place for which Hinbad had set out at first, while he remained to listen to the story.

THE FIRST VOYAGE

I had inherited considerable wealth from my parents and, being young and foolish, I at first squandered it recklessly upon every kind of pleasure. But presently, finding that riches speedily take to themselves wings if managed as badly as I was managing mine, and remembering also that to be old and poor is misery indeed, I began to bethink me of how I could make the best of what still remained to me. I sold all my household goods by public auction and joined a company of merchants who traded by sea, embarked with them at Balsora in a ship which we had fitted out among us.

We set sail and took our course toward the East Indies by the Persian Gulf, having the coast of Persia upon our left hand and upon our right the shores of Arabia Felix. I was at first much troubled by the uneasy motion of the vessel but speedily recovered my health, and since that hour have been no more plagued by seasickness.

From time to time we landed at various islands where we sold or exchanged our merchandise, and one day, when the wind dropped suddenly, we found ourselves becalmed close to a small island which rose only slightly above the surface of the water. Our sails were furled, and the captain gave all who wished permission to land for a while and amuse themselves. I was among the number but when, after strolling about for some time, we lighted a fire and sat down to enjoy the repast which we had brought with us, we were startled by a sudden and

105

violent trembling of the island. At the same moment those left upon the ship set up an outcry, bidding us come on board for our lives, since what we had taken for an island was nothing but the back of a sleeping whale. Those who were nearest to the boat threw themselves into it, others sprang into the sea, but before I could save myself the whale plunged suddenly into the depths of the ocean, leaving me clinging to a piece of wood which we had brought to make our fire.

Meanwhile a breeze had sprung up, and in the confusion that ensued on board our vessel in hoisting the sails and taking up those who were in the boat and clinging to its sides, no one missed me and I was left at the mercy of the waves. All that day I floated up and down, now beaten this way, now that, and when night fell I despaired for my life. But weary and spent as I was, I clung to my frail support, and great was my joy when the morning light showed me that I had drifted against an island.

The cliffs were high and steep, but luckily for me some tree roots protruded in places, and by their aid I climbed up at last and stretched myself upon the turf at the top, where I lay, more dead than alive, till the sun was high in the heavens. By that time I was very hungry, but after some searching I came upon some edible herbs and a spring of clear water, and much refreshed I set out to explore the island. Presently I reached a great plain where a grazing horse was tethered, and as I stood looking at it I heard voices talking, apparently underground. In a moment a man appeared who asked me how I came upon the island.

I told him my adventures and heard in return that he was one of the grooms of Mihrage, the king of the island, and that each year they came to feed their master's horses in this plain. He took me to a cave where his companions were assembled and, when I had eaten the food they set before me, they bade me think myself fortunate to have come upon them when I did, since they were going back to their master on the morrow and, without their aid, I could certainly never have found my way to the inhabited part of the island.

Early the next morning we accordingly set out, and when we reached the capital I was graciously received by the king, to whom I related my adventures. He ordered that I should be well cared for and provided with such things as I needed. Being a merchant I sought out men of my own profession, particularly those who came from foreign countries, as I hoped in this way to hear news from Baghdad and find some means of returning thither; for the capital was situated upon the seashore, and visited by vessels from all parts of the world.

In the meantime I heard many curious things, and answered many questions concerning my own country, for I talked willingly with all who came to me. Also, to while away the time of waiting, I explored a little island named Cassel, which belonged to King Mihrage and was supposed to be inhabited by a spirit named Deggial. Indeed, the sailors assured me that often at night the playing of timbals could be heard upon it. However, I saw nothing strange upon my voyage, saving some fish that were a full two hundred cubits long, but were fortunately even more in dread of us than we of them, and fled from us if we did but strike upon a board to frighten them. Other fishes there were only a cubit long and these had heads like owls.

One day after my return, as I went down to the quay, I saw a ship which had just cast anchor and was discharging her cargo, while the merchants to whom it belonged were busily directing the removal of it to their warehouses. Drawing nearer, I presently noticed that my own name was marked upon some of the packages, and after having carefully examined them, I felt sure that they were indeed those which I had put on board our ship at Balsora. I then recognized the captain of the vessel, but as I was certain that he believed me to be dead, I went up to him and asked who owned the packages at which I was looking.

"There was on board my ship," he replied, "a merchant of Baghdad named Sinbad. One day he and several of my other passengers landed upon what we supposed to be an island but which was really an enormous whale floating asleep upon the waves. No sooner did it feel upon its back the heat of the fire which had been kindled than it

107

plunged into the depths of the sea. Several of the people who were upon it perished in the waters and among others this unlucky Sinbad. This merchandise is his, but I have resolved to dispose of it for the benefit of his family should I ever chance to meet with them."

"Captain," I said, "I am that Sinbad whom you believe to be dead, and these are my possessions!"

When the captain heard these words he cried out in amazement, "Lackaday! What is the world coming to? In these days there is not an honest man to be met with. Did I not with my own eyes see Sinbad drown, and now you have the audacity to tell me that you are he! I should have taken you to be a just man, and yet for the sake of obtaining what does not belong to you, you are ready to invent this horrible falsehood."

"Have patience and do me the favor of hearing my story," said I.

"Speak then," replied the captain, "I'm all attention."

So I told him of my escape and of my fortunate meeting with the king's grooms, and how kindly I had been received at the palace. Very soon I began to see that I had made some impression upon him, and after the arrival of some of the other merchants who showed great joy at once more seeing me alive, he declared that he also recognized me.

Throwing himself upon my neck, he exclaimed, "Heaven be praised that you have escaped from so great a danger. As to your goods, I pray you take them and dispose of them as you please."

I thanked him and praised his honesty, begging him to accept several bales of merchandise in token of my gratitude, but he would take nothing. Of the choicest of my goods I prepared a present for King Mihrage who was at first amazed, having known that I had lost my all. However, when I had explained to him how my bales had been miraculously restored to me, he graciously accepted my gifts and in return gave me many valuable things. I then took leave of him and, exchanging my merchandise for sandal and aloes wood, camphor, nutmegs, cloves, pepper, and ginger, I embarked upon the same vessel and traded so successfully upon our homeward voyage that I arrived in Balsora with about one hundred thousand sequins.

My family received me with as much joy as I felt upon seeing them once more. I bought land and slaves, and built a great house in which I resolved to live happily and in the enjoyment of all the pleasures of life to forget my past sufferings.

Here Sinbad paused and commanded the musicians to play again, while the feasting continued until evening. When the time came for the porter to depart, Sinbad gave him a purse containing one hundred sequins, saying, "Take this, Hinbad, and go home, but tomorrow come again and you shall hear more of my adventures."

The porter retired, quite overcome by so much generosity, and you may imagine that he was well received at home, where his wife and children thanked their lucky stars that he had found such a benefactor.

The next day Hinbad, dressed in his best, returned to the voyager's house and was received with open arms. As soon as all the guests had arrived the banquet began as before, and when they had feasted long and merrily, Sinbad addressed them thus:

"My friends, I beg that you will give me your attention while I relate the adventures of my second voyage, which you will find even more astonishing than the first."

THE SECOND VOYAGE

I had resolved, as you know, on my return from my first voyage, to spend the rest of my days quietly in Baghdad, but very soon I grew tired of such an idle life and longed once more to find myself upon the sea. I procured, therefore, such goods as were suitable for the places I intended to visit and embarked for the second time in a good ship with other merchants whom I knew to be honorable men.

We went from island to island, often making excellent bargains, until one day we landed at a spot which, though covered with fruit trees and abounding in springs of excellent water, appeared to possess neither houses nor people. While my companions wandered here and there gathering flowers and fruit, I sat down in a shady place and, having heartily enjoyed the provisions and the wine I had brought with me, I fell asleep, lulled by the murmur of a clear brook which flowed close by.

How long I slept I know not but, when I opened my eyes and started to my feet, I perceived with horror that I was alone and the ship was gone. I rushed to and fro like one distracted, uttering cries of despair, and when from the shore I saw the vessel under full sail just disappearing upon the horizon, I wished bitterly enough that I had been content to stay at home in safety.

Since wishes could do me no good, I presently took courage and looked about me for a means of escape. When I had climbed a tall tree I first of all directed my anxious glances toward the sea; but, finding nothing hopeful there, I turned landward and my curiosity was excited by a huge dazzling white object, so far off that I could not make out what it might be.

Descending from the tree I hastily collected what remained of my provisions and set off as fast as I could go toward it. As I drew near, it seemed to me to be a white ball of immense size and height, and when I could touch it I found it marvelously smooth and soft. As it was impossible to climb it—for it presented no foothold—I walked round about it, seeking some opening, but there was none. I counted, however, that it was at least fifty paces round.

By this time the sun was near setting, but quite suddenly it fell dark, something like a huge black cloud came swiftly over me and I saw with amazement that it was a bird of extraordinary size which was hovering near. Then I remembered I had often heard the sailors speak of a wonderful bird called a roc, and it occurred to me that the white object which had so puzzled me must be its egg.

110

Sure enough, the bird settled slowly down upon it, covering it with its wings to keep it warm, and I cowered close beside the egg in such a position that one of the bird's feet, which was as large as the trunk of a tree, was just in front of me. Taking off my turban, I bound myself securely to the foot with the linen in the hope that the roc, when it took flight next morning, would bear me away with it from the desolate island. And this was precisely what did happen.

As soon as the dawn appeared the bird rose into the air, carrying me up and up till I could no longer see the earth, and then suddenly it descended so swiftly that I almost lost consciousness. When I became aware that the roc had settled and I was once again upon solid ground, I hastily unbound my turban from its foot and freed myself, and not a moment too soon; for the bird, pouncing upon a huge snake, killed it with a few blows from its powerful beak, and seizing it, rose into the air once more and soon disappeared from my view. When I had looked about me I began to doubt if I had gained anything by quitting the desolate island.

The valley in which I found myself was deep and narrow and surrounded by mountains, which towered into the clouds and were so steep and rocky there was no way of climbing up their sides. As I wandered about, seeking anxiously for some means of escaping from this trap, I observed that the ground was strewn with diamonds, some of them of an astonishing size.

This sight gave me great pleasure, but my delight was speedily dampened when I saw also numbers of horrible snakes so long and so large that the smallest of them could have swallowed an elephant with ease. Fortunately for me they seemed to hide in caverns of the rocks by day, and only came out by night, probably because of their enemy the roc.

All day long I wandered up and down the valley, and when it grew dusk I crept into a little cave. Having blocked up the entrance to it with a stone, I ate part of my little store of food and lay down to sleep, but all through the night the serpents crawled to and fro, hissing horribly, so that I could scarcely close my eyes for terror.

I was thankful when the morning light appeared and, when I judged by the silence that the serpents had retreated to their dens, I came tremblingly out of my cave and wandered up and down the valley once more, kicking the diamonds contemptuously out of my path, for I felt that they were indeed vain things to a man in my situation. At last, overcome with weariness, I sat down upon a rock, but I had hardly closed my eyes when I was startled by something which fell to the ground with a thud close beside me.

It was a huge piece of fresh meat, and as I stared at it several more pieces rolled over the cliffs in different places. I had always thought that the stories the sailors told of the famous valley of diamonds, and of the cunning way which some merchants had devised for getting at the precious stones, were mere travelers' tales invented to give pleasure to the hearers, but now I perceived that they were surely true.

These merchants came to the valley at the time when the eagles, which keep their eyries in the rocks, had hatched their young. The merchants then threw great lumps of meat into the valley. These, falling with so much force upon the diamonds, were sure to take up some of the precious stones with them, when the eagles pounced upon the meat and carried it off to their nests to feed their hungry broods. Then the merchants, scaring away the parent birds with shouts and outcries, would secure their treasures.

Until this moment I had looked upon the valley as my grave, for I had seen no possibility of getting out of it alive, but now I took courage and began to devise a means of escape. I began by picking up all the largest diamonds I could find and storing them carefully in the leathern wallet which had held my provisions; this I tied securely to my belt. I then chose the piece of meat which seemed most suited to my purpose, and with the aid of my turban bound it firmly to my back; this done I lay down upon my face and awaited the coming of the eagles. I soon heard the flapping of their mighty wings above me, and had the satisfaction of feeling one of them seize upon my piece of meat and me with it, and rise slowly toward his nest, into which he presently dropped me.

Luckily for me the merchants were on the watch and, setting up their usual outcries, they rushed to the nest, scaring away the eagle. Their amazement was great when they discovered me, also their disappointment, and with one accord they fell to abusing me for having robbed them of their usual profit.

Addressing myself to the one who seemed most aggrieved, I said, "I am sure, if you knew all I have suffered, you would show more kindness toward me, and as for diamonds, I have enough here of the very best for you and me and all your company." So saying I showed them to him.

The others all crowded round me, wondering at my adventures and admiring the device by which I had escaped from the valley. When they had led me to their camp and examined my diamonds, they assured me that, in all the years they had carried on their trade, they had seen no stones to be compared with them for size and beauty.

I found that each merchant chose a particular nest and took his chance of what he might find in it. So I begged the one who owned the nest to which I had been carried to take as much as he would of my treasure, but he contented himself with one stone and that by no means the largest, assuring me that with such a gem his fortune was made, and he need toil no more. I stayed with the merchants several days, and then as they were journeying homeward I gladly accompanied them.

Our way lay across high mountains infested with frightful serpents, but we had the good luck to escape them and came at last to the seashore. Thence we sailed to the Isle of Roha, where the camphor trees grow to such size a hundred men could shelter under one of them with ease. The sap flows from an incision made high up in the tree into a vessel hung there to receive it and soon hardens into the substance called camphor, but the tree itself withers up and dies when it has been so treated.

In this same island we saw the rhinoceros, an animal which is smaller than the elephant and larger than a buffalo. It has one horn about a cubit long which is solid but has a furrow from the base to the tip. Upon it is traced in white lines the figure of a man. The rhinoceros fights with the elephant and, transfixing him with his horn, carries him off upon his head, but becoming blinded with the blood of his enemy, he falls helpless to the ground. Then comes the roc and clutches them both in his talons and takes them to feed his young.

This doubtless astonishes you but, if you do not believe my tale, go to Roha and see for yourself. For fear of wearying you I pass over in silence many other wonderful things which we saw in this island. Before we left I exchanged one of my diamonds for much goodly merchandise by which I profited greatly on our homeward way. At last we reached Balsora, whence I hastened to Baghdad, where my first action was to bestow large sums of money upon the poor, after which I settled down to enjoy tranquilly the riches I had gained with so much toil and pain.

Having thus related the adventures of his second voyage, Sinbad again bestowed a hundred sequins upon Hinbad, inviting him to come again on the following day and hear how he fared upon his third voyage. The other guests also departed to their homes, but all returned at the same hour next day, including the porter, whose former life of hard work and poverty already seemed to him like a bad dream. Again after the feast was over did Sinbad claim the attention of his guests and began the account of his third voyage.

THE THIRD
VOYAGE

After a very short time the pleasant easy life I led made me quite forget the perils of my two voyages. Moreover, as I was still in the prime of life, it pleased me better to be up and doing. So once more providing myself with the rarest and choicest merchandise of Baghdad, I conveyed it to Balsora and set sail with other merchants of my acquaintance for distant land. We had touched at many ports and made much profit, when one day upon the open sea we were caught by a terrible wind which blew us completely out of our reckoning and, lasting for several days, finally drove us into harbor on a strange island.

"I would rather have come to anchor anywhere than here," quoth our captain. "This island and all adjoining it are inhabited by hairy savages, who are certain to attack us. Whatever these dwarfs may do we dare not resist, since they swarm like locusts, and if one of them is killed the rest will fall upon us and speedily make an end of us."

These words caused great consternation among all the ship's company and only too soon we were to find out that the captain spoke truly. There appeared a vast multitude of hideous savages, not more than two feet high and covered with reddish fur. Throwing themselves into the waves, they surrounded our vessel. Chattering meanwhile in a language we could not understand, and clutching at ropes and gangways, they swarmed up the ship's side with such speed and agility that they almost seemed to fly.

You may imagine the rage and terror that seized us as we watched them, neither daring to hinder them nor able to speak a word to deter them from their purpose, whatever it might be. Of this we were not left long in doubt. Hoisting the sails and cutting the cable of the anchor, they sailed our vessel to an island which lay a little farther off, where they drove us ashore; then taking possession of her, they made off to the place from which they had come, leaving us helpless upon a shore avoided with horror by all mariners for a reason you will soon learn.

Turning away from the sea, we wandered miserably inland, finding as we went various herbs and fruits which we ate, feeling that we might as well live as long as possible though we had no hope of escape. Presently we saw in the far distance what seemed to be a splendid palace toward which we turned our weary steps, but when we reached it we saw that it was a castle, lofty and strongly built. Pushing back the heavy ebony doors, we entered the courtyard, but upon the threshold of the great hall beyond it we paused, frozen with horror, at the sight which greeted us. On one side lay a huge pile of bones—human bones, and on the other numberless spits for roasting!

Overcome with despair we sank trembling to the ground and lay there without speech or motion. The sun was setting when a loud noise aroused us, the door of the hall was violently burst open and a horrible giant entered. He was as tall as a palm tree, perfectly black, and had but one eye, which flamed like a burning coal in the middle of his forehead. His teeth were long and sharp and he grinned horribly, while his lower lip hung down upon his chest, and he had ears like elephant's ears, which covered his shoulders, and nails like the claws of some fierce bird.

At this terrible sight our senses left us and we lay like dead men. When at last we came to ourselves the giant sat examining us attentively with his fearful eye. Presently, when he had looked at us enough, he came toward us and, stretching out his hand, took me by the back of the neck, turning me this way and that, but feeling that I was mere skin and bone he set me down again and went on to the next, whom he treated in the same fashion. At last he came to the captain, and finding him the fattest of us all, he took him up in one hand and stuck him upon a spit and proceeded to kindle a huge fire at which he presently roasted him. After the giant had supped he lay down to sleep, snoring like the loudest thunder, while we lay shivering with horror the whole

The door burst open and a horrible giant entered.

night through. When day broke the giant awoke and went out, leaving us in the castle.

When we believed him to be really gone we started up, bemoaning our horrible fate until the hall echoed with our despairing cries. Though we were many and our enemy was alone it did not occur to us to kill him. Indeed we should have found that a hard task even if we had thought of it, but no plan could we devise to deliver ourselves. So at last, submitting to our sad fate, we spent the day in wandering up and down the island, eating such fruits as we could find, and when night came we returned to the castle, having sought in vain for any other place of shelter.

At sunset the giant returned, supped upon one of our unhappy comrades, slept and snored till dawn, and then left us as before. Our condition seemed to us so frightful that several of my companions thought it would be better to leap from the cliffs and perish in the waves at once, rather than await so miserable an end; but I had a plan of escape which I now unfolded to them, and which they at once agreed to attempt.

"Listen, my brothers," I said, "you know that plenty of driftwood lies along the shore. Let us make several rafts and carry them to a suitable place. If our plot succeeds, we can wait patiently for the chance of some passing ship which would rescue us from this fatal island. If it fails, we must quickly take to our rafts; frail as they are, we have more chance of saving our lives with them than we have if we remain here."

All agreed with me, and we spent the day in building rafts, each capable of carrying three persons. At nightfall we returned to the castle, and very soon in came the giant and one more of our number was sacrificed. But the time of our vengeance was at hand! As soon as he had finished his horrible repast he lay down to sleep as before, and when we heard him begin to snore I, and nine of the boldest of my comrades, rose softly and each took a spit, which we made red-hot in the fire, and then at a given signal we plunged it with one accord into the giant's eye, completely blinding him. Uttering a terrible cry, he sprang to his feet, clutching in all directions to try to seize one of us, but we had all fled different ways as soon as the deed was done and thrown ourselves flat upon the ground in corners where he was not likely to touch us with his feet.

After a vain search he fumbled about till he found the door and fled out of it, howling frightfully. As for us, when he was gone we made haste to leave the fatal castle and, stationing ourselves beside our rafts, we waited to see what would happen.

Our idea was that if, when the sun rose, we saw nothing of the giant and no longer heard his howls, which still came faintly through the darkness, growing more and more distant, we should conclude that he was dead and that we might safely stay upon the island and need not risk our lives upon the frail rafts. But alas! morning light showed us our enemy approaching, supported on either hand by two giants nearly as large and fearful as himself, while a crowd of others followed close upon their heels. Hesitating no longer, we clambered upon our rafts and rowed with all our might out to sea.

The giants, seeing their prey escaping them, seized huge pieces of rock and, wading into the water, hurled them after us with such good aim that all the rafts except the one I was on were swamped and their luckless crews drowned, without our being able to do anything to help them. Indeed I and my two companions had all we could do to keep our own raft beyond the reach of the giants, but by dint of hard rowing we at last gained the open sea. Here we were at the mercy of the winds and waves, which tossed us to and fro all that day and night, but the next morning we found ourselves near an island, upon which we gladly landed.

There we found delicious fruits, and having satisfied our hunger, we presently lay down to rest upon the shore. Suddenly we were aroused by a loud rustling noise and, starting up, saw that it was caused by an immense snake which was gliding toward us over the sand. So swiftly it came that it had seized one of my comrades before he had time to fly and, in spite of his cries and struggles, speedily crushed him in its mighty coils and proceeded to swallow him.

By this time my other companion and I were running for our lives to some place where we might hope to be safe from this new horror. Seeing a tall tree we climbed up into it, having first provided ourselves with a store of fruit off the surrounding bushes. When night came I fell asleep, only to be awakened once more by the terrible snake which, after hissing horribly round the tree, at last reared itself up against it and finding my comrade who was perched just below me, it swallowed him also, and crawled away, leaving me half-dead with terror.

When the sun rose I crept down from the tree, with hardly a hope of escaping the dreadful fate which had overtaken my comrades; but life is sweet, and I determined to do all I could to save myself. All day long I toiled with frantic haste and collected quantities of dry brushwood, reeds and thorns which I bound with fagots and, making a circle of them under my tree, I piled them firmly one upon another until I had a kind of tent in which I crouched, like a mouse in a hole when she sees the cat coming.

You may imagine what a fearful night I passed, for the snake returned eager to devour me, and glided round and round my frail shelter seeking an entrance. Every moment I feared that it would succeed in pushing aside some of the fagots, but happily for me they held together, and when it grew light my enemy retired, baffled and hungry, to his den. As for me I was more dead than alive!

Shaking with fright and half-suffocated by the poisonous breath of the monster, I came out of my tent and crawled down to the sea, feeling that it would be better to plunge from the cliffs and end my life at once than pass another night of such horror. But to my joy and relief I saw a ship sailing by and, by shouting wildly and waving my turban, I managed to attract the attention of her crew.

A boat was sent to rescue me, and very soon I found myself on board surrounded by a wondering crowd of sailors and merchants eager to know by what chance I found myself on that desolate island. After I had told my story they regaled me with the choicest food the ship afforded and the captain, seeing that I was in rags, generously bestowed upon me one of his own coats. After sailing about for some time and touching at many ports we came at last to the Island of Salahat, where sandalwood grows in great abundance.

Here we anchored, and as I stood watching the merchants disembarking their goods and preparing to sell or exchange them, the captain came up to me and said, "I have here, Brother, some merchandise belonging to a passenger of mine who is dead. Will you do me the favor to trade with it, and when I meet with his heirs I shall be able to give them the money, though it will be only just that you shall have a portion for your trouble."

I consented gladly, for I did not like standing by idle. Whereupon he pointed the bales out to me and sent for the person whose duty it was to keep a list of the goods that were upon the ship. When this man came he asked in what name the merchandise was to be registered.

"In the name of Sinbad the Sailor," replied the captain.

At this I was greatly surprised, but looking carefully at him I recognized him to be the captain of the ship upon which I had made my second voyage, though he had altered much since that time. As for him, believing me to be dead, it was no wonder that he had not recognized me.

"So, Captain," said I, "the merchant who owned those bales was called Sinbad?"

"Yes," he replied, "he was so named. He belonged to Baghdad and joined my ship at Balsora, but by mischance he was left behind upon a desert island where we had landed to fill up our water casks, and it was not until four hours later that he was missed. By that time the wind had freshened and it was impossible to put back for him."

"You suppose him to have perished then?" said I.

"Alas, yes," he answered.

"Why, Captain," I cried, "look well at me! I am that Sinbad who fell asleep upon the island and awoke to find himself abandoned."

The captain stared at me in amazement, but was presently convinced that I was indeed speaking the truth and rejoiced greatly at my escape.

"I am glad to have that piece of carelessness off my conscience at any rate," said he. "Now take your goods and the profit I have made for you upon them, and may you prosper in the future."

I took them gratefully, and as we went from one island to another I laid in stores of cloves, cinnamon, and other spices. In one place I saw a tortoise which was twenty cubits long and as many broad, also a fish that was like a cow and had skin so thick it was used to make shields. Another I saw was like a camel in shape and color. So by degrees we came back to Balsora, and I returned to Baghdad with so much money that I could not myself count it, besides treasures without end. I gave largely to the poor and bought much land to add to what I already possessed, and thus ended my third voyage.

When Sinbad had finished his story he gave another hundred sequins to Hinbad, who then departed with the other guests, but next day when they had all reassembled and the banquet was ended, their host continued his adventures.

THE FOURTH VOYAGE

Rich and happy as I was after my third voyage, I could not make up my mind to stay at home altogether. My love of trading and the pleasure I took in anything that was new and strange made me set my affairs in order and begin my journey through some of the Persian provinces, having first sent off stores of goods to await my coming in the different places I intended to visit. I took ship at a distant seaport, and for some time all went well, but at last, being caught in a violent hurricane, our vessel became a total wreck in spite of all our worthy captain could do to save her, and many of our company perished in the waves. I, with a few others, had the good fortune to be washed ashore clinging to pieces of the wreck, for the storm had driven us near an island; and scrambling up beyond the reach of the waves, we threw ourselves down quite exhausted, to wait for morning.

At daylight we wandered inland and soon saw some huts, to which we directed our steps. As we drew near, their inhabitants swarmed out in great numbers and surrounded us, and we were led to their houses and divided among our captors. I with five others was taken into a hut, where we were made to sit upon the ground, and certain herbs were given to us, which our captors made signs to us to eat.

Observing that they themselves did not touch them, I was careful only to pretend to taste my portion; but my companions, being very hungry, rashly ate all that was set before them, and very soon I had the horror of seeing them become perfectly mad. Though they chattered incessantly I could not understand a word they said, nor did they heed when I spoke to them. The savages now produced large bowls full of rice prepared with coconut oil, of which my crazy comrades ate eagerly, but I only tasted a few grains, understanding clearly that the object of our captors was to fatten us speedily for their own eating, and this was exactly what happened.

My unlucky companions, having lost their reason, felt neither anxiety nor fear and ate greedily all that was offered them. So they were soon fat and there was an end of them, but I grew leaner day by day, for I ate but little, and even that little did me no good by reason of my fear of what lay before me. However, as I was so far from being a tempting morsel, I was allowed to wander about freely, and one day, when all the savages had gone off upon some expedition leaving only an old man to guard me, I managed to escape from him and plunged into the forest, running faster the more he cried to me to come back, until I had completely distanced him.

For seven days I hurried on, resting only when the darkness stopped me, and living chiefly upon coconuts, which afforded me both meat and drink, and on the eighth day I reached the seashore and saw a party of men gathering pepper, which grew abundantly all about. Reassured by the nature of their occupation, I advanced toward them and they greeted me in Arabic, asking who I was and whence I came. My delight was great on hearing this familiar speech, and I willingly satisfied their curiosity, telling them how I had been shipwrecked and captured.

"But these savages devour men!" said they. "How did you escape?" I repeated to them what I have just told you, at which they were mightily astonished. I stayed with them until they had collected as much pepper as they wished, and then they took me back to their own country and presented me to their king, by whom I was hospitably received. To him also I had to relate my adventures, which surprised him much, and when I had finished he ordered that I should be supplied with food and raiment and treated with consideration.

The island on which I found myself was full of people and abounded in all sorts of desirable things, and a great deal of traffic went on in the capital, where I soon began to feel at home and contented. Moreover, the king treated me with special favor and in consequence of this everyone, whether at the court or in the town, sought to make life pleasant to me.

One thing I remarked which I thought very strange; from the greatest to the least, all men rode their horses without bridle or stirrups. I one day presumed to ask His Majesty why he did not use them, to which he replied, "You speak to me of things of which I have never before heard!"

This gave me an idea. I found a clever workman and made him cut out, under my direction, the foundation of a saddle, which I wadded and covered with choice leather, adorning it with rich gold embroidery. I then had a locksmith make me a bit and a pair of spurs after a pattern that I drew for him, and when all these things were completed I presented them to the king and showed him how to use them.

When I had saddled one of his horses he mounted it and rode about, quite delighted with the novelty, and to show his gratitude he rewarded me with large gifts. After this I had to make saddles for all the principal officers of the king's household, and as they all gave me rich presents I soon became very wealthy and quite an important person in the city.

One day the king sent for me and said, "Sinbad, I am going to ask a favor of you. Both I and my subjects esteem you, and wish you to end your days among us. Therefore, I desire you to marry a rich and beautiful lady I will find for you and think no more of your own country."

As the king's will was law I accepted the charming bride he presented to me and lived happily with her. Nevertheless, I had every intention of escaping at the first opportunity and going back to Baghdad. Things were thus going prosperously with me when it happened that the wife of one of my neighbors, with whom I had struck up quite a friendship, fell ill and presently died. I went to his house to offer my consolations and found him in the depths of woe.

"Heaven preserve you," said I, "and send you a long life!"

"Alas!" he replied. "What is the good of saying that when I have but an hour left to live!"

"Come, come!" said I. "Surely it is not so bad as all that. I trust that you may be spared to me for many years."

"I hope," answered he, "that your life may be long, but as for me, all is finished. I have set my house in order, and today I shall be buried with my wife. This has been the law upon our island from the earliest ages—the living husband goes to the grave with his dead wife, the living wife with her dead husband. So did our fathers and so must we do. The law changes not and all must submit to it!"

As he spoke the friends and relations of the unhappy pair began to assemble. The body, decked in rich robes and sparkling with jewels, was laid upon an open bier, and the procession started, taking its way to a high mountain at some distance from the city, the wretched husband, clothed from head to foot in a black mantle, following mournfully.

When the place of interment was reached the corpse was lowered, just as it was, into a deep pit. Then the husband, bidding farewell to all his friends, stretched himself upon another bier, upon which were laid seven little loaves of bread and a pitcher of water, and he was also let down, down, down to the depths of the horrible cavern, and then a stone was laid over the opening, and the melancholy company wended its way back to the city.

You may imagine that I was no unmoved spectator of these proceedings. All the others were accustomed to it from their youth up, but I was so horrified that I could not help telling the king how it struck me.

"Sire," I said, "I am more astonished than I can express to you at the strange custom which exists in your dominions of burying the living with the dead. In all my travels I have never before met with so cruel and horrible a law."

"What would you have, Sinbad?" he replied. "It is the law for everybody. I myself should be buried with the queen if she were the first to die."

"But, Your Majesty," said I, "dare I ask if this law applies to foreigners also?"

"Why, yes," replied the king, smiling in what I could but consider a very heartless manner, "they are no exception to the rule if they have married in the country."

When I heard this I went home much cast down, and from that time forward my mind was never easy. If only my wife's little finger ached I fancied she was going to die, and sure enough before very long she fell really ill and in a few days breathed her last.

My dismay was great, for it seemed to me that to be buried alive was even a worse fate than to be devoured by cannibals; nevertheless, there was no escape. The body of my wife, arrayed in her richest robes and decked with all her jewels, was laid upon the bier. I followed it, and after me came a great procession, headed by the king and all his nobles, and in this order we reached the fatal mountain, one of a lofty chain bordering the sea.

126

Here I made one more frantic effort to excite the pity of the king and those who stood by, hoping to save myself even at this last moment, but it was of no avail. No one spoke to me; they even appeared to hasten over their dreadful task, and I speedily found myself descending into the gloomy pit, with my seven loaves and pitcher of water beside me. Almost before I reached the bottom the stone was rolled into its place above my head, and I was left to my fate.

A feeble ray of light shone into the cavern through some chink, and when I had the courage to look about me I could see that I was in a vast vault, bestrewn with the bones of the dead. I even fancied that I heard the expiring sighs of those who, like myself, had come into this dismal place alive. All in vain did I shriek aloud with rage and despair, reproaching myself for the love of gain and adventure which had brought me to such a pass; but at length, growing calmer, I took up my bread and water and, wrapping my face in my mantle, groped my way toward the end of the cavern, where the air was fresher.

Here I lived in darkness and misery until my provisions were exhausted, but just as I was nearly dead from starvation the rock was rolled away overhead and I saw that a bier was being lowered into the cavern, and that the corpse upon it was a man. In a moment my mind was made up; the woman who followed had nothing to expect but a lingering death; I should be doing her a service if I shortened her misery. Therefore when she descended, already insensible from terror, I was ready armed with a huge bone, one blow from which left her dead, and I secured the bread and water which gave me a hope of life.

Several times did I have recourse to this desperate expedient, and I know not how long I had been a prisoner, when one day I fancied that I heard something near me which breathed loudly. Turning to the place from which the sound came I dimly saw a shadowy form which fled at my movement, squeezing itself through a cranny in the wall. I pursued it as fast as I could and found myself in a narrow crack among the rocks, along which I was just able to force my way. I followed it for what seemed to me many miles and, at last, saw before me a glimmer of light which grew clearer every moment until I emerged upon the seashore with a joy which I cannot describe. When I was sure that I was not dreaming, I realized that it was doubtless some little animal which had found its way into the cavern from the sea and when disturbed had fled, showing me a means of escape which I could never have discovered for myself. I hastily surveyed my surroundings and saw that I was safe from all pursuit from the town.

The mountains sloped sheer down to the sea and there was no road across them. Being assured of this I returned to the cavern and amassed a rich treasure of diamonds, rubies, emeralds, and jewels of all kinds which strewed the ground. These I made up into bales, stored them in a safe place upon the beach, and then waited hopefully for the passing of a ship.

I had looked out for two days, however, before a single sail appeared, so it was with much delight that I at last saw a vessel not very far from the shore, and by waving my arms and uttering loud cries succeeded in attracting the attention of her crew. A boat was sent off to me, and in answer to the questions of the sailors as to how I came to be in such a plight, I replied that I had been shipwrecked two days before but had managed to scramble ashore with the bales which I pointed out to them.

Luckily for me they believed my story and, without even looking at the place where they found me, took up my bundles and rowed me back to the ship. Once on board, I soon saw that the captain was too much occupied with the difficulties of navigation to pay much heed to me, though he generously made me welcome and would not even accept the jewels with which I offered to pay my passage.

Our voyage was prosperous, and after visiting many lands, and collecting in each place great store of goodly merchandise, I found myself at last in Baghdad once more with unheard-of riches of every description. Again I gave large sums of money to the poor and enriched all the mosques in the city, after which I gave myself up to my friends and relations, with whom I passed my time in feasting and merriment.

Here Sinbad paused, and all his hearers declared that the adventures of his fourth voyage had pleased them better than anything they had heard before. They then took their leave, followed by Hinbad who had once more received a hundred sequins and with the rest had been bidden to return next day for the story of the fifth voyage.

When the time came all were in their places and, when they had eaten and drunk of all that was set before them, Sinbad began his tale.

THE FIFTH VOYAGE

Not even all that I had gone through could make me contented with a quiet life. I soon wearied of its pleasures and longed for change and adventure. Therefore I set out once more, but this time in a ship of my own, which I built and fitted out at the nearest seaport. I wished to be able to call at whatever port I chose, taking my own time; but as I did not intend carrying enough goods for a full cargo, I invited several merchants of different nations to join me. We set sail with the first favorable wind, and after a long voyage upon the open seas we landed upon an unknown island which proved to be uninhabited.

We determined, however, to explore it, but had not gone far when we found a roc's egg, as large as the one I had seen before and evidently very nearly hatched, for the beak of the young bird had already pierced the shell. In spite of all I could say to deter them, the merchants who were with me fell upon it with their hatchets, breaking the shell, and killing the young roc. Then lighting a fire upon the ground, they hacked morsels from the bird and proceeded to roast them while I stood by aghast.

Scarcely had they finished their ill-omened repast, when the air above us was darkened by two mighty shadows. The captain of my ship, knowing by experience what this meant, cried out to us that the parent birds were coming and urged us to get on board with all speed. This we did, and the sails were hoisted but, before we had made any way, the rocs reached their despoiled nest and hovered about it, uttering frightful cries when they discovered the mangled remains of their young one. For a moment we lost sight of them and were flattering ourselves that we had escaped, when they reappeared and soared into the air directly over our vessel, and we saw that each held in its claws an immense rock ready to crush us.

There was a moment of breathless suspense; then one bird loosed its hold and the huge block of stone hurtled through the air; but thanks to the presence of mind of the helmsman, who turned our ship violently in another direction, it fell into the sea close beside us, cleaving it asunder till we could nearly see the bottom. We had hardly time to draw a breath of relief before the other rock fell with a mighty crash right in the midst of our luckless vessel, smashing it into a thousand fragments, and crushing, or hurling into the sea, passengers and crew.

I myself went down with the rest, but had the good fortune to rise unhurt and, by holding onto a piece of driftwood with one hand and swimming with the other, I kept myself afloat and was presently washed up by the tide onto an island. Its shores were steep and rocky, but I scrambled up safely and threw myself down to rest upon the green turf.

When I had somewhat recovered I began to examine the spot in which I found myself, and truly it seemed to me that I had reached a garden of delights. There were trees everywhere, laden with flowers and fruit, while a crystal stream wandered in and out under their shadow. When night came I slept sweetly in a cozy nook, though the remembrance that I was alone in a strange land made me sometimes start up and look around me in alarm, and then I wished heartily that I had stayed at home.

However, the morning sunlight restored my courage and I once more wandered among the trees, but always with some anxiety as to what I might see next. I had penetrated some distance into the island when I saw an old man, bent and feeble, sitting upon the riverbank. At first I took him to be some shipwrecked mariner like myself. Going up to him I greeted him in a friendly way but he only nodded his head at me in reply. I then asked what he did there, and he made signs to me that he wished to get across the river to gather some fruit and seemed to beg me to carry him on my back.

Pitying his age and feebleness, I took him up and, wading across the stream, I bent down that he might more easily reach the bank and bade him get down. But instead of allowing himself to be set upon his feet (even now it makes me laugh to think of it) this creature, who had seemed to me so decrepit, leaped nimbly upon my shoulders, and hooking his legs round my neck gripped me so tightly that I was well-nigh choked, and so overcome with terror that I fell insensible to the ground.

When I recovered, my enemy was still in his place, though he had released his hold enough to allow me breathing space, and seeing me revive, he prodded me adroitly first with one foot and then with the other, until I was forced to get up and stagger about with him under the trees while he gathered and ate the choicest fruits. This went on all day and even at night, when I threw myself down half-dead with weariness, the terrible old man held on tight to my neck, nor did he fail to greet the first glimmer of morning light by drumming upon me with his heels, until I perforce awoke and resumed my dreary march with rage and bitterness in my heart.

It happened one day that I passed a tree under which lay several dry gourds. Catching one up I amused myself with scooping out its contents and pressing into it the juice of several bunches of the grapes which hung from every vine. When it was full I left it propped in the fork of a tree, and a few days later, carrying the hateful old man that way, I snatched at my gourd as I passed it and had the satisfaction of a draught of excellent wine so good and refreshing that I even forgot my detestable burden and began to sing and caper.

The old monster was not slow to perceive the effect which my draught had produced and that I carried him more lightly than usual, so he stretched out his skinny hand and seizing the gourd first tasted its contents cautiously, then drained them to the very last drop. The wine was strong and the gourd capacious, so he also began to sing, after a fashion. Soon I had the delight of feeling the iron grip of his goblin legs unclasp, and with one vigorous effort I threw him to the ground, from which he did not move again. I was so rejoiced to have at last got rid of this uncanny old man that I ran leaping and bounding down to the seashore where, by the greatest good luck, I met with some mariners who had anchored off the island to enjoy the delicious fruits and to renew their supply of water.

They heard the story of my escape with amazement, saying, "You fell into the hands of the Old Man of the Sea, and it is a mercy that he did not strangle you as he has everyone else upon whose shoulders he has managed to perch himself. This island is well known as the scene of his evil deeds and no merchant or sailor who lands upon it cares to stray far away from his comrades."

After we had talked for a while they took me back with them on board their ship, where the captain received me kindly. We soon set sail, and after several days reached a large and prosperous-looking town where all the houses were built of stone. Here we anchored, and one of the merchants, who had been very friendly to me on the way, took me ashore with him and showed me a lodging set apart for strange merchants. He then provided me with a large sack and pointed out to me a party of others equipped in like manner.

"Go with them," said he, "and do as they do, but beware of losing sight of them, for if you strayed, your life would be in danger."

With that he supplied me with provisions, bade me farewell, and I set out with my new companions. I soon learnt that the object of our expedition was to fill our sacks with coconuts, but when at length I saw

"Pitying his age and feebleness, I carried him on my back."

the trees and noted their immense height and the slippery smoothness of their slender trunks, I did not at all understand how we were to do it. The crowns of the coco palms were alive with monkeys, big and little, which skipped from one to the other with surprising agility, seeming to be curious about us and disturbed at our appearance. I was at first surprised when my companions after collecting stones began to throw them at the lively creatures, which seemed to me quite harmless. But very soon I saw the reason of it and joined them heartily, for the monkeys, annoyed and wishing to pay us back in our own coin, began to tear the nuts from the trees and cast them at us with angry and spiteful gestures, so after very little labor our sacks were filled with the fruit which we could not otherwise have obtained.

As soon as we had as many coconuts as we could carry we went back to the town, where my friend bought my share and advised me to continue the same occupation until I had earned money enough to carry me to my own country. This I did and before long had amassed a considerable sum.

Just then I heard that there was a trading ship ready to sail. Taking leave of my friend, I went on board, carrying with me a goodly store of coconuts; and we sailed first to the islands where pepper grows, then to Comari where the best aloes wood is found, and where men drink no wine by an unalterable law. Here I exchanged my nuts for pepper and good aloes wood, and went fishing for pearls with some of the other merchants, and my divers were so lucky that very soon I had an immense number and those very large and perfect. With all these treasures I came joyfully back to Baghdad, where I disposed of them for large sums of money, of which I did not fail as before to give the tenth part to the poor, and after that I rested from my labors and comforted myself with all the pleasures that my riches could give me.

Having thus ended his story, Sinbad ordered that one hundred sequins should be given to Hinbad, and the guests then withdrew; but after the next day's feast he began the account of his sixth voyage as follows.

THE SIXTH VOYAGE

It must be a marvel to you how, after having five times met with shipwreck and unheard-of perils, I could again tempt fortune and risk fresh troubles. I am even surprised myself when I look back, but evidently it was my fate to rove, and after a year of repose I prepared to make a sixth voyage, regardless of the entreaties of my friends and relations, who did all they could to keep me at home. Instead of going by the Persian Gulf, I traveled a considerable way overland and finally embarked from a distant Indian port with a captain who meant to make a long voyage. And truly he did so, for we fell in with stormy weather which drove us completely off our course, so for many days neither captain nor pilot knew where we were nor where we were going.

When they did at last discover our position we had small ground for rejoicing, for the captain, casting his turban upon the deck and tearing his beard, declared that we were in the most dangerous spot upon the whole wide sea and had been caught by a current which was at that minute sweeping us to destruction. It was too true! In spite of all the sailors could do we were driven with frightful rapidity toward the foot of a mountain which rose sheer out of the sea, and our vessel was dashed to pieces upon the rocks at its base; not, however, before we had managed to scramble on shore, carrying with us the most precious of our possessions.

When we had done this the captain said to us, "Now we are here, we may as well begin to dig our graves at once, since from this fatal spot no shipwrecked mariner has ever returned."

This speech discouraged us much, and we began to lament over our sad fate.

The mountain formed the seaward boundary of a large island, and the narrow strip of rocky shore upon which we stood was strewn with the wreckage of a thousand gallant ships, while the bones of luckless mariners shone white in the sunshine, and we shuddered to think how soon our own would be added to the heap.

All around, too, lay vast quantities of the costliest merchandise, and treasures were heaped in every cranny of the rocks, but all these things only added to the desolation of the scene. It struck me as very strange that a river of clear fresh water, which gushed out from the mountain not far from where we stood, instead of flowing into the sea as rivers generally do, turned off sharply and flowed out of sight under a natural archway of rock; and when I went to examine it more closely I found that inside the cave the walls were thick with diamonds and rubies and masses of crystal and the floor was strewn with ambergris.

Here, then, upon this desolate shore we abandoned ourselves to our fate, for there was no possibility of scaling the mountain, and if a ship had appeared it could only have shared our doom. The first thing our captain did was to divide equally among us all the food we possessed, and then the length of each man's life depended on the time he could make his portion last. I myself could live upon very little.

Nevertheless, by the time I had buried the last of my companions my stock of provisions was so small I hardly thought I should live long enough to dig my own grave, which I set about doing. I regretted bitterly the roving disposition which was always bringing me into such straits and thought longingly of all the comfort and luxury I had left. But luckily for me the fancy took me to stand once more beside the river where it plunged out of sight in the depths of the cavern, and as I did so an idea struck me.

This river which hid itself underground doubtless emerged again at some distant spot. Why should I not build a raft and trust myself to its swiftly flowing waters? If I perished before I could reach the light of day once more I should be no worse off than I was now, for death stared me in the face, while there was always the possibility that, as I was born under a lucky star, I might find myself safe and sound in some desirable land. I decided at any rate to risk it, and speedily built myself a stout raft of driftwood with strong cords, of which enough and to spare lay strewn upon the beach. I then made up many packages of rubies, emeralds, rock crystal, ambergris and precious stuffs, and bound them upon my raft, being careful to preserve the balance. Then I seated myself upon it, having two small oars that I had fashioned laid ready to my hand, and loosed the cord which held it to the bank.

Once out in the current my raft flew swiftly under the gloomy archway, and I found myself in total darkness, carried smoothly forward by the rapid river. On I went as it seemed to me for many nights and days. Once the channel became so small that I had a narrow escape from being crushed against the rocky roof, and after that I took the precaution of lying flat upon my precious bales. Though I only ate what was absolutely necessary to keep myself alive, the inevitable moment came when, after swallowing my last morsel of food, I began to wonder if I must after all die of hunger.

Then, worn out with anxiety and fatigue, I fell into a deep sleep and when I again opened my eyes I was once more in the light of day; a beautiful country lay before me and my raft, which was tied to the river-bank, was surrounded by friendly black men. I rose and saluted them, and they spoke to me in return, but I could not understand a word of their language. Feeling perfectly bewildered by my sudden return to life and light, I murmured to myself in Arabic, "Close thine eyes, and while thou sleepest Heaven will change thy fortune from evil to good."

One of the natives, who understood this tongue, then came forward, saying, "My brother, be not surprised to see us; this is our land, and as we came to get water from the river we noticed your raft floating down it, and one of us swam out and brought you to the shore. We have waited for your awakening; tell us now whence you come and where you were going by that dangerous way?"

I replied that nothing would please me better than to tell them, but that I was starving and would fain eat something first. I was soon supplied with all I needed and, having satisfied my hunger, I told them faithfully all that had befallen me.

They were lost in wonder at my tale when it was interpreted to them and said that adventures so surprising must be related to their king only by the man to whom they had happened. So, procuring a horse, they mounted me upon it, and we set out, followed by several strong men carrying my raft just as it was upon their shoulders. In this order we marched into the city of Serendib, where the natives presented me to their king, whom I saluted in the Indian fashion, prostrating myself at his feet and kissing the ground; but the monarch bade me rise and sit beside him, asking first what was my name.

"I am Sinbad," I replied, "whom men call 'the Sailor,' for I have voyaged much upon many seas."

"And how come you here?" asked the king.

I told my story, concealing nothing, and his surprise and delight were so great that he ordered my adventures to be written in letters of gold and laid up in the archives of his kingdom.

Presently my raft was brought in, the bales opened in his presence, and the king declared that in all his treasury there were no such rubies and emeralds as those which lay in great heaps before him.

Seeing that he looked at them with interest, I ventured to say that I myself and all that I had were at his disposal, but he answered me, smiling, "Nay, Sinbad. Heaven forbid that I should covet your riches; I will rather add to them, for I desire that you shall not leave my kingdom without some tokens of my goodwill."

He then commanded his officers to provide me with a suitable lodging at his expense and sent slaves to wait upon me and carry my raft and my bales to my new dwelling place. You may imagine that I praised his generosity and gave him grateful thanks; nor did I fail to present myself daily in his audience chamber, and for the rest of my time I amused myself in seeing all that was most worthy of attention in the city.

The Island of Serendib being situated on the equinoctial line, the days and nights there are of equal length. The chief city is placed at the end of a beautiful valley, formed by the highest mountain in the world, which is in the middle of the island. I had the curiosity to ascend to its very summit, for this was the place to which Adam was banished out of Paradise. Here are found rubies and many precious things, and rare plants grow abundantly, also cedar trees and coco palms. On the seashore and at the mouths of the rivers the divers seek for pearls, and in some valleys diamonds are plentiful.

After many days I petitioned the king that I might return to my own country, to which he graciously consented. Moreover, he loaded me with rich gifts, and when I went to take leave of him he entrusted me with a royal present and a letter to the Commander of the Faithful, our sovereign lord, saying, "I pray you give these to the Caliph Harun al-Rashid, and assure him of my friendship."

I accepted the charge respectfully and soon embarked upon the vessel which the king himself had chosen for me. The king's letter was written in blue characters upon a rare and precious skin of yellow color, and these were the words of it:

"The King of the Indies, before whom walk a thousand elephants, who lives in a palace the roof of which blazes with a hundred thousand rubies, and whose treasure house contains twenty thousand diamond crowns, to the Caliph Harun al-Rashid sends greeting. Though the offering we present to you is unworthy of your notice, we pray you to accept it as a mark of the esteem and friendship which we cherish for you, and of which we gladly send you this token, and we ask of you a like regard if you deem us worthy of it. Adieu, Brother."

The present consisted of a vase carved from a single ruby, six inches high and as thick as my finger; this was filled with the choicest pearls, large, and of perfect shape and luster; secondly, a huge snakeskin, with scales as large as a sequin, which would preserve from sickness those who slept upon it. Then quantities of aloes wood, camphor and pistachio nuts and, lastly, a beautiful slave girl, whose robes glittered with precious stones.

After a long and prosperous voyage we landed at Balsora, and I made haste to reach Baghdad. Taking the king's letter, I presented myself at the palace gate, followed by the beautiful slave and various members of my own family, bearing the treasure.

As soon as I had declared my errand I was conducted into the presence of the caliph, to whom, after I had made my obeisance, I gave the letter and the king's gift. When he had examined them he demanded of me whether the Prince of Serendib was really as rich and powerful as he claimed to be.

"Commander of the Faithful," I replied, again bowing humbly before him, "I can assure Your Majesty that he has in no way exaggerated his wealth and grandeur. Nothing can equal the magnificence of his palace. When he goes abroad, his throne is prepared upon the back of an elephant, and on either side of him ride his ministers, his favorites, and courtiers. On his elephant's neck sits an officer, his golden lance in his hand, and behind him stands another bearing a pillar of gold, at the top of which is an emerald as long as my hand.

"A thousand men in cloth of gold, mounted upon richly caparisoned elephants, go before him, and as the procession moves onward the officer who guides his elephant cries aloud, 'Behold the mighty monarch, the powerful and valiant Sultan of the Indies, whose palace is covered with a hundred thousand rubies, who possesses twenty thousand diamond crowns. Behold a monarch greater than Solomon and Mihrage in all their glory.'

"Then the one who stands behind the throne answers, 'This king, so great and powerful, must die, must die, must die!'

"And the first takes up the chant again, 'All praise to Him who lives forevermore.'

"Further, my lord, in Serendib no judge is needed, for to the king himself his people come for justice."

The caliph was well satisfied with my report. "From the king's letter," said he, "I judged that he was a wise man. It seems that he

140

is worthy of his people, and his people of him." So saying he dismissed me with rich presents and I returned in peace to my own house.

When Sinbad had done speaking his guests withdrew, Hinbad having first received a hundred sequins; but all returned next day to hear the story of the seventh voyage. Sinbad thus began.

THE SEVENTH VOYAGE

After my sixth voyage I was quite determined that I would go to sea no more. I was now of an age to appreciate a quiet life and I had run risks enough. I only wished to end my days in peace. One day, however, when I was entertaining a number of my friends, I was told that an officer of the caliph wished to speak to me. When he was admitted he bade me follow him into the presence of Harun al-Rashid, which I accordingly did.

After I had saluted him, the caliph said, "I have sent for you, Sinbad, because I need your services. I have chosen you to bear a letter and a gift to the King of Serendib in return for his message of friendship."

The caliph's commandment fell upon me like a thunderbolt. "Commander of the Faithful," I answered, "I am ready to do all that Your Majesty commands, but I humbly pray you to remember that I am utterly disheartened by the unheard-of sufferings I have undergone. Indeed, I have made a vow never again to leave Baghdad."

With this I gave him a long account of some of my strangest adventures, to which he listened patiently.

"I admit," said he, "that you have indeed had some extraordinary experiences, but I do not see why they should hinder you from doing as I wish. You have only to go straight to Serendib and give my message, then you are free to come back and do as you will. But go you must; my honor and dignity demand it."

Seeing there was no help for it, I declared myself willing to obey; and the caliph, delighted at having got his own way, gave me a thousand sequins for the expenses of the voyage. I was soon ready to start and, taking the letter and the present, embarked at Balsora and sailed quickly and safely to Serendib. Here, when I had disclosed my errand, I was well received and brought into the presence of the king, who greeted me with joy.

"Welcome, Sinbad," he cried. "I have thought of you often, and rejoice to see you once more."

After thanking him for the honor he did me, I displayed the caliph's gifts: first a bed with complete hangings of cloth of gold, which cost a thousand sequins, and another like to it of crimson stuff; fifty robes of rich embroidery, a hundred of the finest white linen from Cairo, Suez, Cufa, and Alexandria; then more beds of different fashion; and an agate vase carved with the figure of a man aiming an arrow at a lion; and finally a costly table, which had once belonged to King Solomon.

The King of Serendib received with satisfaction the assurance of the caliph's friendliness toward him, and now my task being accomplished I was anxious to depart, although it was some time before the king would think of letting me go. At last, however, he dismissed me with many presents and I lost no time in going on board a ship, which sailed at once, and for four days all went well.

On the fifth day we had the misfortune to fall in with pirates who seized our vessel, killing all who resisted and making prisoners of those who were prudent enough to submit at once, of whom I was one. When they had despoiled us of all we possessed, they forced us to put on vile raiment and, sailing to a distant island, there sold us for slaves.

I fell into the hands of a rich merchant, who took me home with him, clothed and fed me well, and after some days sent for me and questioned me as to what I could do. I answered that I was a rich merchant, who had been captured by pirates, and therefore knew no trade.

"Tell me," said he, "can you shoot with a bow?"

I replied that this had been one of the pastimes of my youth, and that doubtless with practice my skill would come back to me.

Upon this he provided me with a bow and arrows, and mounting me with him upon his own elephant took the way to a vast forest which lay far from the town. When we had reached the wildest part of it we stopped, and my master said to me, "This forest swarms with elephants. Hide yourself in this great tree and shoot at all that pass you. When you have succeeded in killing one come and tell me."

So saying he gave me a supply of food and returned to the town. I perched myself high up in the tree and kept watch. That night I saw nothing, but just after sunrise the next morning a large herd of elephants came crashing and trampling by. I lost no time in letting fly several arrows, and at last one of the great animals fell to the ground dead. The others retreated, leaving me free to come down from my hiding place and run back to tell my master of my success, for which I was praised and regaled with good things. Then we went back to the forest together and dug a mighty trench in which we buried the elephant I had killed, in order that when it became a skeleton my master might return and secure its tusks.

For two months I hunted thus, and no day passed without my securing an elephant. Of course I did not always station myself in the same tree, but sometimes in one place, sometimes in another. One morning as I watched the coming of the elephants I was surprised to see that, instead of passing the tree I was in, as they usually did, they paused and completely surrounded it, trumpeting horribly and shaking the very ground with their heavy tread. When I saw that their eyes were fixed upon me I was terrified and my arrows dropped from my trembling hand.

I had indeed good reason for my terror when, an instant later, the largest of the animals wound his trunk round the stem of my tree, and with one mighty effort tore it up by the roots, bringing me to the ground entangled in its branches. I thought now my last hour was surely come; but the huge creature, picking me up gently enough, set me upon its back, where I clung more dead than alive, and followed by the whole herd, turned and crashed into the dense forest. It seemed to me a long time before I was once more set upon my feet by the elephant, and I stood as if in a dream watching the herd, which turned and trampled off in another direction and were soon hidden in the dense underwood. Then, recovering myself, I looked about me and found that I was standing upon the side of a great hill, strewn as far as I could see on either hand with bones and tusks of elephants. "This then must be the elephants' burying place," I said to myself, "and they must have brought me here that I might cease to persecute them, seeing that I want nothing but their tusks, and here lie more than I could carry away in a lifetime."

Whereupon I turned and made for the city as fast as I could go, not seeing a single elephant by the way. This convinced me that they had retired deeper into the forest to leave the way open to the Ivory Hill, and I did not know how to admire their sagacity sufficiently. After a day and a night I reached my master's house and was received by him with joyful surprise.

"Ah, poor Sinbad," he cried, "I was wondering what could have become of you. When I went to the forest I found the tree newly uprooted, the arrows lying beside it, and I feared I should never see you again. Pray tell me how you escaped death."

I soon satisfied his curiosity, and the next day we went together to the Ivory Hill and he was overjoyed to find that I had told him nothing but the truth. When we had loaded our elephant with as many tusks as it could carry and were on our way back to the city, he said:

"My brother—since I can no longer treat as a slave one who has enriched me thus—take your liberty and may Heaven prosper you. I will no longer conceal from you that these wild elephants have killed numbers of our slaves every year. No matter what good advice we gave

"This then must be the elephants' burying place."

them, they were caught sooner or later. You alone have escaped the wiles of these animals, therefore you must be under the special protection of Heaven. Now, through you, the whole town will be enriched without further loss of life; therefore you shall not only receive your liberty, but I will also bestow fortune and honors upon you."

To which I replied, "Master, I thank you and wish you all prosperity. For myself I only ask liberty to return to my own country."

"It is well," he answered, "the monsoon will soon bring the ivory ships hither, then I will send you on your way with somewhat to pay your passage."

So I stayed with him till the time of the monsoon, and every day we added to our store of ivory till all his warehouses were overflowing with it. By this time the other merchants knew the secret, but there was enough and to spare for all. When the ships at last arrived, my master himself chose the one in which I was to sail and put on board for me a great store of choice provisions, also ivory in abundance and all the costliest curiosities of the country; for which I could not thank him enough, and so we parted.

I left the ship at the first port we came to, not feeling at ease upon the sea after all that had happened to me by reason of it. Having disposed of my ivory for much gold and bought many rare and costly presents, I loaded my pack animals and joined a caravan of merchants. Our journey was long and tedious, but I bore it patiently, reflecting that at least I had not to fear tempests, nor pirates, nor serpents, nor any of the other perils from which I had suffered before. At length we reached Baghdad.

My first care was to present myself before the caliph and give him an account of my embassy. He assured me that my long absence had disquieted him much, but he had nevertheless hoped for the best. As to my adventure among the elephants he heard it with amazement, declaring that he could not have believed it had not my truthfulness been well known to him.

By his orders this story and the others I had told him were written by his scribes in letters of gold, and laid up among his treasures. I took my leave of him, well satisfied with the honors and rewards he bestowed upon me; and since that time I have rested from my labors and given myself up wholly to my family and my friends.

Thus Sinbad ended the story of his seventh and last voyage. Turning to Hinbad, he added, "Well, my friend, what do you think now? Have you ever heard of anyone who has suffered more, or had more narrow escapes than I have? Is it not just that I should now enjoy a life of ease and tranquillity?"

Hinbad drew near and, kissing his hand respectfully, replied, "Sir, you have indeed known fearful perils; my troubles have been nothing compared to yours. Moreover, the generous use you make of your wealth proves that you deserve it. May you live long and happily in the enjoyment of it."

Sinbad then gave him a hundred sequins and henceforward counted him among his friends. Also he caused him to give up his profession as a porter and to eat daily at his table that he might all his life remember Sinbad the Sailor.

THE
LITTLE
HUNCHBACK

In the kingdom of Kashgar which is, as everybody knows, situated on the frontiers of Great Tartary, there lived long ago a tailor and his wife who loved each other very much. One day when the tailor was hard at work, a little hunchback came and sat at the entrance of the shop and began to sing and play his tambourine. The tailor was amused with his antics and thought he would take him home to divert his wife. The hunchback having agreed to his proposal, the tailor closed his shop and they set off together.

When they reached the house they found the table ready laid for supper, and in a very few minutes all three were sitting before a beautiful fish which the tailor's wife had cooked. But, unluckily, the hunchback happened to swallow a large bone and, in spite of all the tailor and his wife could do to help him, died of suffocation in an instant. Besides being very sorry for the poor man, the tailor and his wife were very much frightened on their own account, for if the police came to hear of it the worthy couple ran the risk of being thrown into prison for wilful murder.

In order to prevent this dreadful calamity they both set about inventing some plan which would throw suspicion on someone else, and at last they made up their minds that they could do no better than select a Jewish doctor, who lived close by, as the author of the crime. So the tailor picked up the hunchback by his head while his wife took his feet and carried him to the doctor's house. Then they knocked at the door which opened directly onto a steep staircase. A servant soon appeared, feeling her way down the dark staircase, and inquired what they wanted.

"Tell your master," said the tailor, "that we have brought a very sick man for him to cure. And," he added, holding out some money, "give him this in advance, so that he may not feel he is wasting his time." The servant remounted the stairs to give the message to the doctor, and the moment she was out of sight the tailor and his wife carried the body swiftly after her, propped it up at the top of the staircase, and ran home as fast as their legs could carry them.

Now the doctor was so delighted at the news of a patient (for he was too young to have had many of them) that he was transported with joy.

"Get a light," he called to the servant, "and follow me as fast as you can!" Rushing out of his room he ran toward the staircase. There he nearly fell over the body of the hunchback and, without knowing what it was, gave it such a kick that it rolled right to the bottom and very nearly dragged the doctor after it. "A light! A light!" he cried again. When it was brought and he saw what he had done, he was almost beside himself with terror.

"Holy Moses!" he exclaimed. "Why did I not wait for the light? I have killed the sick man whom they brought me, and if the sacred Ass of Esdras does not come to my aid I am lost! It will not be long before I am led to jail as a murderer."

Agitated though he was, and with reason, the doctor did not forget to shut the house door, lest some passersby might chance to see what had happened. He then took up the corpse and carried it into his wife's room, nearly driving her crazy with fright.

"It is all over with us," she wailed, "if we cannot find some means

151

of getting the body out of the house. Once let the sun rise, we can hide it no longer! How were you driven to commit such a terrible crime?"

"Never mind that," returned the doctor, "the thing is to find a way out of it."

For a long while the doctor and his wife continued to turn over in their minds a way of escape but could not find any that seemed good enough. At last the doctor gave it up altogether and resigned himself to bear the penalty of his misfortune.

But his wife, who had twice his brains, suddenly exclaimed, "I have thought of something! Let us carry the body to the roof of the house and lower it down the chimney of our neighbor the Mussulman." Now this Mussulman was employed by the sultan and furnished his table with oil and butter. Part of his house was occupied by a great storeroom, where rats and mice held high revel.

The doctor jumped at his wife's plan. They took up the hunchback and, passing cords under his armpits, let him down into the purveyor's bedroom so gently that he really seemed to be leaning against the wall. When they felt he was touching the ground they drew up the cords and left him.

Scarcely had they returned to their own house when the purveyor entered his room. He had spent the evening at a wedding feast and had a lantern in his hand. In the dim light it cast he was astonished to see a man standing in his chimney, but being naturally courageous he seized a stick and made straight for the supposed thief. "Ah," he cried, "so it is you, and not the rats and mice, who steal my butter! I'll take care that you don't want to come back!"

So saying, he struck him several hard blows. The corpse fell on the floor, but the man only redoubled his blows, till at length it occurred to him that it was odd the thief should lie so still and make no resistance. Then, finding he was quite dead, a cold fear took possession of him. "Wretch that I am," said he, "I have murdered a man. Ah, my revenge has gone too far. Without the help of Allah I am undone!

Cursed be the goods which have led me to my ruin." Already he felt the rope round his neck.

But when he had got over the first shock he began to think of some way out of the difficulty and, seizing the hunchback in his arms, he carried him out into the street. Leaning him against the wall of a shop he stole back to his own house without once looking behind him.

A few minutes before the sun rose, a rich Christian merchant, who supplied the palace with all sorts of necessaries, left his house after a night of feasting to go to the bath. Though he was very drunk, he was yet sober enough to know that the dawn was at hand and that all good Mussulmen would shortly be going to prayer. So he hastened his steps lest he should meet someone on his way to the mosque who, seeing his condition, would send him to prison as a drunkard. In his haste he jostled against the hunchback, who fell heavily upon him, and the merchant, thinking he was being attacked by a thief, knocked him down with one blow of his fist. He then called loudly for help, beating the fallen man all the while.

The chief policeman of the quarter came running up and found a Christian ill-treating a Mussulman. "What are you doing?" he asked indignantly.

"He tried to rob me," replied the merchant, "and very nearly choked me."

"Well, you have had your revenge," said the man, catching hold of his arm. "Come, be off with you!"

As he spoke he held out his hand to the hunchback to help him up, but the hunchback never moved. "Oho," the policeman went on, looking closer, "so this is the way a Christian has the impudence to treat a Mussulman!" And seizing the merchant in a firm grasp he took him to the inspector of police, who threw him into prison till the judge should be out of bed and ready to attend to his case. All this brought the merchant to his senses, but the more he thought of it the less he could understand how the hunchback could have died merely from the blows he had received.

The merchant was still pondering on this subject when he was summoned before the chief of police and questioned about his crime, which he could not deny. As the hunchback was one of the sultan's private jesters, the chief of police resolved to defer sentence of death until he had consulted his master.

He went to the palace to demand an audience and told his story to the sultan, who only answered, "There is no pardon for a Christian who kills a Mussulman. Do your duty."

So the chief of police ordered a gallows to be erected and sent criers to proclaim in every street in the city that a Christian was to be hanged that day for having killed a Mussulman.

When all was ready the merchant was brought from prison and led to the foot of the gallows. The executioner knotted the cord firmly round the unfortunate man's neck and was just about to swing him into the air, when the sultan's purveyor dashed through the crowd, and cried, panting, to the hangman, "Stop, stop! Don't be in such a hurry! It was not he who did the murder, it was I."

The chief of police, who was present to see that everything was in order, put several questions to the purveyor, who told him the whole story of the death of the hunchback and how he had carried the body to the place where it had been found by the Christian merchant.

"You are going," he said to the chief of police, "to kill an innocent man, for it is impossible that he should have murdered a creature who was dead already. It is bad enough for me to have slain a Mussulman without having it on my conscience that a Christian who is guiltless should suffer through my fault."

Now the purveyor's speech had been made in a loud voice and was heard by all the crowd. Even if he had wished it, the chief of police could not have escaped setting the merchant free.

"Loose the cords from the Christian's neck," he commanded, turning to the executioner, "and hang this man in his place, seeing that by his own confession he is the murderer."

The hangman did as he was bid and was tying the cord firmly, when

154

he was stopped by the voice of the Jewish doctor beseeching him to pause, for he had something very important to say. The doctor fought his way through the crowd and reached the chief of police.

"Worshipful sir," he began, "this Mussulman whom you desire to hang is unworthy of death; I alone am guilty. Last night a man and a woman who were strangers to me knocked at my door, bringing with them a patient for me to cure. The servant opened it but having no light was hardly able to make out their faces, though she readily agreed to wake me and to hand me the fee for my services. While she was telling me her story they seem to have carried the sick man to the top of the staircase and then left him there. I jumped up in a hurry without waiting for a lantern, and in the darkness I fell against something which tumbled headlong down the stairs and never stopped till it reached the bottom. I hurried down to see what had fallen.

"When I examined the body I found it was quite dead, and the corpse was that of a hunchback Mussulman. Terrified at what we had done, my wife and I took the body on the roof and let it down the chimney of our neighbor, the purveyor you were just about to hang. The purveyor, finding him in his room, naturally thought he was a thief and struck him such a blow that the man fell down and lay motionless on the floor.

"Stooping to examine him, and finding him stone dead, the purveyor supposed that the man had died from the blow he had received; but of course this was a mistake, as you will see from my account, and I only am the murderer. And although I am innocent of any wish to commit a crime, I must suffer for it all the same or else have the blood of two Mussulmen on my conscience. Therefore send away this man, I pray you, and let me take his place, as it is I who am guilty."

On hearing the declaration of the Jewish doctor, the chief of police commanded that he should be led to the gallows and the sultan's purveyor go free. The cord was placed round the neck of the doctor, and his feet had already ceased to touch the ground when the voice of the tailor was heard beseeching the executioner to pause one moment and to listen to what he had to say.

"Oh, my lord," he cried, turning to the chief of police, "how nearly have you caused the death of three innocent people! But if you will only have the patience to listen to my tale, you shall know who is the real culprit. If someone has to suffer it must be me! Yesterday, at dusk, I was working in my shop with a light heart when the little hunchback, who was more than half-drunk, came and sat in the doorway. He sang me several songs, and then I invited him to finish the evening at my house. He accepted my invitation, and we went away together. At supper I helped him to a slice of fish, but in eating it a bone stuck in his throat, and in spite of all we could do he died in a few minutes.

"We felt deeply sorry for his death, but fearing lest we should be held responsible, we carried the corpse to the house of the doctor. I knocked and desired the servant to beg her master to come down as fast as possible and see a sick man whom we had brought for him to cure, and I placed a piece of money in her hand as the doctor's fee. Directly she had disappeared I dragged the body to the top of the stairs and then hurried away with my wife back to our house. In descending the stairs the doctor accidentally knocked over the corpse, and finding him dead believed that he himself was the murderer. But now you know the truth, set him free and let me die in his stead."

The chief of police and the crowd of spectators were lost in astonishment at the strange events to which the death of the hunchback had given rise. "Loosen the doctor," said he to the hangman, "and string up the tailor instead, since he has made confession of this crime. Really, one cannot deny that this is a very singular story, and it deserves to be written in letters of gold."

The executioner speedily untied the knots which confined the doctor and was passing the cord round the neck of the tailor when the Sultan of Kashgar, who had missed his jester, happened to make inquiry of his officers as to what had become of him.

"Sire," replied they, "the hunchback having drunk more than was good for him, escaped from the palace and was seen wandering about the town, where this morning he was found dead. A man was arrested for having caused his death and held in custody till a gallows was erected. At the moment that he was about to suffer punishment, first one man arrived, and then another, each accusing himself of the murder, and this went on for a long time; at the present instant the chief of police is engaged in questioning a man who declares that he alone is the true assassin."

The Sultan of Kashgar no sooner heard these words than he ordered an usher to go to the chief of police and to bring all the persons concerned in the hunchback's death, together with the corpse. The usher hastened on his errand but was only just in time, for the tailor was positively swinging in the air, when his voice fell upon the silence of the crowd, commanding the hangman to cut down the body.

The hangman, recognizing the usher as one of the king's servants, cut down the tailor, and the usher, seeing the man was safe, sought the chief of police and gave him the sultan's message. Accordingly, the chief of police at once set out for the palace, taking with him the tailor, the doctor, the purveyor and the merchant, who bore the dead hunchback on their shoulders; and followed by the large crowd of spectators who had gathered to witness the execution.

When the procession reached the palace the chief of police prostrated himself at the feet of the sultan and related all that he knew of the matter. The sultan listened with an air of pleasure which filled the tailor and his friends with hope; however, just as he was about to turn to his grand vizir with an order, a barber stepped forward from the crowd and knelt humbly at his feet, saying: "Will Your Highness graciously be pleased to let me examine the body?"

"What business is that of yours?" asked the sultan with a smile; but seeing that the barber had some reason for his request, he commanded that the body of the hunchback be laid before him.

The barber then knelt down and took the head on his knees, looking at it attentively. Suddenly he burst into such loud laughter that he fell right over backwards and, when he had recovered himself enough to speak, he turned to the sultan. "The man is no more dead than I am," he said, "watch me." As he spoke he drew a small case of medicines from his pocket and rubbed the neck of the hunchback with some ointment made of balsam. Next he opened his mouth and, with the help of a pair of pincers, drew the bone from his throat. At this the hunchback sneezed, stretched himself, and opened his eyes.

The sultan and all those who saw this operation did not know which to admire most, the constitution of the hunchback who had apparently been dead for a whole night and most of one day, or the skill of the barber, whom everyone now began to look upon as a great man. His Highness now ordered his private historian to write down an exact account of what had passed, so that in the years to come the miraculous escape of the four men who had thought themselves murderers might never be forgotten. And he did not stop there; for in order to wipe out the memory of what they had undergone, he commanded that the tailor, the doctor, the purveyor and the merchant should each be clothed in his presence with a robe from his own wardrobe before they returned home. As for the barber, he bestowed on him a large pension and kept him near his own person.

THE PRINCE
AND
THE PRINCESS

ome twenty days' sail from the coast of Persia lies the Isle of the Children of Khaledan. The island is divided into several provinces, in each of which are large, flourishing towns, and the whole forms an important kingdom. It was governed in former days by a king named Schahzaman who, with good right, considered himself one of the most peaceful, prosperous and fortunate monarchs on the earth. In fact, he had but one grievance; he had no heir.

This distressed him so greatly that one day he confided his grief to the grand vizir who, being a wise counselor, said, "Such matters are indeed beyond human aid. Allah alone can grant your desire, and I should advise you, sire, to send large gifts to those holy men who spend their lives in prayer and to beg for their intercessions. Who knows whether their petitions may not be answered!"

The king took his vizir's advice, and the result of so many prayers for an heir to the throne was that a son was born to him the following year. Schahzaman sent noble gifts as thank offerings to all the mosques and religious houses, and great rejoicings were celebrated in honor of the birth of the little prince, who was so beautiful that he was named Camaralzaman, or "Moon of the Century."

Prince Camaralzaman was brought up with extreme care by an excellent governor and all the cleverest teachers, and he had done such credit to them that a more charming and accomplished young man was not to be found. While he was still a youth the king, who loved him dearly, had some thoughts of abdicating in his favor. As usual he talked over his plans with his grand vizir who, though he did not approve the idea, would not state all his objections.

"Sire," he replied, "the prince is still very young for the cares of state. Your Majesty fears his growing idle and careless, and doubtless you are right. But how would it be if he were first to marry? This would attach him to his home, and Your Majesty might give him a share in your council, so he might gradually learn how to wear a crown, which you can give up to him whenever you find him capable of wearing it."

The vizir's advice once more struck the king as being good, and he sent for his son, who lost no time in obeying the summons and, standing respectfully with downcast eyes before the king, asked for his commands.

"I have sent for you," said the king, "to say that I wish you to marry. What do you think about it?"

The prince was so much overcome by these words that he remained silent for some time. At length he said, "Sire, I beg you to pardon me if I am unable to reply as you wish. I certainly did not expect such a proposal as I am still so young, and I confess that the idea of marrying is distasteful to me. Possibly I may not always be in this mind, but I feel it will require some time to induce me to take the step which Your Majesty desires."

This answer greatly distressed the king who was sincerely grieved by his son's objection to marriage. However, he would not have recourse to extreme measures, so he said, "I do not wish to force you. I will give you time to reflect, but remember that such a step is necessary for a prince such as you, who will someday be called to rule over a great kingdom."

From this time Prince Camaralzaman was admitted to the royal council, and the king showed him every mark of favor.

At the end of a year the king took his son aside, and said, "Well, my son, have you changed your mind on the subject of marriage, or do you still refuse to obey my wish?"

The prince was less surprised but no less firm than on the former occasion and begged his father not to press the subject, adding that it was quite useless to urge him any longer. This answer much distressed the king, who again confided his trouble to his vizir.

"I have followed your advice," he said; "but Camaralzaman declines to marry and is more obstinate than ever."

"Sire," replied the vizir, "much is gained by patience, and Your Majesty might regret any violence. Why not wait another year and then inform the prince in the midst of the assembled council that the good of the state demands his marriage? He cannot possibly refuse again before so distinguished an assemblage and in your immediate presence."

The sultan ardently desired to see his son married at once, but he yielded to the vizir's arguments and decided to wait. He then visited the prince's mother, and after telling her of his disappointment and of the further respite he had given his son, he added, "I know that Camaralzaman confides more in you than he does in me. Pray speak very seriously to him on this subject and make him realize that he will most seriously displease me if he remains obstinate and that he will certainly regret the measures I shall be obliged to take to enforce my will."

So the next time the Sultana Fatima saw her son she told him she had heard of his refusal to marry, adding how distressed she felt that he should have vexed his father so much. She asked what reasons he could have for his objections to obey.

"Madam," replied the prince, "I make no doubt that there are as many good, virtuous, sweet, and amiable women as there are others very much the reverse. Would that all were like you! But what revolts me is the idea of marrying a woman without knowing anything at all about her. My father will ask the hand of the daughter of some neighboring sovereign, who will give his consent to our union. Be she fair or frightful, clever or stupid, good or bad, I must marry her and am left no choice in the matter. How am I to know that she will not be proud, passionate, contemptuous, and recklessly extravagant, or that her disposition will in any way suit mine?"

"But, my son," urged Fatima, "you surely do not wish to be the last of a race which has reigned so long and so gloriously over this kingdom?"

"Madam," said the prince, "I have no wish to survive the king, my father, but should I do so I will try to reign in such a manner as may be considered worthy of my predecessors."

These and similar conversations proved to the sultan how useless it was to argue with his son, and the year elapsed without bringing any change in the prince's ideas.

At length a day came when the sultan summoned him before the council, and there informed him that not only his own wishes but the good of the empire demanded his marriage, and desired him to give his answer before the assembled ministers. At this Camaralzaman grew so angry and spoke with so much heat that the king, naturally irritated at being opposed by his son in full council, ordered the prince to be arrested and locked up in an old tower, where he had nothing but a very little furniture, a few books, and a single slave to wait on him.

Camaralzaman, pleased to be free to enjoy his books, showed himself very indifferent to his sentence. When night came he washed himself, performed his devotions and, having read some pages of the Koran, lay down on a couch without putting out the light near him, and was soon asleep.

Now there was a deep well in the tower in which Prince Camaralzaman was imprisoned, and this well was a favorite resort of the fairy Maimoune, daughter of Damriat, chief of a legion of genii. Toward midnight Maimoune floated lightly up from the well intending, according to her usual habit, to roam about the upper world as curiosity or accident might prompt.

The light in the prince's room surprised her, and without disturbing the slave, who slept across the threshold, she entered the room and, approaching the bed, was still more astonished to find it occupied.

The prince lay with his face half-hidden by the coverlet. Maimoune lifted it a little and beheld the most beautiful youth she had ever seen. What a marvel of beauty he must be when his eyes are open! she thought. What can he have done to deserve to be treated like this?

She could not weary of gazing at Camaralzaman, but at length, having softly kissed his brow, she replaced the coverlet and resumed her flight through the air. As she entered the middle region she heard the sound of great wings coming toward her and shortly met one of the race of bad genii. This genie, whose name was Danhasch, recognized Maimoune with terror, for he knew the supremacy which her goodness gave her over him.

He would gladly have avoided her altogether, but they were so near that he must either be prepared to fight or yield to her, so he at once addressed her in a conciliatory tone. "Good Maimoune, swear to me by Allah to do me no harm, and on my side I will promise not to injure you."

"Accursed genie!" replied Maimoune. "What harm can you do me? But I will grant your power and give the promise you ask. And now tell me what you have seen and done tonight."

"Fair lady," said Danhasch, "you meet me at the right moment to hear something really interesting. I must tell you that I come from the farthest end of China, which is one of the largest and most powerful kingdoms in the world. The present king has one only daughter, who is so lovely that neither you, nor I, nor any other creature could find adequate terms in which to describe her marvelous charms. You must therefore picture to yourself the most perfect features, a brilliant and delicate complexion and an enchanting expression, and even then imagination will fall short of the reality.

"The king, her father, has carefully shielded this treasure from the vulgar gaze and has taken every precaution to keep her from the sight of everyone except the happy mortal he may choose to be her husband. But in order to give her variety in her seclusion he has built her seven palaces such as have never been seen before. They are all most sumptuously furnished, while the gardens surrounding them are laid out with exquisite taste. In fact, neither trouble nor cost has been spared to make this retreat agreeable to the princess.

"The report of her wonderful beauty has spread far and wide, and many powerful kings have sent embassies to ask her hand in marriage. The king has always received these embassies graciously but says that he will never oblige the princess to marry against her will and, as she regularly declines each fresh proposal, the envoys have had to leave as disappointed in the result of their missions as they were gratified by their magnificent receptions.

" 'Sire,' said the princess to her father, 'you wish me to marry, and I know you desire to please me, for which I am grateful. But, indeed, I have no inclination to change my state, for where could I find so happy a life amidst so many beautiful and delightful surroundings? I feel that I could never be as happy with any husband as I am here, and I beg you not to press me to marry.'

"At last an embassy came from a king so rich and powerful that the King of China felt constrained to urge this suit on his daughter. He told her how important such an alliance would be and pressed her to consent. In fact, he pressed her so persistently that the princess at length lost her temper and quite forgot the respect due to her father. 'Sire,' cried she angrily, 'do not speak further of this or any other marriage or I will plunge this dagger in my heart and so escape from all these importunities.'

"The King of China was extremely indignant with his daughter and replied, 'You have lost your senses and you must be treated according-ly.' So he had her confined in one set of rooms in one of her palaces, and only allowed her ten old women, of whom her nurse was the head, to wait on her and keep her company. He next sent letters to all the kings who had sued for the princess' hand, begging they would think of her no longer, as she was insane; and he desired his various envoys to make it known that anyone who could cure her should have her to wife.

"Fair Maimoune," continued Danhasch, "this is the present state of affairs. I never pass a day without going to gaze on this incomparable beauty, and I am sure that if you would only accompany me you would think the sight well worth the trouble and own that you never saw such loveliness before."

The fairy only answered with a peal of laughter, and when at length she had control of her voice she cried, "Oh, come, you are making game of me! I thought you had something really interesting to tell me instead of raving about some unknown damsel. What would you say if you could see a prince whose beauty is really transcendent? That is something worth talking about; you would certainly lose your head."

"Charming Maimoune," asked Danhasch, "may I inquire who is the prince of whom you speak?"

"Know," replied Maimoune, "that he is in much the same case as your princess. The king, his father, wanted to force him to marry, and on the prince's refusal to obey he has been imprisoned in an old tower where I have just seen him."

"I don't like to contradict a lady," said Danhasch, "but you must really permit me to doubt any mortal being as beautiful as my princess. The best plan to test the truth of what I say will be for you to let me take you to see the princess for yourself."

"There is no need for that," retorted Maimoune; "we can satisfy ourselves in another way. Bring your princess here and lay her down beside my prince. We can then compare them at leisure and decide which is in the right."

Danhasch readily consented and, after having the tower where the prince was confined pointed out to him and making a wager with Maimoune as to the result of the comparison, he flew off to China to fetch the princess. In an incredibly short time Danhasch returned, bearing the sleeping princess. Maimoune led him to the prince's room, and the rival beauty was placed beside him.

When the prince and princess lay thus side by side, an animated dispute as to their respective charms arose between the fairy and the genie. Danhasch began by saying, "Now you see that my princess is more beautiful than your prince. Can you doubt any longer?"

"Doubt! Of course I do!" exclaimed Maimoune. "Why, you must be blind not to see how much my prince excels your princess. I do not deny that she is very handsome, but only look and you must own that I am in the right."

"There is no need for me to look longer," said Danhasch, "my first impression will remain the same; but of course, charming Maimoune, I am ready to yield to you if you insist on it."

"By no means," replied Maimoune. "I have no idea of being under any obligation to an accursed genie like you. I refer the matter to an umpire and shall expect you to submit to his verdict."

Danhasch readily agreed, and on Maimoune striking the floor with her foot, it opened and a hideous, humpbacked, lame, squinting genie, with six horns on his head, and hands like claws, emerged. As soon as he beheld Maimoune he threw himself at her feet and asked her commands.

"Rise, Caschcasch," said she. "I summoned you to judge between me and Danhasch. Glance at that couch and say without any partiality whether you think the youth or the maiden lying there the more beautiful."

Caschcasch looked at the prince and princess with every token of surprise and admiration. At length, having gazed long without being able to come to a decision, he said, "Madam, I must confess that I should deceive you were I to declare one to be handsomer than the other. There seems to me only one way in which to decide the matter, and that is to wake one after the other and judge which of them expresses the greater admiration for the other."

This advice pleased Maimoune and Danhasch, and the fairy at once transformed herself into a gnat and, settling on Camaralzaman's throat, stung him so sharply that he awoke. As he did so his eyes fell on the Princess of China. Surprised at finding a lady so near him, he raised himself on one arm to look at her. The youth and beauty of the princess at once awoke a feeling to which his heart had as yet been a stranger, and he could not restrain his delight.

"What loveliness! What charms! Oh, my heart, my soul!" he exclaimed, as he kissed her forehead, her eyes and mouth in a way which would certainly have roused her had not the genie's enchantments kept her asleep.

"How, fair lady!" he cried. "You do not wake at the signs of Camaralzaman's love? Be you who you may, he is not unworthy of you."

Suddenly it occurred to him that perhaps this was the bride his father had destined for him and that the king had probably had her placed in this room in order to see how far Camaralzaman's aversion to marriage would withstand her charms.

"At all events, I will take this ring as a remembrance of her." So saying, he drew off a fine ring which the princess wore on her finger and replaced it by one of his own. After which he lay down again and was soon fast asleep.

Then Danhasch, in his turn, took the form of a gnat and bit the princess on her lip.

She started up and was not a little amazed at seeing a young man beside her. From surprise she soon passed to admiration and then to delight on perceiving how handsome and fascinating he was.

"Why," cried she, "was it you my father wished me to marry? How unlucky that I did not know sooner! I should not have made him so angry. But wake up! Wake up! I know I shall love you with all my heart."

So saying, she shook Camaralzaman so violently that nothing but the spells of Maimoune could have prevented his waking.

168

Caschcasch could not decide which was more beautiful.

"Oh!" cried the princess. "Why are you so drowsy?" So saying, she took his hand and noticed her own ring on his finger, which made her wonder still more. But as he still remained in a profound slumber, she pressed a kiss on his cheek and soon fell fast asleep too.

Then Maimoune, turning to the genie, said, "Well, are you satisfied that my prince surpasses your princess? Another time pray believe me when I assert anything."

Then, turning to Caschcasch, she said, "My thanks to you, and now do you and Danhasch bear the princess back to her own home."

The two genii hastened to obey, and Maimoune returned to her well.

On waking next morning the first thing Prince Camaralzaman did was to look round for the lovely lady he had seen and, next, to question the slave who waited on him about her. But the slave persisted so strongly that he knew nothing of any lady and still less of how she got into the tower that the prince lost all patience, and tied a rope round him and ducked him in the well till the unfortunate man cried out that he would tell everything. Then the prince drew him up all dripping wet, but the slave begged leave to change his clothes first, and as soon as the prince consented, hurried off just as he was to the palace. Here he found the king talking to the grand vizir about the anxiety his son had caused him.

The slave was admitted at once and cried, "Alas, sire! I bring sad news to Your Majesty. There can be no doubt that the prince has completely lost his senses. He declares that he saw a lady sleeping on his couch last night, and the state you see me in proves how violent contradiction makes him." He then gave a minute account of all the prince had said and done.

The king, much moved, begged the vizir to examine into this new misfortune, and the latter at once went to the tower, where he found the prince quietly reading a book. After the first exchange of greetings the vizir said:

"I feel really very angry with your slave for alarming His Majesty by the news he brought him."

170

"What news?" asked the prince.

"Ah," replied the vizir, "something absurd, I feel sure, seeing how I find you."

"Most likely," said the prince, "but now that you are here I am glad of the opportunity to ask you where is the lady who slept in this room last night?"

The grand vizir felt beside himself at this question. "Prince!" he exclaimed. "How would it be possible for any man, much less a woman, to enter this room at night without walking over your slave on the threshold? Pray consider the matter and you will realize that you have been deeply impressed by some dream."

But the prince angrily insisted on knowing who and where the lady was, and was not to be persuaded by all the vizir's protestations to the contrary that the plot had not been one of his making. At last, losing patience, he seized the vizir by the beard and loaded him with blows.

"Stop, Prince," cried the unhappy vizir, "stay and hear what I have to say."

The prince, whose arm was getting tired, paused.

"I confess, Prince," said the vizir, "that there is some foundation for what you say. But you know well that a minister has to carry out his master's orders. Allow me to go and take to the king any message you may choose to send."

"Very well," said the prince; "then go and tell him that I consent to marry the lady whom he sent or brought here last night. Be quick and bring me back his answer."

The vizir bowed to the ground and hastened to leave the room and tower.

"Well," asked the king as soon as he appeared, "and how did you find my son?"

"Alas, sire," was the reply, "the slave's report is only too true!"

He then gave an exact account of his interview with Camaralzaman and of the prince's fury when told that it was not possible for any lady to have entered his room, and of the treatment he himself had received. The king, much distressed, determined to clear up the matter himself and, ordering the vizir to follow him, set out to visit his son.

The prince received his father with profound respect, and the king, making him sit beside him, asked him several questions, to which Camaralzaman replied with much good sense. At last the king said, "My son, pray tell me about the lady who, it is said, was in your room last night."

"Sire," replied the prince, "pray do not increase my distress in this matter but rather make me happy by giving her to me in marriage. However much I may have objected to matrimony formerly, the sight of this lovely girl has overcome all my prejudices and I will gratefully receive her from your hands."

The king was almost speechless on hearing his son, but after a time assured him most solemnly that he knew nothing whatever about the lady in question and had not connived at her appearance. He then desired the prince to relate the whole story to him.

Camaralzaman did so at great length, showed the ring, and implored his father to help to find the bride he so ardently desired.

"After all you tell me," remarked the king, "I can no longer doubt your word; but how and whence the lady came, or why she should have stayed so short a time I cannot imagine. The whole affair is indeed mysterious. Come, my dear son, let us wait together for happier days."

So saying the king took Camaralzaman by the hand and led him back to the palace where the prince took to his bed and gave himself up to despair; and the king, shutting himself up with his son, entirely neglected his duty in the affairs of state.

The prime minister, who was the only person admitted, felt it his duty at last to tell the king how much the court and all the people complained of his seclusion, and how bad it was for the nation. He urged the sultan to remove with the prince to a lovely little island close by, whence he could easily attend public audiences, and where the charming scenery and fine air would do the invalid so much good as to enable him to bear his father's occasional absence.

The king approved the plan, and as soon as the castle on the island could be prepared for their reception he and the prince arrived there, Schahzaman never leaving his son except for the prescribed public audiences twice a week.

While all this was happening in the capital of Schahzaman the two genii had carefully borne the Princess of China back to her own palace and replaced her in bed. On waking next morning she first turned from one side to the other and then finding herself alone, called loudly for her women.

"Tell me," she cried, "where is the young man I love so dearly and who slept near me last night?"

"Princess," exclaimed the nurse, "we cannot tell what you allude to without more explanation."

"Why," continued the princess, "the most charming and beautiful young man lay sleeping beside me last night. I did my utmost to wake him but in vain."

"Your Royal Highness wishes to make game of us," said the nurse. "Is it your pleasure to rise?"

"I am quite in earnest," persisted the princess, "and I want to know where he is."

"But, Princess," expostulated the nurse, "we left you quite alone last night and we have seen no one enter your room since then."

At this the princess lost all patience, and taking the nurse by her hair she boxed her ears soundly, crying out, "You shall tell me, you old witch."

The nurse had no little trouble in escaping and hurried off to the queen, to whom she related the whole story with tears in her eyes. "You see, madam," she concluded, "that the princess must be out of her mind. If only you will come and see her, you will be able to judge for yourself."

The queen hurried to her daughter's apartments and, after tenderly embracing her, asked her why she had treated her nurse so badly.

"Madam," said the princess, "I perceive that Your Majesty wishes

173

to make game of me, but I can assure you I will never marry anyone except the charming young man whom I saw last night. You must know where he is, so pray send for him."

The queen was much surprised by these words, but when she declared that she knew nothing whatever of the matter the princess lost all respect and answered that if she were not allowed to marry as she wished she should kill herself, and it was in vain that the queen tried to pacify her and bring her to reason.

The king himself came to hear the rights of the matter, but the princess only persisted in her story and as a proof showed the ring on her finger. The king hardly knew what to make of it all but ended by thinking that his daughter was more crazy than ever, and without further argument he had her placed in still closer confinement, with only her nurse to wait on her and a powerful guard to keep the door.

Then he assembled his council and, having told them the sad state of things, added, "If any of you can succeed in curing the princess I will give her to him in marriage, and he shall be my heir."

An elderly emir present, fired with the desire to have a young and lovely wife and to rule over a great kingdom, offered to try the magic arts with which he was acquainted.

"You are welcome to try," said the king, "but I make one condition; should you fail, you will lose your life."

The emir accepted the condition, and the king led him to the princess who, veiling her face, remarked, "I am surprised, sire, that you should bring an unknown man into my presence."

"You need not be shocked," said the king, "this is one of my emirs who asks your hand in marriage."

"Sire," replied the princess, "this is not the one you gave me before and whose ring I wear. Permit me to say that I can accept no other."

The emir, who had expected to hear the princess talk nonsense, finding how calm and reasonable she was, assured the king that he could not venture to undertake a cure, but placed his head at His

The princess showed the ring on her finger as proof.

Majesty's disposal. This was the first of many suitors for the princess whose inability to cure her cost them their lives.

Now it happened that after things had been going on in this way for some time the nurse's son Marzavan returned from his travels. He had been in many countries and learnt many things, including astrology. Needless to say that one of the first things his mother told him was the sad condition of the princess, his foster sister. Marzavan asked if she could not manage to let him see the princess without the king's knowledge.

After some consideration his mother consented, and even persuaded the eunuch on guard to make no objection to Marzavan's entering the royal apartment. The princess was delighted to see her foster brother again, and she confided to him all her history and the cause of her imprisonment.

Marzavan listened with downcast eyes and the utmost attention. When she had finished speaking he said, "If what you tell me, Princess, is indeed the case, I do not despair of finding comfort for you. Take patience yet a little longer. I will set out at once to explore other countries, and when you hear of my return be sure that he for whom you sigh is not far off." So saying, he took his leave and started next morning on his travels.

Marzavan journeyed from city to city and from one island and province to another, and wherever he went he heard people talk of the strange story of Princess Badoura, as the Princess of China was named.

After four months he reached a large populous seaport named Torf, and here he heard no more of the Princess Badoura but a great deal of Prince Camaralzaman, who was reported ill, and whose story sounded very similar to that of the Princess Badoura.

Marzavan was rejoiced and set out at once for Prince Camaralzaman's residence. The ship on which he embarked had a prosperous voyage till she got within sight of the capital of King Schahzaman, but when just about to enter the harbor, she suddenly struck on a rock and foundered within sight of the palace where the prince was living with his father and the grand vizir.

Marzavan, who swam well, threw himself into the sea and managed to land close to the palace, where he was kindly received, and after having a change of clothing given him was brought before the grand vizir. The vizir was at once attracted by the young man's superior air and intelligent conversation, and perceiving that he had gained much experience in the course of his travels, he said, "Ah, how I wish you had learnt some secret which might enable you to cure a malady which has plunged this court into affliction for some time past!"

Marzavan replied that if he knew what the illness was he might possibly be able to suggest a remedy, on which the vizir related to him the whole history of Prince Camaralzaman. On hearing this Marzavan rejoiced inwardly, for he felt sure that he had at last discovered the object of the Princess Badoura's infatuation. However, he said nothing but begged to be allowed to see the prince.

On entering the royal apartment the first thing which struck him was the prince himself, who lay stretched out on his bed with his eyes closed. The king sat near him, but without paying any regard to his presence, Marzavan exclaimed, "Heavens! What a striking likeness!" And, indeed, there was a good deal of resemblance between the features of Camaralzaman and those of the Princess of China.

These words caused the prince to open his eyes with languid curiosity, and Marzavan seized this moment to pay him his compliments, contriving at the same time to express the condition of the Princess of China in terms unintelligible, indeed, to the sultan and his vizir, but which left the prince in no doubt that his visitor could give him some welcome information.

The prince begged his father to allow him the favor of a private interview with Marzavan, and the king was only too pleased to find his son taking an interest in anyone or anything. As soon as they were left alone Marzavan told the prince the story of the Princess Badoura and her sufferings, adding, "I am convinced that you alone can cure her;

177

but before starting on so long a journey you must be well and strong, so do your best to recover as quickly as may be."

These words produced a great effect on the prince, who was so much cheered by the hopes held out that he declared he felt able to get up and be dressed. The king was overjoyed at the result of Marzavan's interview and ordered public rejoicings in honor of the prince's recovery.

Before long the prince was quite restored to his original state of health, and as soon as he felt himself really strong he took Marzavan aside and said, "Now is the time to perform your promise. I am so impatient to see my beloved princess once more that I am sure I shall fall ill again if we do not start soon. The one obstacle is my father's tender care of me, for as you may have noticed, he cannot bear me out of his sight."

"Prince," replied Marzavan, "I have already thought over the matter and this is what seems to me the best plan. You have not been out-of-doors since my arrival. Ask the king's permission to go with me for two or three days' hunting, and when he has given leave order two good horses to be held ready for each of us. Leave all the rest to me."

Next day the prince seized a favorable opportunity for making his request, and the king gladly granted it on condition that only one night should be spent out for fear of too great fatigue after such a long illness.

Next morning Prince Camaralzaman and Marzavan were off betimes, attended by two grooms leading the two extra horses. They hunted a little by the way but took care to get as far from the towns as possible. At nightfall they reached an inn, where they supped and slept till midnight. Then Marzavan awoke and roused the prince without disturbing anyone else. He begged the prince to give him the coat he had been wearing and to put on another which they had brought with them. They mounted their second horses, and Marzavan led one of the grooms' horses by the bridle.

By daybreak the travelers found themselves where four crossroads met in the middle of the forest. Here Marzavan begged the prince to wait for him, and leading the groom's horse into a dense part of the wood he cut its throat, dipped the prince's coat in its blood and, having rejoined the prince, threw the coat on the ground where the roads parted.

In answer to Camaralzaman's inquiries as to the reason for this, Marzavan replied that the only chance they had of continuing their journey was to divert attention by creating the idea of the prince's death. "Your father will doubtless be plunged in the deepest grief," he went on, "but his joy at your return will be all the greater."

The prince and his companion now continued their journey by land and sea, and as they had brought plenty of money to defray their expenses they met with no needless delays. At length they reached the capital of China, where they spent three days in a suitable lodging to recover from their fatigues.

During this time Marzavan had an astrologer's dress prepared for the prince. They then went to the baths, after which the prince put on the astrologer's robe and was conducted within sight of the king's palace by Marzavan, who left him there and went to consult his mother, the princess' nurse.

Meantime the prince, according to Marzavan's instructions, advanced close to the palace gates and there proclaimed aloud, "I am an astrologer and I come to restore health to the Princess Badoura, daughter of the high and mighty King of China, on the conditions laid down by his majesty of marrying her should I succeed, or of losing my life if I fail."

It was some little time since anyone had presented himself to run the terrible risk involved in attempting to cure the princess, and a crowd soon gathered round the prince. On perceiving his youth, good looks, and distinguished bearing, everyone felt pity for him.

"What are you thinking of, sir," exclaimed some, "why expose yourself to certain death? Are not the heads you see exposed on the town wall sufficient warning? For mercy's sake give up this mad idea and retire while you can."

179

But the prince remained firm and only repeated his cry with greater assurance, to the horror of the crowd.

"He is resolved to die!" they cried. "May heaven have pity on him!"

Camaralzaman now called out for the third time, and at last the grand vizir himself came out and fetched him in. The prime minister led the prince to the king, who was much struck by the noble air of this new adventurer, and felt such pity for the fate so evidently in store for him, that he tried to persuade the young man to renounce his project.

Camaralzaman politely yet firmly persisted in his intentions, and at length the king desired the eunuch who had the guard of the princess' apartments to conduct the astrologer to her presence.

The eunuch led the way through long passages, and Camaralzaman followed rapidly, in haste to reach the object of his desires. At last they came to a large hall which was the anteroom to the princess' chamber, and here Camaralzaman said to the eunuch, "Now you shall choose. Shall I cure the princess in her own presence, or shall I do it from here without seeing her?"

The eunuch, who had expressed many contemptuous doubts as they came along of the newcomer's powers, was much surprised and said, "If you really can cure, it is immaterial where you do it. Your fame will be equally great."

"Very well," replied the prince, "then, impatient though I am to see the princess, I will effect the cure where I stand, the better to convince you of my power." He accordingly drew out his writing case and wrote as follows:

"Adorable Princess! The enamored Camaralzaman has never forgotten the moment when, contemplating your sleeping beauty, he gave you his heart. As he was at that time deprived of the happiness of conversing with you, he ventured to give you his ring as a token of his love and to take yours in exchange, which he now encloses in this letter. Should you deign to return it to him he will be the happiest of mortals; if not, he will cheerfully resign himself to death, seeing he does so for love of you. He awaits your reply in your anteroom."

Having finished this note, the prince carefully enclosed the ring in it without letting the eunuch see it, and gave him the letter, saying, "Take this to your mistress, my friend, and if on reading it and seeing its contents she is not instantly cured, you may call me an impudent impostor."

The eunuch at once passed into the princess' room and, handing her the letter, said, "Madam, a new astrologer has arrived, who declares that you will be cured as soon as you have read this letter and seen what it contains."

The princess took the note and opened it with languid indifference. But no sooner did she see her ring than, barely glancing at the writing, she rose hastily and with one bound reached the doorway and pushed back the hangings. Here she and the prince recognized each other, and in a moment they were locked in each other's arms. They tenderly embraced, wondering how they came to meet at last after so long a separation. The nurse, who had hastened after her charge, drew them back to the inner room, where the princess restored her ring to Camaralzaman.

"Take it back," she said, "I could not keep it without returning yours to you, and I am resolved to wear that as long as I live."

Meanwhile the eunuch had hastened back to the king. "Sire," he cried, "all the former doctors and astrologers were mere quacks. This man has cured the princess without even seeing her."

He then told all to the king who, overjoyed, hastened to his daughter's apartments, where, after embracing her, he placed her hand in that of the prince, saying, "Happy stranger, I keep my promise and give you my daughter to wife, be you who you may. But, if I am not much mistaken, your condition is above what you appear to be."

The prince thanked the king in the warmest and most respectful terms and said, "As regards my person, Your Majesty has rightly guessed that I am not an astrologer. It is but a disguise which I assumed in order to merit your illustrious alliance. I am myself a prince, my name is Camaralzaman and my father is Schahzaman, King of the

Isle of the Children of Khaledan." He then told his whole history, including the extraordinary manner of his first seeing and loving the Princess Badoura.

When he had finished, the king exclaimed, "So remarkable a story must not be lost to posterity. It shall be inscribed in the archives of my kingdom and published everywhere abroad."

The wedding took place next day amidst great pomp and rejoicings. Marzavan was not forgotten but was given a lucrative post at court, with a promise of further advancement. The prince and princess were now entirely happy, and months slipped by in the enjoyment of each other's society.

One night, however, Prince Camaralzaman dreamt that he saw his father lying at the point of death and saying, "Alas! My son, whom I loved so tenderly, has deserted me and is now causing my death."

The prince awoke with such a groan as to startle the princess, who asked what was the matter. "Ah," cried the prince, "at this very moment my father is perhaps no more!' And he told his dream.

The princess said but little at the time, but next morning she went to the king and, kissing his hand, said, "I have a favor to ask of Your Majesty, and I beg you to believe that it is in no way prompted by my husband. It is that you will allow us both to visit my father-in-law, King Schahzaman."

Sorry though the king felt at the idea of parting with his daughter, he felt her request to be so reasonable that he could not refuse it and made but one condition, which was that she should only spend one year at the court of King Schahzaman, suggesting that in future the young couple should visit their respective parents alternately.

The princess brought this good news to her husband who thanked her tenderly for this fresh proof of her affection.

All preparations for the journey were now pressed forward, and when all was ready the king accompanied the travelers for some days, after which he took an affectionate leave of his daughter and, charging the prince to take every care of her, returned to his capital.

The prince and princess journeyed on and at the end of a month reached a huge meadow interspersed with clumps of big trees which cast a most pleasant shade. As the heat was great Camaralzaman thought it well to encamp in this cool spot. Accordingly, the tents were pitched, and the princess, entering hers while the prince was giving his further orders, removed her girdle, which she placed beside her and, desiring her women to leave her, lay down and was soon asleep.

When the camp was all in order the prince entered the tent and, seeing the princess asleep, sat down near her without speaking. His eyes fell on the girdle which he took up, and while inspecting the precious stones set in it he noticed a little pouch sewn to the girdle and fastened by a loop. He touched it and felt something hard within.

Curious as to what this might be, he opened the pouch and found a carnelian engraved with various figures and strange characters. This carnelian must be something very precious, thought he, or my wife would not wear it on her person with so much care. In truth it was a talisman which the Queen of China had given her daughter, telling her it would ensure her happiness as long as she carried it about her.

The better to examine the stone, the prince stepped to the open doorway of the tent. As he stood there holding it in the open palm of his hand, a bird suddenly swooped down, picked the stone up in its beak and flew away with it. Imagine the prince's dismay at losing a jewel by which his wife evidently set such store!

The bird, having secured its prey, flew off some yards and alighted on the ground, holding the talisman in its beak. Prince Camaralzaman advanced, hoping the bird would drop it, but as soon as he approached the thief fluttered on a little farther still. He continued his pursuit till the bird suddenly swallowed the stone and took a longer flight than before. The prince then hoped to kill it with a stone, but the more hotly he pursued the farther flew the bird. In this fashion he was led on by hill and dale through the entire day, and when night came the tiresome creature roosted on the top of a very high tree where it could rest in safety.

A bird swooped down and flew off with the talisman.

The prince, in despair at all his useless trouble, began to think whether he had better return to the camp. But, thought he, how shall I find my way back? Must I go uphill or down? I should certainly lose my way in the dark, even if my strength held out. Overwhelmed by hunger, thirst, fatigue and sleep, he ended by spending the night at the foot of the tree.

Next morning Camaralzaman woke up before the bird left its perch, and no sooner did it take flight than he followed it again with as little success as the previous day, only stopping to eat some herbs and fruit he found by the way. In this fashion he spent ten days, following the bird all day and spending the night at the foot of a tree, while it roosted on the topmost bough. On the eleventh day the bird and the prince reached a large town, and as soon as they were close to its walls the bird took a sudden and higher flight and was shortly completely out of sight. Camaralzaman felt despair at having to give up all hopes of ever recovering the talisman of the Princess Badoura.

184

Much cast down, he entered the town, which was built near the sea and had a fine harbor. He walked about the streets for a long time, not knowing where to go, but at length as he walked near the seashore he found a garden door open and walked in.

The gardener, a good old man who was at work, happened to look up and, seeing a stranger whom he recognized by his dress as a Mussulman, told him to come in at once and shut the door. Camaralzaman did as he was bid and inquired why this precaution was taken.

"Because," said the gardener, "I see that you are a stranger and a Mussulman, and this town is almost entirely inhabited by idolaters who hate and persecute all of our faith. It seems almost a miracle that has led you to this house, and I am indeed glad that you have found a place of safety."

Camaralzaman warmly thanked the kind old man for offering him shelter and was about to say more, but the gardener interrupted him. "Leave compliments alone. You are weary and must be hungry. Come in, eat, and rest." So saying, he led the prince into his cottage and, after satisfying his hunger, begged to learn the cause of his arrival.

Camaralzaman told him all without disguise and ended by inquiring the shortest way to his father's capital. "For," added he, "if I tried to rejoin the princess, how should I find her after eleven days' separation. Perhaps, indeed, she may be no longer alive!" At this terrible thought he burst into tears.

The gardener informed Camaralzaman that they were quite a year's land journey to any Muhammadan country. But there was a much shorter route by sea to the Ebony Island, from whence the Isles of the Children of Khaledan could be easily reached, and a ship sailed once a year for the Ebony Island by which he might get so far as his very home.

"If only you had arrived a few days sooner," he said, "you might have embarked at once. As it is you must now wait till next year, but if you care to stay with me I offer you my house, such as it is, with all my heart."

Prince Camaralzaman thought himself lucky to find some place of refuge, and gladly accepted the gardener's offer. He spent his days working in the garden and his nights thinking of and sighing for his beloved wife.

Let us now see what had become of the Princess Badoura. On first waking she was much surprised not to find the prince near her. She called her women and asked if they knew where he was and while they were telling her that they had seen him enter the tent but had not noticed his leaving it, she took up her belt and perceived that the little pouch was open and the talisman gone.

She at once concluded that her husband had taken it and would shortly bring it back. She waited for him till evening rather impatiently and wondered what could have kept him from her so long. When night came without him she felt in despair and abused the talisman and its maker roundly. In spite of her grief and anxiety, however, she did not lose her presence of mind, but decided on a courageous, though very unusual step.

Only the princess and her women knew of Camaralzaman's disappearance, for the rest of the party were sleeping or resting in their tents. Fearing some treason, should the truth be known, she ordered her women not to say a word which would give rise to any suspicion and proceeded to change her dress for one of her husband's, to whom, as has been already said, she bore a strong likeness.

In this disguise she looked so like the prince that when she gave orders next morning to break up the camp and continue the journey no one suspected the change. She made one of her women enter her litter, while she herself mounted on horseback and the march began.

After a protracted journey by land and sea, the princess, still under the name and disguise of Prince Camaralzaman, arrived at the capital of the Ebony Island whose king was named Armanos.

No sooner did the king hear that the ship which was just in port had on board the son of his old friend and ally than he hurried to meet the supposed prince, and had him and his retinue brought to the palace, where they were lodged and entertained sumptuously.

After three days, finding that his guest, to whom he had taken a great fancy, talked of continuing his journey, King Armanos said to him, "Prince, I am now an old man, and unfortunately I have no son to whom to leave my kingdom. It has pleased Heaven to give me only one daughter, who possesses such great beauty and charm that I could only give her to a prince as highly born and as accomplished as yourself. Instead, therefore, of returning to your own country, take my daughter and my crown and stay with us. I shall feel that I have a worthy successor, and shall cheerfully retire from the fatigues of government."

The king's offer was naturally rather embarrassing to the Princess Badoura. She felt that it was equally impossible to confess that she had deceived him, or to refuse the marriage on which he had set his heart; a refusal which might turn all his kindness to hatred and persecution.

All things considered, she decided to accept and, after a few moment's silence, said with a blush, which the king attributed to modesty, "Sire, I feel so great an obligation for the good opinion Your Majesty has expressed for my person and of the honor you do me that, though I am quite unworthy of it, I dare not refuse. But, sire, I can only accept such an alliance if you give me your promise to assist me with your counsels."

The marriage being thus arranged, the ceremony was fixed for the following day, and the princess employed the intervening time in informing the officers of her suite of what had happened, assuring them that the Princess Badoura had given her full consent to the marriage. She also told her women and bade them keep her secret well.

King Armanos, delighted with the success of his plans, lost no time in assembling his court and council, to whom he presented his successor, and placing his future son-in-law on the throne, made everyone do homage and take oaths of allegiance to the new king.

At night the whole town was filled with rejoicings, and with much

187

pomp the Princess Haiatelnefous, which was the name of the king's daughter, was conducted to the palace of the Princess Badoura.

Now Badoura had thought much of the difficulties of her first interview with King Amanos' daughter, and she felt the only thing to do was at once to take her into her confidence.

Accordingly, as soon as they were alone she took Haiatelnefous by the hand and said, "Princess, I have a secret to tell you and must throw myself on your mercy. I am not Prince Camaralzaman, but a princess like yourself and his wife. I beg you to listen to my story, then I am sure you will forgive my imposture in consideration of my sufferings."

She then related her whole history, and at its close Haiatelnefous embraced her warmly and assured her of her entire sympathy and affection. The two princesses now planned out their future action, and agreed to combine to keep up the deception and to let Badoura continue to play a man's part until such time as there might be news of the real Camaralzaman.

While these things were passing in the Ebony Island Prince Camaralzaman continued to find shelter in the gardener's cottage in the town of the idolaters.

Early one morning the gardener said to the prince, "Today is a public holiday, and the people of the town not only do not work themselves but forbid others to do so. You had better therefore take a good rest while I go to see some friends, and as the time is near for the arrival of the ship of which I told you I will make inquiries about it and try to bespeak a passage for you."

He then put on his best clothes and went out, leaving the prince, who strolled into the garden and was soon lost in thoughts of his dear wife and their sad separation. As he walked up and down he was suddenly disturbed in his reverie by the noise two large birds were making in a tree.

Camaralzaman stood still and, looking up, saw that the birds were fighting so savagely with beaks and claws that before long one fell dead to the ground, while the conqueror spread his wings and flew away. Almost immediately two other larger birds, who had been watching the duel, flew up and alighted, one at the head and the other at the feet of the dead bird. They stood there some time sadly shaking their heads and then dug up a grave with their claws in which they buried him.

As soon as they had filled in the grave the birds flew off, but ere long returned with the murderer, whom they held, one by a wing and the other by a leg, with their beaks. The prisoner was screaming and struggling with rage and terror; but the two held tight and, having brought him to his victim's grave, proceeded to kill him. Then they tore his body and scattered it, and once more flew away.

The prince, who had watched the whole scene with much interest, now drew near the spot where it happened, and glancing at the dead bird he noticed something red lying near. He picked it up, and what was his surprise when he recognized the Princess Badoura's talisman which had been the cause of his many misfortunes. It would be impossible to describe his joy; he kissed the talisman repeatedly, wrapped it up, and carefully tied it round his arm. For the first time since his separation from the princess he had a good night, and next morning he was up at daybreak and went cheerfully to ask what work he should do.

The gardener told him to cut down an old fruit tree which had died, and Camaralzaman took an axe and fell to vigorously. As he was hacking at one of the roots the axe struck something hard. On pushing away the earth he discovered a large slab of bronze, under which was disclosed a staircase with ten steps. He went down them and found himself in a cave in which stood fifty large bronze jars, each with a cover on it. The prince uncovered one after another and found them all filled with gold dust. Delighted with his discovery, he left the cave, replaced the slab and, having finished cutting down the tree, waited for the gardener's return.

The gardener had heard the night before that the ship about which he was inquiring would start ere long, but the exact date not being yet known, he had been told to return next day for further information. He had gone therefore to inquire and came back with good news beaming in his face.

"My son," he said, "rejoice and hold yourself ready to start in three days' time. The ship is to set sail, and I have arranged all about your passage with the captain."

"You could not bring me better news," replied Camaralzaman, "and in return I have something pleasant to tell you. Follow me and see the good fortune which has befallen you."

He then led the gardener to the cave and, having shown him the treasure stored up there, said how happy it made him that Heaven should in this way reward his kind host's many virtues and compensate him for the privations of many years.

"What do you mean?" asked the gardener. "Do you imagine that I should appropriate this treasure? It is yours and I have no right whatever to it. For the last eighty years I have dug up the ground here without discovering anything. It is clear that these riches are intended for you, and they are much more needed by a prince like yourself than by an old man like me, who am near my end and require nothing. This treasure comes just at the right time, when you are about to return to your own country, where you will make good use of it."

But the prince would not hear of this suggestion, and finally after much discussion they agreed to divide the gold.

When this was done the gardener said, "My son, the great thing is to arrange how you can best carry off this treasure as secretly as possible for fear of losing it. There are no olives in the Ebony Island and those imported from here fetch a high price. As you know, I have a good stock of the olives which grew in this garden. Now you must take fifty jars, fill each half-full of gold dust and then fill them up with the olives. We will then have them taken on board ship when you embark."

The prince took his advice and spent the rest of the day filling the fifty jars, and fearing lest the precious talisman might slip from his arm and be lost again, he took the precaution of putting it in one of the jars, on which he made a mark so as to be able to recognize it. When night came the jars were all ready, and the prince and his host went to bed.

Whether in consequence of his great age, or of the fatigues and excitement of the previous day, I do not know, but the gardener passed a very bad night. He was worse next day, and by the morning of the third day was dangerously ill. At daybreak the ship's captain and some of his sailors knocked at the garden door and asked for the passenger who was to embark.

"I am he," said Camaralzaman, who had opened the door. "The gardener who took my passage is ill and cannot see you, but please come in and take these jars of olives and my bag, and I will follow as soon as I have taken leave of him."

The sailors did as he asked, and the captain, before leaving, charged Camaralzaman to lose no time, as the wind was fair and he wished to set sail at once. As soon as they were gone the prince returned to the cottage to bid farewell to his old friend and to thank him once more for all his kindness. But the old man was at his last gasp and had barely murmured his confession of faith when he expired.

Camaralzaman was obliged to stay and pay him the last offices, so having dug a grave in the garden, he wrapped the kind old man up and buried him. He then locked the door, gave up the key to the owner of the garden, and hurried to the quay only to hear that the ship had sailed long ago, after waiting three hours for him.

It may well be believed that the prince felt in despair at this fresh misfortune which obliged him to spend another year in a strange and distasteful country. Moreover, he had once more lost the Princess Badoura's talisman, which he feared he might never see again. There was nothing left for him but to hire the garden as the old man had done and to live on in the cottage. As he could not well cultivate the garden by himself, he engaged a lad to help him, and to secure the rest of the treasure he put the remaining gold dust into fifty more jars, filling them up with olives so as to have them ready for transport.

191

While the prince was settling down to this second year of toil and privation, the ship made a rapid voyage and arrived safely at the Ebony Island.

As the palace of the new king, or rather of the Princess Badoura, overlooked the harbor, she saw the ship entering it and asked what vessel it was coming in so gaily decked with flags, and was told that it was a ship from the Island of the Idolaters which yearly brought rich merchandise.

The princess, ever on the lookout for any chance of news of her beloved husband, went down to the harbor attended by some officers of the court, and arrived just as the captain was landing. She sent for him and asked many questions as to his country, voyage, what passengers he had, and what his vessel was laden with. The captain answered all her questions, and said that his passengers consisted entirely of traders who brought rich stuffs from various countries, fine muslins, precious stones, musk, amber, spices, drugs, olives, and many other things.

As soon as he mentioned olives, the princess, who was very partial to them, exclaimed, "I will take all you have on board. Have them unloaded and we will make our bargain at once, and tell the other merchants to let me see all their best wares before showing them to other people."

"Sire," replied the captain, "I have on board fifty very large pots of olives. They belong to a merchant who was left behind, as in spite of waiting for him he delayed so long that I was obliged to set sail without him."

"Never mind," said the princess, "unload them all the same, and we will arrange the price."

The captain accordingly sent his boat off to the ship and it soon returned laden with the fifty pots of olives. The princess asked what they might be worth.

"Sire," replied the captain, "the merchant is very poor. Your

Majesty will not overpay him if you give him a thousand pieces of silver."

"In order to satisfy him and as he is so poor," said the princess, "I will order a thousand pieces of gold to be given you, which you will be sure to remit to him."

So saying she gave orders for the payment and returned to the palace, having the jars carried before her. When evening came the Princess Badoura retired to the inner part of the palace and going to the apartments of the Princess Haiatelnefous, she had the fifty jars of olives brought to her. She opened one to let her friend taste the olives and to taste them herself, but great was her surprise when, on pouring some into a dish, she found them all powdered with gold dust. "What an adventure! How extraordinary!" she cried.

Then she had the other jars opened, and was more and more surprised to find the olives in each jar mixed with gold dust. But when at length her talisman was discovered in one of the jars, her emotion was so great that she fainted away. The Princess Haiatelnefous and her women hastened to restore her, and as soon as she recovered consciousness she covered the precious talisman with kisses.

Then, dismissing the attendants, she said to her friend, "You will have guessed, my dear, that it was the sight of this talisman which has moved me so deeply. This was the cause of my separation from my dear husband, and now, I am convinced, it will be the means of our reunion."

As soon as it was light next day the Princess Badoura sent for the captain, and made further inquiries about the merchant who owned the olive jars she had bought. In reply the captain told her all he knew of the place where the young man lived and how, after engaging his passage, he came to be left behind.

"If that is the case," said the princess, "you must set sail at once and go back for him. He is a debtor of mine and must be brought here at once, or I will confiscate all your merchandise. I shall now give orders to have all the warehouses where your cargo is placed under the royal seal, and they will only be opened when you have brought the man I ask for. Go at once and obey my orders."

The captain had no choice but to do as he was bid, so hastily provisioning his ship he started that same evening on his return voyage. When after a rapid passage he gained sight of the Island of Idolaters, he judged it better not to enter the harbor but, casting anchor at some distance, he embarked at night in a small boat with six active sailors and landed near Camaralzaman's cottage.

The prince was not asleep and, as he lay awake moaning over all the sad events which had separated him from his wife, he thought he heard a knock at the garden door. He went to open it, and was immediately seized by the captain and sailors who, without a word of explanation, forcibly bore him off to the boat, which took them back to the ship without loss of time. No sooner were they on board than they weighed anchor and set sail.

Camaralzaman, who had kept silence till then, now asked the captain, whom he had recognized, the reason for this abduction.

"Are you not a debtor of the King of the Ebony Island?" asked the captain.

"I? Why, I never even heard of him before and never set foot in his kingdom!" was the answer.

"Well, you must know better than I," said the captain. "You will soon see him now, and meantime be content where you are and have patience."

The return voyage was as rapid as the former one, and though it was night when the ship entered the harbor, the captain lost no time in landing with his passenger, whom he conducted to the palace where he begged an audience with the king.

Directly the Princess Badoura saw the prince she recognized him in spite of his shabby clothes. She longed to throw herself on his neck, but restrained herself, feeling it was better for them both that she should play her part a little longer. She therefore desired one of her officers to take care of him and to treat him well. Next she ordered another officer to remove the seals from the warehouse, while she presented the captain with a costly diamond, and told him to keep the thousand pieces of gold paid for the olives, as she would arrange matters with the merchant himself.

She then returned to her private apartments, where she told the Princess Haiatelnefous all that had happened, as well as her plans for the future, and begged her assistance, which her friend readily promised.

Next morning she ordered the prince to be taken to the bath and clothed in a manner suitable to an emir or governor of a province. He was then introduced to the council, where his good looks and grand air drew the attention of all on him.

Princess Badoura, delighted to see him looking himself once more, turned to the other emirs, saying, "My lords, I introduce to you a new colleague, Camaralzaman, whom I have known on my travels and who, I can assure you, well deserves your regard and admiration."

Camaralzaman was much surprised at hearing the king—whom he never suspected of being a woman in disguise—asserting their acquaintance, whom he felt sure he had never seen before.

However, he received all the praises bestowed on him with becoming modesty, and prostrating himself, said, "Sire, I cannot find words in which to thank Your Majesty for the great honor conferred on me. I can but assure you that I will do all in my power to prove myself worthy of it."

On leaving the council the prince was conducted to a splendid house which had been prepared for him, where he found a full establishment and well-filled stables at his orders. On entering his study his steward presented him with a coffer filled with gold pieces for his current expenses. He felt more and more puzzled by such good fortune, and little guessed that the Princess of China was the cause of it.

After a few days the Princess Badoura promoted Camaralzaman to the post of grand treasurer, an office which he filled with so much integrity and benevolence as to win universal esteem. He would now have thought himself the happiest of men had it not been for that separation which he never ceased to bewail. He had no clue to the mystery of his present position, for the princess, out of compliment to the old king, had taken his name and was generally known as King Armanos the younger, few people remembering that on her first arrival she went by another name.

At length the princess felt the time had come to put an end to her own and the prince's suspense and, having arranged all her plans with the Princess Haiatelnefous, she informed Camaralzaman that she wished his advice on some important business and, to avoid being disturbed, desired him to come to the palace that evening.

The prince was punctual and was received in the private apartment. Then, having ordered her attendants to withdraw, the princess took from a small box the talisman and, handing it to Camaralzaman, said, "Not long ago an astrologer gave me this talisman. As you are universally well informed, you can perhaps tell me what is its use."

Camaralzaman took the talisman and, holding it to the light, cried with surprise, "Sire, you ask me the use of this talisman. Alas! Hitherto it has been only a source of misfortune to me, being the cause of my separation from the one I love best on earth. The story is so sad and strange that I am sure Your Majesty will be touched by it if you will permit me to tell it you."

"I will hear it some other time," replied the princess. "Meanwhile I fancy it is not quite unknown to me. Wait here for me. I will return shortly."

So saying she retired to another room, where she hastily changed her masculine attire for that of a woman and, after putting on the girdle she wore the day they parted, returned to Camaralzaman.

The prince recognized her at once and, embracing her with the utmost tenderness, cried, "Ah, how can I thank the king for this delightful surprise?"

"Do not expect ever to see the king again," said the princess, as she wiped the tears of joy from her eyes. "In me you see the king. Let us sit down, and I will tell you all about it."

She then gave a full account of all her adventures since their parting and dwelt much on the charms and noble disposition of the Princess Haiatelnefous, to whose friendly assistance she owed so much. When she had done she asked to hear the prince's story, and in this manner they spent most of the night.

Next morning, as soon as she was dressed, the princess desired the chief eunuch to beg King Armanos to come to her apartments. When he arrived, great was his astonishment at finding a strange lady in company of the grand treasurer, who had no actual right to enter the private apartments. Seating himself, he asked for the king.

"Sire," said the princess, "yesterday I was the king, today I am only the Princess of China and wife to the real Prince Camaralzaman, son of King Schahzaman, and I trust when Your Majesty shall have heard our story you will not condemn the innocent deception I have been obliged to practice."

The king consented to listen, and did so with marked surprise.

At the close of her narrative the princess said, "Sire, as our religion allows a man to have more than one wife, I would beg Your Majesty to give your daughter, the Princess Haiatelnefous, in marriage to Prince Camaralzaman. I gladly yield to her the precedence and title of Queen in recognition of the debt of gratitude which I owe her."

King Armanos heard the princess with surprise and admiration. Turning to Camaralzaman, he said, "My son, as your wife, the Princess Badoura, whom I have hitherto looked on as my son-in-law, consents to share your hand and affections with my daughter, I have only to ask if this marriage is agreeable to you, and if you will consent to accept

197

the crown which the Princess Badoura deserves to wear all her life, but which she prefers to resign for love of you."

"Sire," said Camaralzaman, "I can refuse Your Majesty nothing."

Accordingly Camaralzaman was duly proclaimed king and married with all pomp to the Princess Haiatelnefous, with whose beauty, talents, and affection he had every reason to be pleased.

The two queens lived in true sisterly harmony together, and after a time each presented King Camaralzaman with a son, whose births were celebrated throughout the kingdom with the utmost rejoicing.

ALADDIN AND THE WONDERFUL LAMP

here once lived a poor tailor who had a son called Aladdin, a careless, idle boy who would do nothing but play all day long in the streets with little idle boys like himself. This so grieved the father that he died; yet, in spite of his mother's tears and prayers, Aladdin did not mend his ways. One day, when he was playing in the streets as usual, a stranger asked him his age, and if he were not the son of Mustapha the tailor.

"I am, sir," replied Aladdin; "but he died a long while ago."

On this the stranger, who was a famous African magician, fell on his neck and kissed him, saying, "I am your uncle and I knew you from your likeness to my brother. Go to your mother and tell her I am coming."

Aladdin ran home and told his mother of his newly found uncle.

"Indeed, child," she said, "your father had a brother, but I always thought he was dead."

However, she prepared supper and bade Aladdin seek his uncle, who came laden with wine and fruit. He presently knelt and kissed the place where Mustapha used to sit, bidding Aladdin's mother not to be surprised at not having seen him before, as he had been forty years out of the country.

He then turned to Aladdin and asked him his trade, at which the boy hung his head, while his mother burst into tears. On learning that Aladdin was idle and would learn no trade, he offered to take a shop for him and stock it with merchandise. Next day he bought Aladdin a fine suit of clothes and took him all over the city, showing him the sights, and brought him home at nightfall to his mother, who was overjoyed to see her son so fine.

Next day the magician led Aladdin into some beautiful gardens a long way outside the city gates. They sat down by a fountain, and the magician pulled a cake from his girdle, which he divided between them. They then journeyed onward till they almost reached the mountains. Aladdin was so tired that he begged to go back, but the magician beguiled him with pleasant stories and led him on in spite of himself.

At last they came to two mountains divided by a narrow valley. "We will go no farther," said the false uncle. "I will show you something wonderful; only do you gather up sticks while I kindle a fire."

When the fire was lit the magician threw on it a powder he had with him, at the same time saying some magical words. The earth trembled a little and opened in front of them, disclosing a square flat stone with a brass ring in the middle to raise it by. Aladdin tried to run away, but the magician caught him and gave him a blow that knocked him down.

"What have I done, Uncle?" he said piteously.

Whereupon the magician said more kindly, "Fear nothing, but obey me. Beneath this stone lies a treasure which is to be yours, and no one else may touch it, so you must do exactly as I tell you."

At the word *treasure*, Aladdin forgot his fears and grasped the ring as he was told, saying the names of his father and grandfather. The stone came up quite easily and some steps appeared.

"Go down," said the magician. "At the foot of those steps you will find an open door leading into three large halls. Tuck up your gown and go through them without touching anything, or you will die instantly. These halls lead into a garden of fine fruit trees. Walk on till you come to a niche in a terrace where stands a lighted lamp. Pour out the oil it contains and bring it to me." He drew a ring from his finger and gave it to Aladdin, bidding him prosper.

Aladdin found everything as the magician had said, gathered some fruit off the trees and, having got the lamp, arrived at the mouth of the cave.

The magician cried out in a great hurry, "Make haste and give me the lamp." This Aladdin refused to do until he was out of the cave. The magician flew into a terrible passion, and throwing some more powder on the fire, he said something, and the stone rolled back into its place.

The magician left Persia forever, which plainly showed that he was no uncle of Aladdin's, but a cunning sorcerer who had read in his magic books of a wonderful lamp which would make him the most powerful man in the world. Though he alone knew where to find it, he could only receive it from the hand of another. He had picked out the foolish Aladdin for this purpose, intending to get the lamp and kill him afterward.

For two days Aladdin remained in the dark, crying and lamenting. At last he clasped his hands in prayer, and in so doing rubbed the ring, which the magician had forgotten to take from him.

Immediately an enormous and frightful genie rose out of the earth, saying, "What wouldst thou with me? I am the slave of the ring and will obey thee in all things."

Aladdin fearlessly replied, "Deliver me from this place," whereupon the earth opened, and he found himself outside. As soon as his eyes could bear the light he went home, but fainted on the threshold. When he came to himself he told his mother what had passed, and showed her the lamp and the fruits he had gathered in the garden, which were in reality precious stones. He then asked for some food.

"Alas, child," she said, "I have nothing in the house, but I have spun a little cotton and will go and sell it."

Aladdin bade her keep her cotton, for he would sell the lamp instead. As it was very dirty she began to rub it, that it might fetch a higher price. Instantly a hideous genie appeared and asked what she would have.

She fainted away, but Aladdin, snatching the lamp, said boldly, "Fetch me something to eat!"

The genie returned with a silver bowl, twelve silver plates containing rich meats, two silver cups, and a bottle of wine.

Aladdin's mother, when she came to herself, said, "Whence comes this splendid feast?"

"Ask not, but eat," replied Aladdin.

So they sat at breakfast till it was dinnertime, and Aladdin told his mother about the lamp. She begged him to sell it and have nothing to do with genii.

"No," said Aladdin, "since chance has made us aware of its virtues, we will use it and the ring likewise, which I shall always wear on my finger." When they had eaten all the genie had brought, Aladdin sold one of the silver plates, and so on, till none were left. He then had recourse to the genie, who gave him another set of plates, and thus they lived for many years.

One day Aladdin heard an order from the sultan proclaiming that everyone was to stay at home and close his shutters while the princess, his daughter, went to and from the bath. Aladdin was seized by a desire to see her face, which was very difficult, as she always went veiled. He hid himself behind the door of the bath and peeped through a chink.

The princess lifted her veil as she went in, and looked so beautiful that Aladdin fell in love with her at first sight. He went home so changed that his mother was frightened. He told her he loved the princess so deeply he could not live without her and meant to ask her in marriage of her father. His mother, on hearing this, burst out laughing, but Aladdin at last prevailed upon her to go before the sultan and carry his request. She fetched a napkin and laid in it the magic fruits from the enchanted garden, which sparkled and shone like the most beautiful jewels. She took these with her to please the sultan and set out, trusting in the lamp. The grand vizir and the lords of council had just gone in as she entered the hall and placed herself in front of the sultan. He, however, took no notice of her. She went every day for a week and stood in the same place.

When the council broke up on the sixth day the sultan said to his vizir, "I see a certain woman in the audience chamber every day, carrying something in a napkin. Call her next time that I may find out what she wants."

Next day, at a sign from the vizir, she went up to the foot of the throne and remained kneeling till the sultan said to her, "Rise, good woman, and tell me what you want."

She hesitated, so the sultan sent away all but the vizir and bade her speak freely, promising to forgive her beforehand for anything she might say. She then told him of her son's violent love for the princess.

"I prayed him to forget her," she said, "but in vain; he threatened to do some desperate deed if I refused to go and ask Your Majesty for the hand of the princess. Now I pray you to forgive not me alone but my son Aladdin."

The sultan asked her kindly what she had in the napkin, whereupon she unfolded the jewels and presented them.

He was thunderstruck, and turning to the vizir, said, "What sayest thou? Ought I not to bestow the princess on one who values her at such a price?"

The vizir, who wanted her for his own son, begged the sultan to withhold her for three months, in the course of which he hoped his son would contrive to make him a richer present. The sultan granted this and told Aladdin's mother that, though he consented to the marriage, she must not appear before him again for three months.

Aladdin waited patiently for nearly three months, but after two had elapsed his mother, going into the city to buy oil, found everyone rejoicing and asked what was going on.

"Do you not know," was the answer, "that the son of the grand vizir is to marry the sultan's daughter tonight?"

Breathless, she ran and told Aladdin, who was overwhelmed at first, but presently bethought him of the lamp. He rubbed it, and the genie appeared, saying, "What is thy will?"

Aladdin replied, "The sultan, as thou knowest, has broken his promise to me, and the vizir's son is to have the princess. My command is that tonight you bring hither the bride and bridegroom."

"Master, I obey," said the genie.

Aladdin then went to his chamber where, sure enough at midnight, the genie transported the bed containing the vizir's son and the princess.

"Take this new-married man," Aladdin said, "and put him outside in the cold and return at daybreak."

Whereupon the genie took the vizir's son out of bed, leaving Aladdin with the princess.

"Fear nothing," Aladdin said to her; "you are my wife, promised to me by your unjust father, and no harm shall come to you."

The princess was too frightened to speak and passed the most miserable night of her life, while Aladdin lay down beside her and slept soundly. At the appointed hour the genie fetched in the shivering bridegroom, laid him in his place, and transported the bed back to the palace.

Presently the sultan came to wish his daughter good morning. The unhappy vizir's son jumped up and hid himself, while the princess would not say a word and was very sorrowful.

The sultan sent her mother to her, who said, "How comes it, child, that you will not speak to your father? What has happened?"

The princess sighed deeply, and at last told her mother how, during the night, the bed had been carried into some strange house, and what had passed there. Her mother did not believe her in the least but bade her rise and consider it an idle dream.

The following night exactly the same thing happened, and next morning, on the princess' refusing to speak, the sultan threatened to cut off her head. She then confessed all, bidding him ask the vizir's son if it were not so. The sultan told the vizir to ask his son, who owned the truth; adding that, dearly as he loved the princess, he had rather die than go through another such fearful night and that he wished to be separated from her. His wish was granted, and there was an end of feasting and rejoicing.

When the three months were over, Aladdin sent his mother to remind the sultan of his promise. She stood in the same place as before, and the sultan, who had forgotten Aladdin, at once remembered him and sent for her. On seeing her poverty the sultan felt less inclined than ever to keep his word and asked the vizir's advice, who counseled him to set so high a value on the princess that no man living could come up to it.

The sultan then turned to Aladdin's mother, saying, "Good woman, a sultan must remember his promises and I will remember mine, but your son must first send me forty basins of gold brimful of jewels, carried by forty black slaves, led by as many white ones, splendidly dressed. Tell him that I await his answer."

The mother of Aladdin bowed low and went home, thinking all was lost. She gave Aladdin the message, adding, "He may wait long enough for your answer!"

"Not so long, Mother, as you think," her son replied. "I would do a great deal more than that for the princess." He summoned the genie, and in a few moments the eighty slaves arrived and filled up the small house and garden.

Aladdin made them set out to the palace, two and two, followed by his mother. They were so richly dressed, with such splendid jewels in their girdles, that everyone crowded to see them and the basins of gold they carried on their heads.

They entered the palace and, after kneeling before the sultan, stood in a half-circle round the throne with their arms crossed, while Aladdin's mother presented them to the sultan.

He hesitated no longer but said, "Good woman, return and tell your son that I wait for him with open arms."

She lost no time in telling Aladdin, bidding him make haste. But Aladdin first called the genie.

"I want a scented bath," he said, "a richly embroidered habit, a horse surpassing the sultan's, and twenty slaves to attend me. Besides this I desire six slaves, beautifully dressed, to wait on my mother; and lastly, ten thousand pieces of gold in ten purses."

No sooner said than done. Aladdin mounted his horse and passed through the streets, the slaves strewing gold as they went. Those who had played with him in his childhood knew him not, he had grown so handsome.

When the sultan saw him, he came down from his throne, embraced him, and led him into a hall where a feast was spread, intending to marry him to the princess that very day. But Aladdin refused, saying, "I must build a palace fit for her," and took his leave.

Once home, he said to the genie, "Build me a palace of the finest marble, set with jasper, agate, and other precious stones. In the middle you shall build me a large hall with a dome, its four walls of massy gold and silver, each side having six windows whose lattices, all except one, which is to be left unfinished, must be set with diamonds and rubies. There must be stables and horses and grooms and slaves. Go and see about it!"

The palace was finished by next day, and the genie carried him there and showed him all his orders faithfully carried out, even to the laying of a velvet carpet from Aladdin's palace to the sultan's. Aladdin's mother then dressed herself carefully and walked to the palace with her slaves. The sultan sent musicians with trumpets and cymbals to meet them and the air resounded with music and cheers.

Aladdin's mother was taken to the princess, who saluted her and treated her with great honor. At night the princess said good-bye to her father and set out on the carpet for Aladdin's palace, with his mother at her side, and followed by the hundred slaves. She was charmed at the sight of Aladdin who ran to receive her.

"Princess," he said, "blame your beauty for my boldness if I have displeased you."

She told him that, having seen him, she willingly obeyed her father in this matter. After the wedding had taken place, Aladdin led her into the hall where a feast was spread, and she supped with him, after which they danced till midnight.

Next day Aladdin invited the sultan to see the palace. On entering the hall with the four-and-twenty windows, with their rubies, diamonds, and emeralds, he cried, "It is a world's wonder! There is only one thing that surprises me. Was it by accident that one window was left unfinished?"

"No, sir, by design," returned Aladdin. "I wished Your Majesty to have the glory of finishing this palace."

The sultan was pleased and sent for the best jewelers in the city. He showed them the unfinished window and bade them fit it up like the others.

"Sir," replied their spokesman, "we cannot find jewels enough."

The sultan had his own fetched, which they soon used, but to no purpose, for in a month's time the work was not half done. Aladdin, knowing that their task was vain, bade them undo their work and carry the jewels back, and the genie finished the window at his command. The sultan was surprised to receive his jewels again and visited Aladdin, who showed him the window finished. The sultan embraced him, the envious vizir meanwhile hinting that it was the work of enchantment.

Aladdin had won the hearts of the people by his gentle bearing. He was made captain of the sultan's armies and won several battles for him, but remained modest and courteous as before and lived thus in peace and content for several years.

But far away in Africa the magician remembered Aladdin, and by his magic arts discovered that Aladdin, instead of perishing miserably in the cave, had escaped and had married a princess, with whom he was living in great honor and wealth. He knew that the poor tailor's son could only have accomplished this by means of the lamp and traveled night and day till he reached the capital of China, bent on Aladdin's ruin. As he passed through the town he heard people talking everywhere about a marvelous palace.

"Forgive my ignorance," he asked, "what is this palace you speak of?"

"Have you not heard of Prince Aladdin's palace," was the reply, "the greatest wonder of the world? I will direct you if you have a mind to see it."

The magician thanked him who spoke and, having seen the palace, knew that it had been raised by the genie of the lamp and became half-mad with rage. He determined to get hold of the lamp and again plunge Aladdin into the deepest poverty.

Unluckily, Aladdin had gone hunting for eight days, which gave the magician plenty of time. He bought a dozen copper lamps, put them into a basket, and went to the palace, crying, "New lamps for old!" followed by a jeering crowd.

The princess, sitting in the hall of four-and-twenty windows, sent a slave to find out what the noise was about. The slave came back laughing, so the princess scolded her.

"Madam," replied the slave, "who can help laughing to see an old fool offering to exchange fine new lamps for old ones?"

Another slave, hearing this, said, "There is an old one on the cornice there which he can have."

Now this was the magic lamp, which Aladdin had left there, as he could not take it out hunting with him. The princess, not knowing its value, laughingly bade the slave take it and make the exchange. She went and said to the magician, "Give me a new lamp for this."

He snatched it and bade the slave take her choice, amid the jeers of the crowd. Little he cared, but left off crying his lamps, and went out of the city gates to a lonely place, where he remained till nightfall, when he pulled out the lamp and rubbed it. The genie appeared and at the magician's command carried him, together with the palace and the princess in it, to a lonely place in Africa.

Next morning the sultan looked out of the window toward Aladdin's palace and rubbed his eyes, for it was gone. He sent for the vizir and asked what had become of the palace. The vizir looked out, too, and was lost in astonishment. He again put it down to enchantment and this time the sultan believed him and sent thirty men on horse-back to fetch Aladdin in chains. They met him riding home, bound him, and forced him to go with them on foot.

The people, however, who loved him, followed, armed, to see that he came to no harm. He was carried before the sultan, who ordered the executioner to cut off his head. The executioner made Aladdin kneel down, bandaged his eyes, and raised his scimitar to strike. At that instant the vizir, who saw that the crowd had forced their way into the courtyard and were scaling the walls to rescue Aladdin, called to the executioner to stay his hand. The people, indeed, looked so threaten-ing that the sultan gave way and ordered Aladdin to be unbound, and pardoned him in the sight of the crowd.

Aladdin now begged to know what he had done.

"False wretch!" said the sultan, "come hither," and showed him from the window the place where his palace had stood. Aladdin was so amazed that he could not say a word.

"Where is the palace and my daughter?" demanded the sultan. "For the first I am not so deeply concerned, but my daughter I must have and you must find her or lose your head."

Aladdin begged for forty days in which to find her, promising if he failed, to return and suffer death at the sultan's pleasure. His prayer was granted, and he went forth sadly from the sultan's presence. For three days he wandered about like a madman, asking everyone what had become of his palace, but they only laughed and pitied him.

He came to the banks of a river and knelt down to say his prayers before throwing himself in. In so doing he rubbed the magic ring he still wore. The genie he had seen in the cave appeared and asked his will.

"Save my life, genie," said Aladdin, "and bring my palace back."

"That is not in my power," said the genie. "I am only the slave of the ring, you must ask the slave of the lamp."

"Even so," said Aladdin, "but thou canst take me to the palace, and set me down under my dear wife's window." He at once found himself in Africa, under the window of the princess, where he fell asleep from sheer weariness.

He was awakened by the singing of the birds and his heart was lighter. He saw plainly that all his misfortunes were owing to the loss of the lamp and vainly wondered who had robbed him of it.

That morning the princess rose earlier than she had since she had been carried into Africa by the magician, whose company she was forced to endure once a day. She, however, treated him so harshly that he dared not live there altogether. As she was dressing, one of her women looked out and saw Aladdin. The princess ran and opened the window, and at the noise she made Aladdin looked up. She called him to come to her, and great was their joy at seeing each other again.

After he had kissed her Aladdin said, "I beg of you, Princess, before we speak of anything else, for your own sake and mine, tell me what has become of an old lamp I left on the cornice in the hall of four-and-twenty windows, when I went hunting."

"Alas," she said, "I am the innocent cause of our sorrows," and told him of the exchange of the lamp.

"Now I know," cried Aladdin, "that we have to thank the African magician for this! Where is the lamp?"

"He carries it about with him," said the princess, "I know, for he pulled it out of his robe to show me. He wishes me to break my faith with you and marry him, saying that you were beheaded by my father's command. He is forever speaking ill of you, but I only reply by my tears. If I persist, I doubt not that he will use violence."

Aladdin comforted her and left her for a while. He changed clothes with the first person he met in the town and, having bought a certain powder, returned to the princess, who let him in by a little side door.

"Put on your most beautiful dress," he said to her, "and receive the magician with smiles, leading him to believe that you have forgotten me. Invite him to sup with you and say you wish to taste the wine of his country. He will go for some and while he is gone I will tell you what to do."

She listened carefully to Aladdin and, when he left her, arrayed herself gaily for the first time since she left China. She put on a girdle and headdress of diamonds, and seeing in a glass that she looked more beautiful than ever, received the magician, saying to his great amazement, "I have made up my mind that Aladdin is dead and that all my tears will not bring him back to me, so I am resolved to mourn no more and therefore invite you to sup with me. But I am tired of the wines of China and would fain taste those of Africa."

The magician flew to his cellar and the princess put the powder Aladdin had given her in her cup. When he returned she asked him to drink her health in the wine of Africa, handing him her cup in exchange for his as a sign she was reconciled to him.

Before drinking, the magician made her a speech in praise of her beauty, but the princess cut him short, saying, "Let me drink first, and you shall say what you will afterward." She set her cup to her lips while the magician drained his to the dregs and fell back lifeless.

The princess then opened the door to Aladdin and flung her arms round his neck, but Aladdin put her away, bidding her to leave him, as he had more to do. He then went to the dead magician, took the lamp out of his vest, and bade the genie carry the palace and all in it back to China. This was done, and the princess in her chamber only felt two slight shocks and little thought she was at home again.

The sultan, who was sitting in his closet, mourning for his lost daughter, happened to look up and rubbed his eyes, for there stood the palace as before! He hastened thither, and Aladdin received him in the hall of the four-and-twenty windows, with the princess at his side. Aladdin told him what had happened and showed him the dead body of the magician, that he might believe. A ten days' feast was proclaimed, and it seemed as if Aladdin might now live the rest of his life in peace; but it was not to be.

The African magician had a younger brother, who was, if possible, more wicked and cunning than himself. He traveled to China to avenge his brother's death and went to visit a pious woman called Fatima, thinking she might be of use to him. He entered her cell and clapped a dagger to her breast, telling her to rise and do his bidding on pain of death. He changed clothes with her, colored his face like hers, put on her veil, and murdered her that she might tell no tales.

Then he went toward the palace of Aladdin, and all the people, thinking he was the holy woman, gathered round him, kissing his hands and begging his blessing. When he reached the palace there was such a noise round him that the princess bade her slave look out of the window and ask what was the matter. The slave said it was the holy woman, curing people of their ailments by her touch, whereupon the princess, who had long desired to see Fatima, sent for her.

On coming to the princess, the magician offered up a prayer for her health and prosperity. When he had done the princess made him sit by her and begged him to stay with her always. The false Fatima, who wished for nothing better, consented but kept his veil down for fear of discovery. The princess showed him the hall and asked him what he thought of it.

"It is truly beautiful," said the false Fatima. "In my mind it wants but one thing."

"And what is that?" said the princess.

"If only a roc's egg," replied he, "were hung up from the middle of this dome, it would be the wonder of the world."

After this the princess could think of nothing but a roc's egg, and when Aladdin returned from hunting he found her in a very ill humor. He begged to know what was amiss, but she told him that all her pleasure in the hall was spoilt for the want of a roc's egg hanging from the dome.

"If that is all," replied Aladdin, "you shall soon be happy."

He left her and rubbed the lamp, and when the genie appeared commanded him to bring a roc's egg. The genie gave such a loud and terrible shriek that the hall shook.

"Wretch," he cried, "is it not enough that I have done everything for you, but you must command me to bring my master and hang him up in the midst of this dome? You and your wife and your palace deserve to be burnt to ashes, but this request does not come from you but from the brother of the African magician whom you destroyed. He is now in your palace disguised as the holy woman—whom he murdered. He it was who put that wish into your wife's head. Take care of yourself, for he means to kill you." So saying the genie disappeared.

Aladdin went back to the princess, saying his head ached and requesting that the holy Fatima should be fetched to lay her hands on it. But when the magician came near, Aladdin, seizing his dagger, pierced him to the heart.

"What have you done?" cried the princess. "You have killed the holy woman!"

"Not so," replied Aladdin, "but a wicked magician," and told her of how she had been deceived.

After this Aladdin and his wife lived in peace. He succeeded the sultan when he died, and reigned for many years, leaving behind him a long line of kings.

THE CALIPH OF BAGHDAD

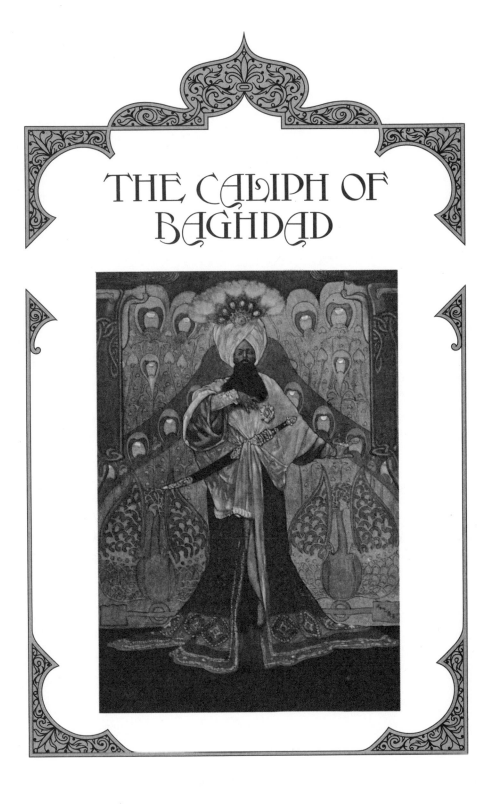

he Caliph Harun al-Rashid sat in his palace, wondering if there was anything left in the world that could possibly give him a few hours' amusement, when Giafar, the grand vizir, his old and tried friend, suddenly appeared before him. Bowing low, he waited, as was his duty, till his master spoke, but Harun al-Rashid merely turned his head and looked at him, and sank back into his former weary posture.

Now Giafar had something of importance to say to the caliph and had no intention of being put off by mere silence, so with another low bow in front of the throne, he began to speak.

"Commander of the Faithful," said he, "I have taken on myself to remind Your Highness that you have undertaken secretly to observe for yourself the manner in which justice is done and order is kept throughout the city. This is the day you have set apart to devote to this object, and perhaps in fulfilling this duty you may find some distraction from the melancholy to which, I see to my sorrow, you are a prey."

"You are right," returned the caliph, "I had forgotten all about it. Go and change your coat, and I will change mine."

A few moments later they both reentered the hall disguised as foreign merchants, and passed through a secret door out into the open country. Here they turned toward the Euphrates and, crossing the river in a small boat, walked through that part of the town which lay along the farther bank without seeing anything to call for their interference. Much pleased with the peace and good order of the city, the caliph and his vizir made their way to a bridge which led straight back to the palace, and had already crossed it, when they were stopped by an old, blind man who begged for alms.

The caliph gave him a piece of money and was passing on, but the blind man seized his hand and held him fast.

"Charitable person," he said, "whoever you may be, grant me yet another prayer. Strike me, I beg of you, one blow. I have deserved it richly, and even a more severe penalty."

The caliph, much surprised at this request, replied gently, "My good man, that which you ask is impossible. Of what use would my alms be if I treated you so ill?" And as he spoke he tried to loosen the grasp of the blind beggar.

"My lord," answered the man, "pardon my boldness and my persistence. Take back your money or give me the blow which I crave. I have sworn a solemn oath that I will receive nothing without receiving chastisement, and if you knew all, you would feel that the punishment is not a tenth part of what I deserve."

Moved by these words and perhaps still more by the fact that he had other business to attend to, the caliph yielded and struck the beggar lightly on the shoulder. Then he continued his road, followed by the blessing of the blind man. When they were out of earshot, he said to the vizir, "There must be something very odd to make that man act so—I should like to find out what is the reason. Go back to him, tell him who I am and order him to come without fail to the palace tomorrow after the hour of evening prayer."

So the grand vizir went back to the bridge, gave the blind beggar first a piece of money and then a blow, delivered the caliph's message, and rejoined his master.

The next day after evening prayer, the caliph entered the hall and was followed by the vizir bringing with him the man expected. They bowed low before the throne and then the caliph bade them rise and asked the blind man his name.

"Baba-Abdalla, Your Highness," said he.

"Baba-Abdalla," returned the caliph, "your way of asking alms yesterday seemed to me so strange that I almost commanded you then and there to cease from causing such a public scandal. But I have sent for you to inquire what was your motive in making such a curious vow. When I know the reason I shall be able to judge whether you can be permitted to continue to practise it, for I cannot help thinking that it sets a very bad example to others. Tell me therefore the whole truth and conceal nothing."

These words troubled the heart of Baba-Abdalla, who prostrated himself at the feet of the caliph. Then rising, he answered, "Commander of the Faithful, I crave your pardon humbly for my persistence in an action which appears on the face of it to be without any meaning. No doubt, in the eyes of men, it has none; but I look on it as a slight expiation for a fearful sin of which I have been guilty, and if Your Highness will deign to listen to my tale, you will see that no punishment could atone for the crime."

THE BLIND
BABA-ABDALLA

I was born, Commander of the Faithful, in Baghdad and was left an orphan while I was yet a very young man, for my parents died within a few days of each other. I had inherited from them a small fortune, which I worked hard night and day to increase, till at last I found myself the owner of eighty camels. These I hired out to traveling merchants, whom I frequently accompanied on their various journeys and always returned with large profits.

One day I was coming back from Balsora, whither I had taken a supply of goods intended for India, and halted at noon in a lonely place which promised rich pasture for camels. I was resting in the shade under a tree when a dervish, going on foot toward Balsora, sat down by my side. I inquired whence he had come and to what place he was going. We soon made friends and, after we had asked each other the usual questions, produced the food we had with us and satisfied our hunger.

While we were eating, the dervish happened to mention that in a spot only a little way off from where we were sitting, there was hidden a treasure so great that if my eighty camels were loaded till they could carry no more, the hiding place would seem as full as if it had never been touched.

At this news I became almost beside myself with joy and greed and flung my arms round the neck of the dervish, exclaiming, "Good dervish, I see plainly that the riches of this world are nothing to you, therefore of what use is the knowledge of this treasure to you? Alone and on foot, you could carry away a mere handful. But tell me where it is, and I will load my eighty camels with it and give you one of them as a token of my gratitude."

Certainly my offer does not sound very magnificent, but it was great to me, for at his words a wave of covetousness had swept over my heart, and I almost felt as if the seventy-nine camels that were left were nothing in comparison.

The dervish saw quite well what was passing in my mind, but he did not show what he thought of my proposal.

"My brother," he answered quietly, "you know as well as I do that you are behaving unjustly. It was open to me to keep my secret and to reserve the treasure for myself. But the fact that I have told you of its existence shows that I had confidence in you and hoped to earn your gratitude forever, by making your fortune as well as mine. But before I reveal to you the secret of the treasure, you must swear that, after we have loaded the camels with as much as they can carry, you will give half to me and let us go our own ways. I think you will see that this is fair, for if you present me with forty camels, I on my side will give you the means of buying a thousand more."

I could not of course deny that what the dervish said was perfectly reasonable but, in spite of that, the thought he would be as rich as I was unbearable to me. Still, there was no use in discussing the matter, and I had to accept his conditions or bewail to the end of my life the loss of immense wealth. So I collected my camels and set out under the guidance of the dervish. After walking some time, we reached what looked like a valley but with such a narrow entrance my camels could only pass one by one. The little valley, or open space, was shut in by two mountains, whose sides were formed of straight cliffs which no human being could climb.

When we were exactly between these mountains the dervish stopped. "Make your camels lie down in this open space," he said, "so we can easily load them; then we will go to the treasure."

I did what I was bid and rejoined the dervish, who was trying to kindle a fire out of some dry wood. As soon as it was alight, he threw on it a handful of perfumes and pronounced a few words that I did not understand; immediately a thick column of smoke rose high into the air. He separated the smoke into two columns, and then I saw a rock which stood like a pillar between the two mountains slowly open and a splendid palace appear within.

But, Commander of the Faithful, the love of gold had taken such possession of my heart I could not even stop to examine the riches, but fell upon the first pile of gold within my reach and began to heap it into a sack I had brought with me.

The dervish likewise set to work, but I soon noticed that he confined himself to collecting precious stones, and I felt I should be wise to follow his example. At length the camels were loaded with as much as they could carry, and nothing remained but to seal up the treasure and go our ways.

Before, however, this was done, the dervish went up to a great golden vase, beautifully engraved, and took from it a small wooden box, which he hid in the bosom of his dress, merely saying that it contained a special kind of ointment. Then he once more kindled the fire, threw on the perfume, murmured the unknown spell, and the rock closed and stood whole as before.

The next thing was to divide the camels, after which we each took command of our own and marched out of the valley, till we reached the place in the high road where the routes diverge. Then we parted, the dervish going toward Balsora and I to Baghdad. We embraced each other tenderly, and I poured out my gratitude for the honor he had done me in singling me out for this great wealth, and having said a hearty farewell we turned our backs and hastened after our camels.

I had hardly come up with mine when the demon of envy filled my soul. "What does a dervish want with riches like that?" I said to myself. "He alone has the secret of the treasure and can always get as much as he wants." I halted my camels by the roadside and ran back after him.

I was a quick runner and it did not take me very long to come up with him. "My brother," I exclaimed as soon as I could speak, "almost at the moment of our leave-taking, a reflection occurred to me which is perhaps new to you. You are a dervish by profession and live a very quiet life, only caring to do good and careless of the things of this world. You do not realize the burden that you lay upon yourself when you gather into your hands such great wealth, besides the fact that no one who is not accustomed to camels from his birth can ever manage the stubborn beasts. If you are wise you will not encumber yourself with more than thirty, and you will find those trouble enough."

"You are right," replied the dervish, who understood me quite well but did not wish to quarrel over the matter. "I confess I had not thought about it. Choose any ten you like and drive them before you."

I selected ten of the best camels, and we proceeded along the road to rejoin those I had left behind. I had got what I wanted, but I had found the dervish so easy to deal with that I regretted I had not asked for ten more. I looked back. He had only gone a few paces, and I called after him.

"My brother," I said, "I am unwilling to part from you without pointing out what I think you scarcely grasp, that large experience of camel-driving is necessary to anybody who intends to keep together a troop of thirty. In your own interest, I feel sure you would be much happier if you entrusted ten more of them to me, for with my practise it is all one to me if I take two or a hundred."

As before, the dervish made no difficulties, and I drove off ten camels in triumph, leaving him with only twenty for his share. I had now sixty and anyone might have imagined that I should be content.

But, Commander of the Faithful, there is a proverb that says, "the more one has, the more one wants." So it was with me. I could not rest as long as one solitary camel remained to the dervish. Returning to him, I redoubled my prayers and promises of eternal gratitude till the last twenty were in my hands.

"Make good use of them, my brother," said the holy man. "Remember riches sometimes have wings if we keep them for ourselves, and the poor are at our gates expressly that we may help them."

My eyes were so blinded by gold that I paid no heed to his wise counsel and only looked about for something else to grasp. Suddenly I remembered the little box of ointment the dervish had hidden, which most likely contained a treasure more precious than all the rest, and I observed, "What are you going to do with that little box of ointment? It seems hardly worth taking with you; you might as well let me have it. Really, a dervish who has given up the world has no need of ointment."

Oh, if he had only refused my request! But then, supposing he had, I should have got possession of it by force, so great was the madness that had laid hold upon me. However, far from refusing it, the dervish at once held it out, saying gracefully, "Take it, my friend, and if there is anything else I can do to make you happy you must let me know."

Directly the box was in my hands I wrenched off the cover. "As you *are* so kind," I said, "tell me, I pray you, what are the virtues of this ointment?"

"They are most curious and interesting," replied the dervish. "If you apply a little of it to your left eye you will behold in an instant all the treasures hidden in the earth. But beware lest you touch your right eye with it, or your sight will be destroyed forever."

His words excited my curiosity to the highest pitch. "Make trial on me, I implore you," I cried, holding out the box to the dervish. "You will know how to do it better than I! I am burning with impatience to test its charms."

The dervish took the box I had extended to him and, bidding me shut my left eye, touched it gently with the ointment. When I opened it again I saw spread out, as it were before me, treasures of every kind and without number. But as all this time I had been obliged to keep my right eye closed, which was very fatiguing, I begged the dervish to apply the ointment to that eye also.

"If you insist upon it I will do it," answered the dervish, "but you must remember what I told you just now—if the ointment touches your right eye you will become blind."

Unluckily, in spite of my having proved the truth of the dervish's

223

words in so many instances, I was firmly convinced that he was now keeping concealed from me some hidden and precious virtue of the ointment. So I turned a deaf ear to all he said.

"My brother," I replied smiling, "I see you are joking. It is not natural that the same ointment should have two such exactly opposite effects."

"It is true all the same," answered the dervish, "and it would be well for you if you believed my word."

But I would not believe and, dazzled by greed of avarice, I thought that if one eye could show me riches, the other might teach me how to get possession of them. And I continued to press the dervish to anoint my right eye, but this he resolutely declined to do.

"After having conferred such benefits on you," said he, "I am loath indeed to work you such evil. Think what it is to be blind and do not force me to do what you will repent as long as you live."

It was of no use. "My brother," I said firmly, "pray say no more but do what I ask. You have most generously responded to my wishes up to this time, do not spoil my recollection of you for a thing of such little consequence. Let what will happen. I take it on my own head and will never reproach you."

"Since you are determined upon it," he answered with a sigh, "there is no use talking." And taking the ointment he laid some on my right eye, which was tight shut. When I tried to open it heavy clouds of darkness floated before me. I was as blind as you see me now!

"Miserable dervish," I shrieked, "so it is true after all! Into what a bottomless pit has my lust after gold plunged me. Ah, now that my eyes are closed they are really opened. I know that all my sufferings are caused by myself alone! But, good brother, you who are so kind and charitable and know the secrets of such vast learning, have you nothing that will give me back my sight?"

"Unhappy man," replied the dervish, "it is not my fault that this has befallen you, but it is a just chastisement. The blindness of your heart has wrought the blindness of your eyes. Yes, I have secrets; that you have seen in the short time we have known each other. But I have none that will give you back your sight. You have proved yourself unworthy of the riches that were given you. Now they have passed into my hands, whence they will flow into the hands of others less greedy and ungrateful than you."

The dervish said no more and left me, speechless with shame and confusion and so wretched that I stood rooted to the spot, while he collected the eighty camels and proceeded on his way to Balsora. It was in vain that I entreated him not to leave me but at least to take me within reach of the first passing caravan. He was deaf to my prayers and cries, and I should soon have been dead of hunger and misery if some merchants had not come along the track the following day and kindly brought me back to Baghdad.

From a rich man I had in one moment become a beggar and up to this time I have lived solely on the alms that have been bestowed on me. But in order to expiate the sin of avarice, which was my undoing, I ask each passerby to give me a blow. This, Commander of the Faithful, is my story.

When the blind man had ended, the caliph addressed him, "Baba-Abdalla, truly your sin is great but you have suffered enough. Henceforth repent in private, for I will see that enough money is given you day by day for all your wants."

At these words Baba-Abdalla flung himself at the caliph's feet and prayed that honor and happiness might be his portion forever.

THE MERCHANT
OF BAGHDAD

n the reign of Harun al-Rashid, there lived in Baghdad a merchant named Ali Cogia who, having neither wife nor child, contented himself with the modest profits produced by his trade. He had spent some years quite happily in the house his father had left him when, three nights running, he dreamed that an old man had appeared to him and reproached him for having neglected the duty of a good Mussulman in delaying so long his pilgrimage to Mecca.

Ali Cogia was much troubled by this dream, as he was unwilling to give up his shop and lose all his customers. He had shut his eyes for some time to the necessity of performing this pilgrimage and tried to atone to his conscience by an extra number of good works, but the dream seemed to him a direct warning, and he resolved to put off the journey no longer.

The first thing he did was to sell his furniture and the wares he had in his shop, only reserving to himself such goods as he might trade with on the road. The shop itself he sold also and easily found a tenant for his private house. The only matter he could not settle satisfactorily was the safe custody of a thousand pieces of gold which he wished to leave behind him.

After some thought, Ali Cogia hit upon a plan which seemed a safe one. He took a large vase, and placing the money in the bottom of it, filled up the rest with olives. After corking the vase tightly, he carried it to one of his friends, a merchant like himself, and said to him:

"My brother, you have probably heard that I am starting with a caravan in a few days for Mecca. I have come to ask whether you would do me the favor to keep this vase of olives for me till I come back?"

The merchant replied readily, "Look, this is the key of my shop; take it and put the vase wherever you like. I promise that you shall find it in the same place on your return."

A few days later, Ali Cogia mounted the camel that he had laden with merchandise, joined the caravan, and arrived in due time at Mecca. Like the other pilgrims he visited the sacred Mosque, and after all his religious duties were performed, he set out his goods to the best advantage, hoping to gain some customers among the passersby.

Very soon two merchants stopped and, when they had turned over the goods, one said to the other, "If this man was wise he would take these things to Cairo where he would get a much better price than is likely here."

Ali Cogia heard the words and lost no time in following the advice. He packed up his wares and, instead of returning to Baghdad, joined a caravan that was going to Cairo. The results of the journey gladdened his heart. He sold everything almost directly and bought a large stock of Egyptian curiosities, which he intended selling at Damascus. But as the caravan with which he would have to travel would not be starting for another six weeks, he took advantage of the delay to visit the Pyramids and some of the cities along the banks of the Nile.

Now the attractions of Damascus so fascinated the worthy Ali he could hardly tear himself away, but at length he remembered he had a home in Baghdad. He would return by way of Aleppo and, after he had crossed the Euphrates, follow the course of the Tigris.

But when he reached Mossoul, Ali had made friends with some Persian merchants and they persuaded him to accompany them to their native land and even as far as India. So it came to pass that seven years had slipped by since he had left Baghdad, and during all that time the friend with whom he had left the vase of olives had never once thought of him or of it. In fact, it was only a month before Ali Cogia's actual return that the affair came into his head at all, owing to his wife's remarking one day that it was a long time since she had eaten any olives and she would like some.

"That reminds me," said the husband, "before Ali Cogia went to Mecca seven years ago he left a vase of olives in my care. But really, by this time he must be dead, and there is no reason we should not eat the olives if we like. Give me a light, and I will fetch them and see how they taste."

"My husband," answered the wife, "beware, I pray, of your doing anything so base! Supposing seven years have passed without news of Ali Cogia, he need not be dead, for all that, and may come back any day. How shameful it would be to have to confess you had betrayed your trust and broken the seal of the vase! Pay no attention to my idle words; I really have no desire for olives now, and probably after all this while they are no longer good. I have a presentiment that Ali Cogia will return, and what will he think of you? Give it up, I entreat."

The merchant, however, refused to listen to her advice, sensible though it was. He took a light and a dish and went into his shop.

"If you will be so obstinate," said his wife, "I cannot help it; but do not blame me if it turns out ill."

When the merchant opened the vase he found the topmost olives were rotten, and in order to see if the under ones were in better condition he shook some out into the dish. As they fell out, a few of the gold pieces fell out too.

The sight of the money roused all the merchant's greed. He looked into the vase, and saw that all the bottom was filled with gold. He then replaced the olives and returned to his wife.

"My wife," he said as he entered the room, "you were quite right; the olives are rotten, and I have recorked the vase so well that Ali Cogia will never know it has been touched."

"You would have done better to believe me," replied the wife. "I trust that no harm will come of it."

These words made no more impression on the merchant than the others had done and he spent the whole night in wondering how he could manage to keep the gold if Ali Cogia should come back and claim his vase. Very early next morning he went out and bought fresh new olives; then he threw away the old ones, took out the gold and hid it, and filled up the vase with the olives he had bought. This done he recorked the vase and put it in the same place where it had been left by Ali Cogia.

A month later Ali Cogia reentered Baghdad, and as his house was still let he went to an inn. The following day he set out to see his friend, the merchant, who received him with open arms and many expressions of surprise. After a few moments given to inquiries Ali Cogia begged the merchant to hand him over the vase that he had taken care of for so long.

"Oh, certainly," said he, "I am only glad I could be of use to you in the matter. Here is the key of my shop; you will find the vase in the place where you put it."

Ali Cogia fetched his vase and carried it to his room at the inn, where he opened it. He thrust down his hand but could feel no money, but still he was persuaded it must be there. So he emptied out the olives. To no purpose. The gold was not there. He was dumb with horror, then, lifting up his hands, he exclaimed, "Can my old friend really have committed such a crime?"

In great haste he went back to the house of the merchant. "My friend," he cried, "you will be astonished to see me again, but I can find nowhere in this vase the thousand pieces of gold I placed in the bottom under the olives. Perhaps you may have taken a loan of them for your business purposes; if that is so you are most welcome. I will only ask you to give me a receipt and you can repay the money at your leisure."

The merchant, who had expected something of the sort, had his reply all ready. "Ali Cogia," he said, "when you brought me the vase of olives did I ever touch it? I gave you the key of my shop and you put it yourself where you liked, and did you not find it in exactly the same spot and in the same state? If you placed any gold in it, it must be there still. I know nothing about that; you only told me there were olives. You can believe me or not, but I have not laid a finger on the vase."

Ali Cogia still tried every means to persuade the merchant to admit the truth. "I love peace," he said, "and shall deeply regret having to resort to harsh measures. Once more, think of your reputation. I shall be in despair if you oblige me to call in the aid of the law."

"Ali Cogia," answered the merchant, "you allow that it was a vase of olives you placed in my charge. You fetched it and removed it yourself, and now you tell me it contained a thousand pieces of gold and that I must restore them to you! Did you ever say anything about them before? Why, I did not even know the vase had olives in it! You never showed them to me. I wonder you have not demanded pearls or diamonds. Retire, I pray you, lest a crowd should gather in front of my shop."

By this time not only the casual passersby but also the neighboring merchants were standing round, listening to the dispute and trying every now and then to smooth matters between them. But at the merchant's last words Ali Cogia resolved to lay the cause of the quarrel before them and told them the whole story. They heard him to the end and inquired of the merchant what he had to say.

The accused man admitted that he had kept Ali Cogia's vase in his shop; but he denied having touched it and swore that as to what it contained he only knew what Ali Cogia had told him, calling them all to witness the insult that had been put upon him.

"You have brought it on yourself," said Ali Cogia, taking him by the arm, "and as you appeal to the law, the law you shall have! Let us see if you will dare to repeat your story before the cadi."

Now as a good Mussulman the merchant was forbidden to refuse this choice of a judge, so he accepted the test, and said to Ali Cogia, "Very well; I should like nothing better. We shall soon see which of us is in the right."

So the two men presented themselves before the cadi, and Ali Cogia again repeated his tale. The cadi asked what witnesses he had. Ali Cogia replied that he had not taken this precaution, as he had considered the man his friend and up to that time had always found him honest.

The merchant, on his side, stuck to his story and offered to swear solemnly that not only had he never stolen the thousand gold pieces, but that he did not even know they were there. The cadi allowed him to take the oath and pronounced him innocent.

Ali Cogia, furious at having to suffer such loss, protested against the verdict, declaring that he would appeal to the Caliph Harun al-Rashid himself. But the cadi paid no attention to his threats and was quite satisfied that he had done what was right.

Judgment being given, the merchant returned home triumphant, and Ali Cogia went back to his inn to draw up a petition to the caliph. The next morning he placed himself on the road along which the caliph must pass after midday prayer and stretched out his petition to the officer who walked before the caliph, whose duty it was to collect such things and, on entering the palace, to hand them to his master. There Harun al-Rashid studied them carefully.

Knowing this custom, Ali Cogia followed the caliph into the public hall of the palace and awaited the result. After some time the officer appeared and told him that the caliph had read his petition and had appointed an hour the next morning to give him audience. He then inquired the merchant's address, so that he might be summoned to attend also.

That very evening, the caliph, his grand vizir, Giafar, and Mesrour, chief of the eunuchs, all three disguised, as was their habit, went out to take a stroll through the town.

Going down one street, the caliph's attention was attracted by a noise and looking through a door which opened into a court he perceived ten or twelve children playing in the moonlight. He hid himself in a dark corner and watched them.

"Let us play at being the cadi," said the brightest and quickest of them all. "I will be the cadi. Bring before me Ali Cogia and the merchant who robbed him of the thousand pieces of gold."

The boy's words recalled to the caliph the petition he had read that morning, and he waited with interest to see what the children would do.

The proposal was hailed with joy by the other children, who had heard a great deal of talk about the matter, and they quickly settled the part each one was to play. The cadi took his seat gravely and an officer introduced first Ali Cogia, the plaintiff, and then the merchant who was the defendant.

Ali Cogia made a low bow and pleaded his case point by point, concluding by imploring the cadi not to inflict on him such a heavy loss. The cadi, having heard his case, turned to the merchant and inquired why he had not repaid Ali Cogia the sum in question. The boy merchant repeated the reasons the real merchant had given to the Cadi of Baghdad and also offered to swear that he had told the truth.

"Stop a moment!" said the little cadi, "before we come to oaths, I should like to examine the vase with the olives. Ali Cogia," he added, "have you the vase with you?" Finding he had not, the cadi continued, "Go and get it; bring it to me."

So Ali Cogia disappeared for an instant, and then pretended to lay a vase at the feet of the cadi, declaring it was his vase, which he had given to the accused for safe custody; and in order to be quite correct, the cadi asked the merchant if he recognized it as the same vase. By his silence the merchant admitted the fact, and the cadi then commanded to have the vase opened. Ali Cogia made a movement as if he was taking off the lid, and the little cadi on his part made a pretence of peering into a vase.

"What beautiful olives!" he said, "I should like to taste one," and pretending to put one in his mouth, he added, "they are really excellent! But," he went on, "it seems to me odd that olives seven years old should be as good as that! Send for some dealers in olives, and let us hear what they say!"

Two children were presented to him as olive merchants, and the cadi addressed them. "Tell me," he said, "how long can olives be kept so as to be pleasant eating?"

"My lord," replied the merchants, "however much care is taken to preserve them they never last beyond the third year. They lose both taste and color and are only fit to be thrown away."

"If that is so," answered the little cadi, "examine this vase and tell me how long the olives have been in it."

The olive merchants pretended to examine the olives and taste them, then reported to the cadi that they were fresh and good.

"You are mistaken," said he. "Ali Cogia declares he put them in that vase seven years ago."

"My lord," returned the olive merchants, "we can assure you that the olives are those of the present year. And if you consult all the merchants in Baghdad you will not find one to give a contrary opinion."

The accused merchant opened his mouth as if to protest but the cadi gave him no time. "Be silent," he said, "you are a thief. Take him away and hang him." So the game ended, the children clapping their hands in applause and leading the criminal away to be hanged.

Harun al-Rashid was lost in astonishment at the wisdom of the child, who had given so wise a verdict on the case which he himself was to hear on the morrow. "Is there any other verdict possible?" he asked the grand vizir, who was as much impressed as himself. "I can imagine no better judgment."

"If the circumstances are really such as we have heard," replied the grand vizir, "it seems to me Your Highness could only follow the example of this boy in the method of reasoning and also in your conclusions."

"Then take careful note of this house," said the caliph, "and bring me the boy tomorrow that the affair may be tried by him in my presence. Summon also the cadi, to learn his duty from the mouth of a child. Bid Ali Cogia bring his vase of olives and see that two dealers in olives are present." So saying, the caliph returned to the palace.

The next morning early, the grand vizir went back to the house where they had seen the children playing and asked for the mistress and her children. Three boys appeared, and the grand vizir inquired which had represented the cadi in their game of the previous evening. The eldest and tallest, changing color, confessed that it was he and, to his mother's great alarm, the grand vizir said that he had strict orders to bring him into the presence of the caliph.

"Does he want to take my son from me?" cried the poor woman. The grand vizir hastened to calm her, assuring her that she should have the boy again in an hour and she would be quite satisfied when she knew the reason of the summons. So she dressed the boy in his best clothes, and the two left the house.

When the grand vizir presented the child to the caliph, he was a little awed and confused, and Harun al-Rashid proceeded to explain why he had sent for him. "Approach, my son," he said kindly. "I think it was you who judged the case of Ali Cogia and the merchant last night? I overheard you by chance and was very pleased with the way you conducted the trial. Today you will see the real Ali Cogia and the real merchant. Seat yourself at once next to me."

The caliph being seated on his throne with the boy next him, the parties to the suit were ushered in. One by one they prostrated themselves and touched the carpet at the foot of the throne with their foreheads. When they rose up, the caliph said, "Now speak. This child will give you justice and if more should be wanted I will see to it myself."

Ali Cogia and the merchant pleaded one after the other but, when the merchant offered to swear the same oath that he had taken before the cadi, he was stopped by the child, who said that before this was done he must first see the vase of olives.

At these words, Ali Cogia presented the vase to the caliph and uncovered it. The caliph took one of the olives, tasted it, and ordered the expert merchants to do the same. They pronounced the olives good, and fresh that year. The boy informed them that Ali Cogia declared it was seven years since he had placed them in the vase; to which they returned the same answer as the children had done.

The accused merchant saw by this time that his condemnation was certain and tried to allege something in his defence. The boy had too much sense to order him to be hanged and looked at the caliph, saying, "Commander of the Faithful, this is not a game now; it is for Your Highness to condemn him and not for me."

Then the caliph, convinced that the man was a thief, bade them take him away and hang him, which was done, but not before he had confessed his guilt and the place in which he had hidden Ali Cogia's money. The caliph ordered the cadi to learn how to deal out justice from the mouth of a child, and sent the boy home with a purse containing a hundred pieces of gold as a mark of his favor.

THE
ENCHANTED
HORSE

t was the Feast of the New Year, the oldest and most splendid of all the feasts in the Kingdom of Persia, and the day had been spent by the king in the city of Schiraz, taking part in the magnificent spectacles prepared by his subjects to do honor to the festival. The sun was setting, and the monarch was about to give his court the signal to retire when suddenly an Indian appeared before his throne, leading a horse richly harnessed, and looking in every respect exactly like a real one.

"Sire," said he, prostrating himself as he spoke, "although I make my appearance so late before Your Highness, I can confidently assure you that none of the wonders you have seen during the day can be compared to this horse, if you will deign to cast your eyes upon him."

"I see nothing in it," replied the king, "except a clever imitation of a real horse; any skilled workman might do as much."

"Sire," returned the Indian, "it is not of his outward form that I would speak but of the use I can make of him. I have only to mount him and wish myself in some special place and, no matter how distant it may be, in a very few moments I shall find myself there. It is this, sire, that makes the horse so marvelous, and if Your Highness will allow me, you can prove it for yourself."

The King of Persia, who was interested in everything out of the common and had never before come across a horse with such qualities, bade the Indian mount the animal and show what he could do. In an instant the man had vaulted on his back and inquired where the monarch wished to send him.

"Do you see that mountain?" asked the king, pointing to a huge mass that towered into the sky about three leagues from Schiraz. "Go and bring me the leaf of a palm that grows at the foot."

The words were hardly out of the king's mouth when the Indian turned a screw placed in the horse's neck close to the saddle, and the animal bounded like lightning up into the air and was soon beyond the sight even of the sharpest eyes. In a quarter of an hour the Indian was seen returning, bearing in his hand the palm. Guiding his horse to the foot of the throne, he dismounted and laid the leaf before the king.

Now the monarch had no sooner proved the astounding speed of which the horse was capable than he longed to possess it himself. Indeed, so sure was he that the Indian would be quite ready to sell it, he looked upon it as his own already.

"I never guessed from his mere outside how valuable an animal he was," he remarked to the Indian, "and I am grateful to you for having shown me my error. If you will sell it, name your own price."

"Sire," replied the Indian, "I never doubted that a sovereign so wise and accomplished as Your Highness would do justice to my horse, when he once knew its power; I even went so far as to think it probable that you might wish to possess it. Greatly as I prize it, I will yield it up to Your Highness on one condition. The horse was not constructed by me, but it was given me by the inventor in exchange for my only daughter, who made me take a solemn oath that I would never part with it, except for some object of equal value."

"Name anything you like," cried the monarch, interrupting him. "My kingdom is large and filled with fair cities. You have only to choose which you would prefer, to become its ruler to the end of your life."

"Sire," answered the Indian, to whom the proposal did not seem nearly so generous as it appeared to the king, "I am most grateful to Your Highness for your princely offer and beseech you not to be offended with me if I say I can only deliver up my horse in exchange for the hand of the princess, your daughter."

A shout of laughter burst from the courtiers as they heard these words, and Prince Firouz Schah, the heir apparent, was filled with anger at the Indian's presumption. The king, however, thought that it would not cost him much to part from the princess in order to gain such a delightful toy and while he was hesitating as to his answer the prince broke in.

"Sire," he said, "it is not possible that you can doubt for an instant what reply you should give to such insolence. Consider what you owe to yourself and to the blood of your ancestors."

"My son," replied the king, "you speak nobly, but you do not realize either the value of the horse, or the fact that if I reject the proposal of the Indian he will only make the same to some other monarch, and I should be filled with despair at the thought that anyone but myself should own this seventh wonder of the world. Of course I do not say that I shall accept his conditions, and perhaps he may be brought to reason. Meanwhile I should like you to examine the horse and, with the owner's permission, to make trial of its powers."

The Indian, who had overheard the king's speech, thought that he saw in it signs of yielding to his proposal, so he joyfully agreed to the monarch's wishes. He came forward to help the prince mount the horse and show him how to guide it. But, before he had finished, the young man turned the screw and was soon out of sight.

They waited some time, expecting that every moment the prince might be seen returning in the distance, but at length the Indian grew frightened. Prostrating himself before the throne, he said to the king, "Sire, Your Highness must have noticed that the prince, in his impatience, did not allow me to tell him what it was necessary to do in order to return to the place from which he started. I implore you not to punish me for what was not my fault and not to blame me for any misfortune that may occur."

"But why," cried the king in a burst of fear and anger, "why did you not call him back when you saw him disappearing?"

"Sire," replied the Indian, "the rapidity of his movements took me so by surprise that he was out of hearing before I recovered my speech. But we must hope that he will perceive and turn a second screw, which will have the effect of bringing the horse back to earth."

"But supposing he does," answered the king, "what is to hinder the horse from descending straight into the sea or dashing him to pieces on the rocks?"

"Have no fears, Your Highness," said the Indian; "the horse has the gift of passing over seas and of carrying his rider wherever he wishes to go."

"Well, your head shall answer for it," returned the monarch, "if in three months he is not safe back with me or at any rate does not send me news of his safety; your life shall pay the penalty." So saying, he ordered his guards to seize the Indian and throw him into prison.

Meanwhile, Prince Firouz Schah had gone gaily up into the air and for the space of an hour continued to ascend higher and higher, till the very mountains were not distinguishable from the plains. Then he began to think it was time to come down and took for granted that, in order to do this, it was only needful to turn the screw the reverse way; but to his surprise and horror he found that, turn as he might, he did not make the smallest impression. He then remembered that he had never waited to ask how he was to get back to earth again and understood the danger in which he stood. Luckily, he did not lose his head, and set about examining the horse's neck with great care; at last, to his intense joy, he discovered a tiny little peg, much smaller than the other, close to the right ear. This he turned and found himself dropping to the earth, though more slowly than he had left it.

It was now dark and, as the prince could see nothing, he was obliged, not without some feeling of disquiet, to allow the horse to direct his own course. Midnight was already passed before Prince Firouz Schah again touched the ground, faint and weary from his long ride and from the fact that he had eaten nothing since early morning.

The first thing he did on dismounting was to try to find out where he was, and as far as he could discover in the thick darkness, he found himself on the terraced roof of a huge palace, with a balustrade of marble running round it. In one corner of the terrace stood a small door, opening on to a staircase which led down into the palace.

Some people might have hesitated before exploring further, but not so the prince. "I am doing no harm," he said, "and whoever the owner may be, he will not touch me when he sees I am unarmed," and in dread of making a false step, he went cautiously down the staircase. On a landing he noticed an open door, beyond which was a faintly lighted hall.

Before entering, the prince paused and listened, but he heard nothing except the sound of men snoring. By the light of a lantern suspended from the roof, he perceived a row of black guards sleeping, each with a naked sword lying by him, and he understood that the hall must form the anteroom to the chamber of some queen or princess.

Standing quite still, Prince Firouz Schah looked about him till his eyes grew accustomed to the gloom and he noticed a bright light shining through a curtain in one corner. He then made his way softly toward it and, drawing aside its folds, passed into a magnificent chamber full of sleeping women, all lying on low couches, except one who was on a sofa. This one, he knew, must be the princess.

Gently stealing up to the side of her bed, he looked at her and saw that she was more beautiful than any woman he had ever beheld. But, fascinated though he was, he was well aware of the danger of his position, as one cry of surprise would awake the guards and cause his certain death.

So sinking quietly on his knees, he took hold of the princess' sleeve

244

and drew her arm lightly toward him. The princess opened her eyes, and seeing before her a handsome well-dressed man, she remained speechless with astonishment.

This favorable moment was seized by the prince who, bowing low while he knelt, thus addressed her. "You behold, madam, a prince in distress, son to the King of Persia, who, owing to an adventure so strange that you will scarcely believe it, finds himself here, a suppliant for your protection. But yesterday, I was in my father's court, engaged in the celebration of our most solemn festival; today, I am in an unknown land in danger of my life."

Now, the princess whose mercy Prince Firouz Schah implored was the eldest daughter of the King of Bengal, and was enjoying rest and change in the palace her father had built her at a little distance from the capital.

She listened kindly to what Firouz Schah had to say, and then answered, "Prince, be not uneasy; hospitality and humanity are prac-

The prince gently sank to his knees at her bedside.

245

tised as widely in Bengal as they are in Persia. The protection you ask will be given you by all. You have my word for it." As the prince was about to thank her, she added quickly, "However great may be my curiosity to learn by what means you have traveled here so speedily, I know that you must be faint for want of food, so I shall give orders to my women to take you to one of my chambers, where you will be provided with supper and left to repose."

By this time the princess' attendants were all awake and listening to the conversation. At a sign from their mistress they rose, dressed themselves hastily, and snatching up some tapers which lighted the room, conducted the prince to a large and lofty room, where two of the number prepared his bed and the rest went down to the kitchen from which they soon returned with all sorts of dishes. Then, showing him cupboards filled with dresses and linen, they quitted the room.

During their absence the Princess of Bengal, who had been greatly struck by the beauty of the prince, tried in vain to go to sleep again. It was of no use; she felt wide awake and when her women entered the room she inquired eagerly if the prince had all he wanted and what they thought of him.

"Madam," they replied, "it is of course impossible for us to tell what impression this young man has made on you. For ourselves, we think you would be fortunate if the king your father should allow you to marry anyone so amiable. Certainly there is no one in the Court of Bengal who can be compared with him."

These flattering observations were by no means displeasing to the princess but, as she did not wish to betray her own feelings, she merely said, "You are all a set of chatterboxes; go back to bed and let me sleep."

When she dressed the following morning her maids noticed that, contrary to her usual habit, the princess was very particular about her toilette and insisted on her hair being dressed two or three times over. "For," she said to herself, "if my appearance was not displeasing to the prince when he saw me in the condition I was, how much more will he be struck with me when he beholds me with all my charms."

Then she placed in her hair the largest and most brilliant diamonds she could find and arrayed herself with a necklace, bracelets and girdle, all of precious stones. And over her shoulders her ladies put a robe of the richest stuff in all the Indies that no one was allowed to wear except members of the royal family. When she was fully dressed according to her wishes, she sent to know if the Prince of Persia was awake and ready to receive her, as she desired to present herself before him.

When the princess' messenger entered his room Prince Firouz Schah was in the act of leaving it, to inquire if he might be allowed to pay his homage to her mistress. On hearing the princess' wishes, he at once gave way. "Her will is my law," he said, "I am only here to obey her orders."

In a few moments the princess herself appeared and, after the usual compliments had passed between them, the princess sat down on a sofa and began to explain to the prince her reasons for not giving him an audience in her own apartments. "Had I done so," she said, "we might have been interrupted at any hour by the chief of the eunuchs, who has the right to enter whenever it pleases him, whereas this is forbidden ground. I am all impatience to learn the wonderful accident which has procured the pleasure of your arrival and that is why I have come to you here, where no one can intrude upon us. Begin then, I entreat you, without delay."

So the prince began at the beginning and told all the story of the festival of Nedrouz held yearly in Persia and of the splendid spectacles celebrated in its honor. But when he came to the enchanted horse, the princess declared that she could never have imagined anything half so surprising. "Well then," continued the prince, "you can easily understand how the king, my father, who has a passion for all curious things, was seized with a violent desire to possess this horse and asked the Indian what sum he would take for it.

"The man's answer was absolutely absurd, as you will agree, when I tell you that it was nothing less than the hand of the princess, my sister. But though all the bystanders laughed and mocked and I was beside myself with rage, I saw to my despair that my father could not make up his mind to treat the insolent proposal as it deserved. I tried to argue with him but in vain. He only begged me to examine the horse with a view, as I quite understood, of making me more sensible of its value.

"To please my father, I mounted the horse and, without waiting for any instructions from the Indian, turned the peg as I had seen him do. In an instant I was soaring upward, much quicker than an arrow could fly, and felt as if I must be getting so near the sky that I should soon hit my head against it! I could see nothing beneath me and for some time was so confused I did not even know in what direction I was traveling. At last, when it was growing dark, I found another screw; on turning it, the horse began slowly to sink toward the earth. I was forced to trust to chance and to see what fate had in store, and it was already past midnight when I found myself on the roof of this palace. I crept down the little staircase and made directly for a light which I perceived through an open door. I peeped cautiously in and saw, as you will guess, the eunuchs lying asleep on the floor. I knew the risks I ran but my need was so great I paid no attention to them and stole safely past your guards to the curtain which concealed your doorway.

"The rest, Princess, you know. It only remains for me to thank you for the kindness you have shown me and to assure you of my gratitude. By the law of nations I am already your slave, and I have only my heart that is my own to offer you. But what am I saying? My own? Alas, madam, it was yours from the moment I first beheld you!"

The air with which he said these words could have left no doubt on the mind of the princess as to the effect of her charms, and the blush which mounted to her face only increased her beauty.

"Prince," returned she, as soon as her confusion permitted her to speak, "you have given me the greatest pleasure, and I have followed you closely in all your adventures. Though you are positively sitting before me, I even trembled at your danger in the upper regions of the air! Let me say what a debt I owe to the chance which led you to my house; you could have entered none which would have given you a warmer welcome. As to your being a slave, of course that is merely a joke, and my reception must itself have assured you that you are as free here as at your father's court.

"As to your heart," continued she in tones of encouragement, "I am quite sure that must have been disposed of long ago to some princess who is well worthy of it, and I could not think of being the cause of your unfaithfulness to her."

Prince Firouz Schah was about to protest there was no lady with prior claims, but he was stopped by the entrance of one of the princess' attendants, who announced that dinner was served, and neither was sorry for the interruption.

Dinner was laid in a magnificent apartment, the table was covered with delicious fruits, and during the repast richly dressed girls sang softly and sweetly to stringed instruments. After the prince and princess had dined, they passed into a small room hung with blue and gold, looking out into a garden stocked with flowers and trees quite different from any that were to be found in Persia.

"Princess," observed the young man, "till now I had always believed that Persia could boast finer palaces and more lovely gardens than any kingdom upon earth. But my eyes have been opened, and I begin to perceive that wherever there is a great king he will surround himself with buildings worthy of him."

"Prince," replied the Princess of Bengal, "I have no idea what a Persian palace is like, so I am unable to make comparisons. I do not wish to depreciate my own palace but I can assure you it is very poor beside that of the king, my father, as you will agree when you have been there to greet him, which I hope you will shortly do."

Now the princess hoped that by bringing about a meeting between the prince and her father, the king would be so struck with the young man's distinguished air and fine manners he would offer him his daughter to wife. But the reply of the Prince of Persia to her suggestion was not quite what she wished.

"Madam," he said, "by taking advantage of your proposal to visit the palace of the King of Bengal, I should satisfy not merely my curiosity, but also the sentiments of respect with which I regard him. But, Princess, I am persuaded you will feel with me that I cannot possibly present myself before so great a sovereign without the attendants suitable to my rank. He would think me an adventurer."

"If that is all," she answered, "you can get as many attendants here as you please. There are plenty of Persian merchants and, as for money, my treasury is always open to you. Take what you please."

Prince Firouz Schah guessed what prompted so much kindness on the part of the princess and was much touched by it. Still, his passion, which increased every moment, did not make him forget his duty.

So he replied without hesitation, "I do not know, Princess, how to express my gratitude for your obliging offer, which I would accept at once if it were not for the recollection of all the uneasiness the king, my father, must be suffering on my account. I should be unworthy indeed of all the love he showers upon me if I did not return to him at the first possible moment. For, while I am enjoying the society of the most amiable of all princesses, he is, I am quite convinced, plunged in the deepest grief, having lost all hope of seeing me again. I am sure you will understand my position and will feel that to remain away one instant longer than is necessary would not only be ungrateful on my part but perhaps even a crime, for how do I know if my absence may not break his heart?

"But," continued the prince, "having obeyed the voice of my conscience, I shall count the moments when, with your gracious permission, I may present myself before the King of Bengal, not as a wanderer but as a prince, to implore the favor of your hand. My father has always informed me that in my marriage I shall be left quite free, but I am persuaded that I have only to describe your generosity for my wishes to become his own."

The Princess of Bengal was too reasonable not to accept the explanation offered by Prince Firouz Schah, but she was much disturbed at his intention of departing at once, for she feared that, no sooner had he left her, the impression she had made on him would fade away. So she made one more effort to keep him and, after assuring him that she entirely approved of his anxiety to see his father, begged him to give her a day or two more of his company.

In common politeness the prince could hardly refuse this request, and the princess set about inventing every kind of amusement for him and succeeded so well that two months slipped by almost unnoticed, in balls, spectacles and in hunting, of which, when unattended by danger, the princess was passionately fond. But at last one day the prince declared seriously he could neglect his duty no longer and entreated her to put no further obstacles in his way, promising at the same time to return as soon as he could, with all the magnificence due both to her and to himself.

"Princess," he added, "it may be that in your heart you class me with those false lovers whose devotion cannot stand the test of absence. If you do, you wrong me. Were it not for fear of offending you, I would beseech you to come with me, for my life can only be happy when passed with you. As for your reception at the Persian Court, it will be as warm as your merits deserve; and as for what concerns the King of Bengal, he must be much more indifferent to your welfare than you have led me to believe if he does not give his consent to our marriage."

The princess could not find words in which to reply to the arguments of the Prince of Persia, but her silence and her downcast eyes spoke for her and declared that she had no objection to accompanying him on his travels. The only difficulty that occurred to her was that Prince Firouz Schah did not know how to manage the horse, and she dreaded lest they might find themselves in the same plight as before.

251

But the prince soothed her fears so successfully she soon had no other thought than to arrange for their flight so secretly that no one in the palace should suspect it.

This was done, and early the following morning, when the whole palace was wrapped in sleep, she stole up onto the roof where the prince was already awaiting her, with his horse's head toward Persia. He mounted first and helped the princess up behind. Then, when she was firmly seated, with her hands holding tightly to his belt, he touched the screw and the horse began to leave the earth quickly behind him.

He traveled with his accustomed speed, and Prince Firouz Schah guided him so well that in two hours and a half from the time of starting he saw the capital of Persia lying beneath him. He determined to alight neither in the great square from which he had started, nor in the sultan's palace, but at a country house a little distance from the town. Here he showed the princess a beautiful suite of rooms and begged her to rest, while he informed his father of their arrival and prepared a public reception worthy of her rank. Then he ordered a horse to be saddled and set out.

All the way through the streets he was welcomed with shouts of joy by the people, who had long lost all hope of seeing him again. On reaching the palace he found the sultan surrounded by his ministers, all clad in the deepest mourning, and his father almost went out of his mind with surprise and delight at the mere sound of his son's voice. When he had calmed down a little he begged the prince to relate his adventures.

The prince at once seized the opening thus given him and told the whole story of his treatment by the Princess of Bengal, not even concealing the fact that she had fallen in love with him. "And, sire," he added, "having given my royal word that you would not refuse your consent to our marriage, I persuaded her to return with me on the Indian's horse. I have left her in one of Your Highness' country houses, where she is waiting anxiously to be assured that I have not promised in vain."

As he said this the prince was about to throw himself at the feet of the sultan, but his father prevented him, and embracing him again, said eagerly, "My son, not only do I gladly consent to your marriage with the Princess of Bengal, but I will hasten to pay my respects to her and thank her in my own person for the benefits she has conferred on you. I will then bring her back with me and make all arrangements for the wedding to be celebrated today."

So the sultan gave orders that the mourning worn by the people should be thrown off and there should be a concert of drums, trumpets and cymbals. Also that the Indian should be taken from prison and brought before him.

His commands were obeyed, and the Indian was led into his presence, surrounded by guards. "I have kept you locked up," said the sultan, "in case my son was lost, that your life should pay the penalty. He has now returned, so take your horse and begone for ever."

The Indian hastily quitted the presence of the sultan, and when he was outside he inquired of the man who had taken him out of prison where the prince had really been all this time, and what he had been doing. They told him the whole story and how the Princess of Bengal was even then awaiting in the country palace the consent of the sultan, which at once put into the Indian's head a plan of revenge for the treatment he had received. Going straight to the country house, he informed the doorkeeper who was left in charge that he had been sent by the sultan and by the Prince of Persia to bring the princess and the enchanted horse to the palace.

The doorkeeper knew the Indian by sight and was of course aware that nearly three months before he had been thrown into prison by the sultan. Seeing him at liberty, the man took for granted that he was speaking the truth and made no difficulty about leading him before the Princess of Bengal; while on her side, hearing that he had come from the prince, the lady gladly consented to do what he wished.

The Indian, delighted with the success of his scheme, mounted the horse, assisted the princess to mount behind him, and turned the peg

253

at the very moment the prince was leaving the palace in Schiraz for the country house, followed closely by the sultan and all the court. Knowing this, the Indian deliberately steered the horse right above the city, in order that his revenge for his unjust imprisonment might be all the quicker and sweeter.

When the Sultan of Persia saw the horse and its riders, he stopped short in astonishment and horror and broke out into oaths, which the Indian heard quite unmoved, knowing that he was perfectly safe from pursuit. But mortified and furious as the sultan was, his feelings were nothing to those of Prince Firouz Schah on seeing the object of his passionate devotion being borne rapidly away. And while he was struck speechless with grief and remorse at not having guarded her better, she vanished swiftly out of his sight. What was he to do? Should he follow his father into the palace and there give up to his despair? Both his love and his courage forbade it; and he continued his way to the country house.

The sight of the prince showed the doorkeeper of what folly he had been guilty and, flinging himself at his master's feet, he implored his pardon. "Rise," said the prince, "I am the cause of this misfortune, not you. Go and find me the dress of a dervish but beware of saying it is for me."

At a short distance from the country house a convent of dervishes was situated, and the superior, or scheih, was the doorkeeper's friend. So it was easy enough to obtain a dervish's dress, which the prince at once put on instead of his own. Disguised like this and concealing about him a box of pearls and diamonds he had intended as a present to the princess, he left the house at nightfall, uncertain where he should go but firmly resolved not to return without her.

Meanwhile the Indian had turned the horse in such direction that, before many hours had passed, it had entered a wood close to the capital of the kingdom of Cashmere. Feeling very hungry and supposing that the princess also might be in want of food, he brought his steed down to the earth and left the princess in a shady place on the banks of a clear stream.

At first, when the princess found herself alone, the idea occurred to her of trying to escape and hide herself. But as she had eaten scarcely anything since she had left Bengal, she felt too weak to venture far and was obliged to abandon her design. On the return of the Indian with meats of various kinds she began to eat voraciously and soon had regained sufficient courage to reply with spirit to his insolent remarks. Goaded by his threats she sprang to her feet, calling loudly for help, and luckily her cries were heard by a troop of horsemen, who rode up to inquire what was the matter.

Now the leader of these horsemen was the Sultan of Cashmere, returning from the chase, and he instantly turned to the Indian to inquire who he was and who the lady was he had with him. The Indian rudely answered that it was his wife and there was no occasion for anyone else to interfere between them.

The princess who, of course, was ignorant of the rank of her deliverer, denied altogether the Indian's story. "My lord," she cried, "whoever you may be, put no faith in this impostor. He is an abominable magician, who has this day torn me from the Prince of Persia, my destined husband, and has brought me here on this enchanted horse." She would have continued but her tears choked her, and the Sultan of Cashmere, convinced by her beauty and her distinguished air of the truth of her tale, ordered his followers to cut off the Indian's head, which was done immediately.

But rescued though she was from one peril, it seemed as if she had only fallen into another. The sultan commanded a horse to be given her and conducted her to his own palace, where he led her to a beautiful apartment, selected female slaves to wait on her and eunuchs to be her guard. Then, without allowing her time to thank him for all he had done, he bade her repose, saying she should tell him her adventures on the following day.

"My lord," she cried, "put no faith in this impostor."

The princess fell asleep, flattering herself that she had only to relate her story for the sultan to be touched by compassion and restore her to the prince without delay. But a few hours were to undeceive her.

When the Sultan of Cashmere had quitted her presence the evening before, he resolved that the sun should not set again without the princess becoming his wife. At daybreak, proclamation of his intention was made throughout the town by the sound of drums, trumpets, cymbals and other instruments calculated to fill the heart with joy. The Princess of Bengal was early awakened by the noise, but she did not for one moment imagine it had anything to do with her, till the sultan, arriving as soon as she was dressed to inquire after her health, informed her that the trumpet blasts she heard were part of the solemn marriage ceremonies, for which he begged her to prepare. This unexpected announcement caused the princess such terror that she sank down in a dead faint.

The slaves that were in waiting ran to her aid, and the sultan himself did his best to bring her back to consciousness, but for a long while it was all to no purpose. At length her senses began slowly to come back to her and then, rather than break faith with the Prince of Persia by consenting to such a marriage, she determined to feign madness. So she began by saying all sorts of absurdities and using all kinds of strange gestures, while the sultan stood watching her with sorrow and surprise. But as this sudden seizure showed no signs of abating, he left her to her women, ordering them to take the greatest care of her. Still, as the day went on, the malady seemed to become worse and by night it was almost violent.

Days passed in this manner, till at last the sultan decided to summon all the doctors of his court to consult together over her sad state. Their answer was that madness is of so many different kinds it was impossible to give an opinion on the case without seeing the princess, so the sultan gave orders they were to be introduced into her chamber, one by one, every man according to his rank.

This decision had been foreseen by the princess, who knew quite well that once she allowed the physicians to feel her pulse the most ignorant of them would discover that she was in perfectly good health and her madness was feigned, so as each man approached she broke out into such violent paroxysms that not one dared to lay a finger on her. A few, who pretended to be cleverer than the rest, declared they could diagnose sick people without seeing them and ordered her certain potions, which she made no difficulty about taking as she was persuaded they were all harmless.

When the Sultan of Cashmere saw that the court doctors could do nothing toward curing the princess, he called in those of the city, who fared no better. Then he had recourse to the most celebrated physicians in the other large towns but, finding the task was beyond their science, he finally sent messengers into the other neighboring states, with a memorandum containing full particulars of the princess' madness, offering at the same time to pay the expenses of any physician who would come and see for himself, and a handsome reward to the one who should cure her. In answer to this proclamation many foreign professors flocked into Cashmere, but they naturally were not more successful than the rest had been as the cure depended neither on them, nor their skill, but only on the princess herself.

It was during this time that Prince Firouz Schah, wandering sadly and hopelessly from place to place, arrived in a large city of India, where he heard a great deal of talk about the Princess of Bengal who had gone out of her senses on the very day that she was to have been married to the Sultan of Cashmere. This was quite enough to induce him to take the road to Cashmere and to inquire the full particulars of the story at the first inn at which he lodged in the capital. When he knew that he had at last found the princess whom he had so long lost, he set about devising a plan for her rescue.

The first thing he did was to procure a doctor's robe, that his dress, added to the long beard he had allowed to grow on his travels, might unmistakably proclaim his profession. He then lost no time in going to the palace, where he obtained an audience of the chief usher and while apologizing for his boldness in presuming to think he could cure the princess, where so many others had failed, declared he had the secret of certain remedies which had hitherto never failed of their effect.

The chief usher assured him that he was heartily welcome and the sultan would receive him with pleasure; and in case of success, he would gain a magnificent reward.

When the Prince of Persia, in the disguise of a physician, was brought before him, the sultan wasted no time in talking, beyond remarking that the mere sight of a doctor threw the princess into transports of rage. He then led the prince up to a room under the roof, which had an opening through which he might observe the princess, without himself being seen.

The prince looked and beheld the princess reclining on a sofa, with tears in her eyes, singing softly to herself a song bewailing her sad destiny which had deprived her, perhaps forever, of a being she so tenderly loved. The young man's heart beat fast as he listened, for he needed no further proof that her madness was feigned and that it was love of him which had caused her to resort to this trick. He softly left his hiding place and returned to the sultan, to whom he reported that he was sure from certain signs the princess' malady was not incurable but he must see her and speak with her alone.

The sultan made no difficulty in consenting to this and commanded that he should be ushered in to the princess' apartment. The moment she caught sight of his physician's robe, she sprang from her seat in a fury, and heaped insults upon him. The prince took no notice of her behavior and, approaching quite close so his words might be heard by her alone, he said in a low whisper, "Look at me, Princess, and you will see that I am no doctor but the Prince of Persia, who has come to set you free."

At the sound of his voice, the Princess of Bengal suddenly grew calm, and an expression of joy overspread her face, such as only comes when what we wish for most and expect the least suddenly happens to us. For some time she was too enchanted to speak, and Prince Firouz Schah took advantage of her silence to explain to her all that had occurred: his despair at watching her disappear before his very eyes, the oath he had sworn to follow her over the world, and his rapture at finally discovering her in the palace at Cashmere. When he had finished, he begged in his turn that the princess would tell him how she had come there, so he might the better devise some means of rescuing her from the tyranny of the sultan.

It needed but a few words from the princess to make him acquainted with the whole situation, and how she had been forced to play the part of a madwoman in order to escape from a marriage with the sultan, who had not had sufficient politeness even to ask her consent. If necessary, she added, she had resolved to die sooner than permit herself to be forced into such a union and so break faith with the prince she loved.

The prince then inquired if she knew what had become of the enchanted horse since the Indian's death, but the princess could only reply that she had heard nothing about it. Still she did not suppose that the horse could have been forgotten by the sultan after all she had told him of its value.

To this the prince agreed, and they consulted together over a plan by which she might be able to make her escape and return with him into Persia. As the first step, she was to dress herself with care and receive the sultan with civility when he visited her next morning.

The sultan was transported with delight on learning the result of the interview, and his opinion of the doctor's skill was raised still higher when, on the following day, the princess behaved toward him in such a way as to persuade him her complete cure would not be long delayed. However, he contented himself with assuring her how happy he was to see her health so much improved and exhorted her to make every use of so clever a physician and to repose entire confidence in him. Then he retired, without awaiting any reply from the princess.

The Prince of Persia left the room at the same time and asked if he might be allowed humbly to inquire by what means the Princess of Bengal had reached Cashmere, which was so far distant from her father's kingdom, and how she came to be there alone. The sultan thought the question very natural and related the same story the Princess of Bengal had told him, adding that he had ordered the enchanted horse to be taken to his treasury as a curiosity, though he was quite ignorant how it could be used.

"Sire," replied the physician, "Your Highness' tale has supplied me with the clue I needed to complete the recovery of the princess. During her voyage hither on an enchanted horse a portion of its enchantment has by some means been communicated to her person, and it can only be dissipated by certain perfumes of which I possess the secret.

"If Your Highness will deign to consent and to give the court and the people one of the most astonishing spectacles they have ever witnessed, command the horse to be brought into the big square outside the palace, and leave the rest to me. I promise that in a very few moments, in the presence of all the assembled multitude, you shall see the princess as healthy both in mind and body as ever she was in her life. And in order to make the spectacle as impressive as possible, I would suggest that she should be richly dressed and covered with the noblest jewels of the crown."

The sultan readily agreed to all the prince proposed, and the following morning he desired that the enchanted horse should be taken from the treasury and brought into the great square of the palace. Soon the rumor began to spread through the town that something extraordinary was about to happen, and such a crowd began to collect that the guards had to be called out to keep order and to make a way for the enchanted horse.

When all was ready the sultan appeared and took his place on a platform, surrounded by the chief nobles and officers of his court. When they were seated the Princess of Bengal was seen leaving the palace, accompanied by the ladies who had been assigned to her by the sultan. She slowly approached the enchanted horse and, with the help of her ladies, mounted on its back. Directly she was in the saddle, with her feet in the stirrups and the bridle in her hand, the physician placed around the horse some large braziers full of burning coals, into each of which he threw a perfume composed of all sorts of delicious scents. Then he crossed his hands over his breast, and with lowered eyes walked three times round the horse, muttering the while certain words.

Soon there arose from the burning braziers a thick smoke which almost concealed both the horse and princess; this was the moment for which the prince had been waiting. Springing lightly up behind the lady, he leaned forward and turned the peg, and as the horse darted

261

up into the air, he cried aloud so that his words were heard by all present, "Sultan of Cashmere, when you wish to marry princesses who have sought your protection, learn first to gain their consent."

It was in this way that the Prince of Persia rescued the Princess of Bengal and returned with her to Persia, where they descended this time before the palace of the king himself. The marriage was only delayed long enough to make the ceremony as brilliant as possible, and as soon as the rejoicings were over, an ambassador was sent to the King of Bengal to inform him of what had passed and to ask his approbation of the alliance between the two countries, which he heartily gave.

THE JEALOUS SISTERS

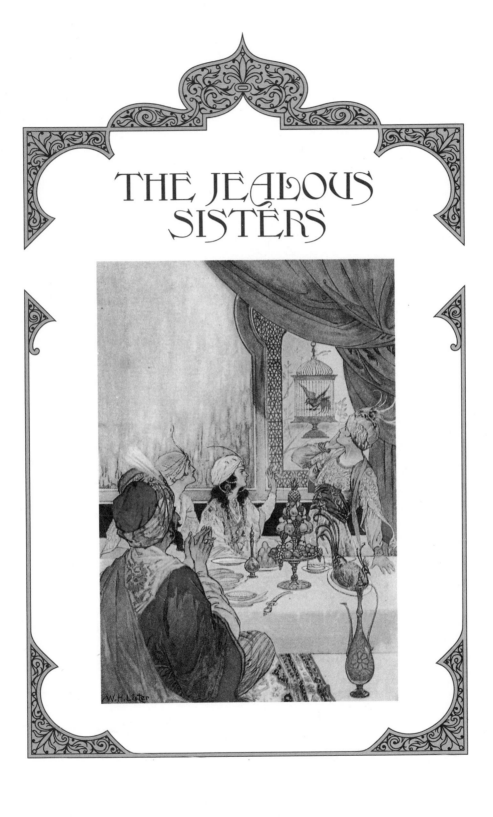

W. H. Lister

nce upon a time there reigned over Persia a sultan named Kosrouschah, who from his boyhood had been fond of putting on a disguise and seeking adventures in all parts of the city, accompanied by one of his officers, disguised like himself. And no sooner was his father buried and the ceremonies over that marked his accession to the throne than the young man hastened to throw off his robes of state and, calling to his vizir to make ready likewise, stole out in the simple dress of a private citizen into the less known streets of the capital.

Passing down a lonely street, the sultan heard women's voices in loud discussion; and peeping through a crack in the door, he saw three sisters sitting on a sofa in a large hall, talking in a very lively and earnest manner. Judging from the few words that reached his ear, they were each explaining what sort of men they wished to marry.

"I ask nothing better," cried the eldest, "than to have the sultan's baker for a husband. Think of being able to eat as much as one wanted of delicious bread that is baked for His Highness alone! Let us see if your wish is as good as mine."

"I," replied the second sister,

"should be quite content with the sultan's head cook. What delicate stews I should feast upon! And, as I am persuaded that the sultan's bread is used all through the palace, I should have that into the bargain. You see, my dear sister, my taste is as good as yours."

It was now the turn of the youngest sister, who was by far the most beautiful of the three, and had, besides, more sense than the other two. "As for me," she said, "I should take a higher flight; if we are to wish for husbands, nothing less than the sultan himself will do for me."

The sultan was so much amused by the conversation he had overheard that he made up his mind to gratify their wishes. Turning to the grand vizir, he bade him note the house and, on the following morning, bring the ladies into his presence.

The grand vizir fulfilled his commission and, hardly giving them time to change their dresses, desired the three sisters to follow him to the palace. Here they were presented one by one and, when they had bowed before the sultan, the sovereign abruptly put the question to them.

"Tell me, do you remember what you wished for last night when you were making merry? Fear nothing, but answer me the truth."

These words, which were so unexpected, threw the sisters into great confusion, their eyes fell, and the blushes of the youngest did not fail to make an impression on the heart of the sultan. All three remained silent, and he hastened to continue, "Do not be afraid, I have not the slightest intention of giving you pain, and let me tell you at once that I know the wishes formed by each one. You," he said, turning to the youngest, "who desired to have me for a husband, shall be satisfied this very day. And you," he added, addressing himself to the other two, "shall be married at the same moment to my baker and my chief cook."

When the sultan had finished speaking, the three sisters flung themselves at his feet, and the youngest faltered out, "Oh, sire, since you know my foolish words, believe, I pray you, that they were only said in a joke. I am unworthy of the honor you propose to do me, and I can only ask your pardon for my boldness."

The other sisters also tried to excuse themselves, but the sultan would hear nothing. "No, no," he said, "my mind is made up. Your wishes shall be accomplished."

So the three weddings were celebrated that same day but with a great difference. That of the youngest was marked by all the magnificence customary at the marriage of the Shah of Persia, while the festivities attending the nuptials of the sultan's baker and his chief cook were only such as were suitable to their conditions.

This, though quite natural, was highly displeasing to the elder sisters, who fell into a passion of jealousy which, in the end, caused a great deal of trouble and pain to several people. And the first time they had opportunity of speaking to each other, which was not till several days later at a public bath, they did not attempt to disguise their feelings.

"Can you possibly understand what the sultan saw in that little cat," said one to the other, "for him to be so fascinated by her?"

"He must be quite blind," returned the wife of the chief cook. "As for her looking a little younger than we do, what does that matter? You would have made a far better sultana than she."

"Oh, I say nothing of myself," replied the elder, "and if the sultan had chosen you it would have been all very well; but it really grieves me that he should have selected a wretched little creature like that. However, I will be revenged on her somehow, and I beg you will give me your help in the matter. Tell me anything you can think of that is likely to mortify her."

In order to carry out their wicked scheme, the two sisters met constantly to talk over their ideas, though all the while they pretended to be as friendly as ever toward the sultana who, on her part, invariably treated them with kindness. For a long time no plan occurred to the two plotters that seemed in the least likely to meet with success, but at length the expected birth of an heir gave them the chance for which they had been hoping.

They obtained permission of the sultana to take up their abode in the palace for some weeks and never left their sister night or day. When at last a little boy, beautiful as the sun, was born, they laid him in his cradle and carried it down to a canal which passed through the grounds of the palace. Then, leaving it to its fate, they informed the sultan that instead of the son he had so fondly desired, the sultana had given birth to a puppy. At this dreadful news the sultan was so overcome with rage and grief that it was with great difficulty that the grand vizir managed to save the sultana from his wrath.

Meanwhile the cradle continued to float peacefully along the canal till on the outskirts of the royal gardens it was suddenly perceived by the intendant, one of the highest and most respected officials in the kingdom.

The wicked sisters sent the cradle floating down a canal.

"Go," he said to a gardener who was working near, "and get that cradle for me."

The gardener did as he was bid and soon placed the cradle in the hands of the intendant.

The official was much astonished to see that the cradle, that he had supposed to be empty, contained a baby which, young though it was, already gave promise of great beauty. Having no children himself, although he had been married some years, it at once occurred to him that here was a child he could bring up as his own. And, bidding the man pick up the cradle and follow him, he turned toward home.

"My wife," he exclaimed as he entered the room, "Heaven has denied us any children but here is one that has been sent in their place. Send for a nurse, and I will do what is needful publicly to recognize it as my son."

The wife accepted the baby with joy, and though the intendant saw quite well that it must have come from the royal palace he did not think it was his business to inquire further into the mystery.

The following year another prince was born and sent adrift. But happily for the baby, the intendant of the gardens again was walking by the canal and carried it home as before.

The sultan, naturally enough, was still more furious the second time than the first, but when the same curious accident was repeated in the third year he could control himself no longer and, to the great joy of the jealous sisters, commanded that the sultana should be executed. But the poor lady was so much beloved at court that not even the dread of sharing her fate could prevent the grand vizir and the courtiers from throwing themselves at the sultan's feet and imploring him not to inflict so cruel a punishment for what, after all, was not her fault.

"Let her live," entreated the grand vizir, "and banish her from your presence for the rest of her days. That in itself will be punishment enough."

His first passion spent, the sultan had regained his self-command. "Let her live then," he said, "since you have it so much at heart. But

I grant her life only on one condition which shall make her daily pray for death. Let a box be built for her at the door of the principal mosque and let the window of the box be always open. There she shall sit, in the coarsest clothes, and every Mussulman who enters the mosque shall spit in her face in passing. Anyone who refuses to obey shall be exposed to the same punishment himself. You, vizir, will see that my orders are carried out."

The grand vizir saw that it was useless to say more, and full of triumph the sisters watched the building of the box and then listened to the jeers of the people at the helpless sultana sitting inside. But the poor lady bore herself with so much dignity and meekness that it was not long before she had won the sympathy of the best among the crowd.

But it is now time to return to the fate of the third baby, this time a princess. Like its brothers, it was found by the intendant of the gardens and adopted by him and his wife, and all three were brought up with the greatest care and tenderness.

As the children grew older their beauty and air of distinction became more and more marked, and their manners had all the grace and ease proper to people of high birth. The princes had been named by their foster father Bahman and Perviz, after two of the ancient kings of Persia, while the princess was called Parizade, or the child of the genii.

The intendant was careful to bring them up as befitted their real rank and soon appointed a tutor to teach the young princes how to read and write. And the princess, determined not to be left behind, showed herself so anxious to learn with her brothers that the intendant consented to her joining in their lessons, and it was not long before she knew as much as they did.

From that time all their studies were in common. They had the best masters for the fine arts, geography, poetry, history and music, and even those sciences which are learned by few, and every branch seemed so easy to them that their teachers were astonished at the progress they made. The princess had a passion for music, and could sing and play upon all sorts of instruments; she could also ride and drive as well as her brothers, shoot with a bow and arrow, and throw a javelin with the same skill as they, and sometimes even better.

In order to set off these accomplishments, the intendant resolved that his foster children should not be pent up any longer in the narrow borders of the palace gardens where he had always lived, so he bought a splendid country house a few miles from the capital, surrounded by an immense park. This park he filled with wild beasts of various sorts, so the princes and princess might hunt as much as they pleased.

When everything was ready, the intendant threw himself at the sultan's feet and, after referring to his age and his long services, begged His Highness' permission to resign his post. This was granted by the sultan in a few gracious words, and he then inquired what reward he could give to his faithful servant. But the intendant declared he wished for nothing except the continuance of His Highness' favor and, prostrating himself once more, he retired from the sultan's presence.

Five or six months passed away in the pleasures of the country, when death attacked the intendant so suddenly that he had no time to reveal the secret of their birth to his adopted children. His wife had long been dead, so it seemed as if the princes and the princess would never know that they had been born to a higher station than the one they filled. Their sorrow for their father was very deep, and they lived quietly on in their new home, without feeling any desire to leave it for court gaieties or intrigues.

One day the princes went out to hunt as usual, but their sister remained alone in her apartments. While they were gone an old Mussulman devotee appeared at the door and asked leave to enter, as it was the hour of prayer. The princess sent orders at once that the old woman was to be taken to the private oratory in the grounds, and when she had finished her prayers was to be shown the house and gardens and then to be brought before her.

Although the old woman was very pious, she was not at all indifferent to the magnificence of all around her, which she seemed to

270

understand as well as to admire, and when she had seen it all she was led by the servants before the princess, who was seated in a room which surpassed in splendor all the rest.

"My good woman," said the princess, pointing to a sofa, "come and sit beside me. I am delighted at the opportunity of speaking for a few moments with so holy a person." The old woman made some objections to so much honor being done her, but the princess refused to listen and insisted that her guest should take the best seat and, as she thought she must be tired, ordered refreshments.

While the old woman was eating, the princess put several questions to her as to her mode of life and the pious exercises she practised, and then inquired what she thought of the house now that she had seen it.

"Madam," replied the pilgrim, "one must be hard indeed to please in order to find any fault. It is beautiful, comfortable and well ordered, and it is impossible to imagine anything more lovely than the garden. But since you ask me, I must confess that it lacks three things to make it absolutely perfect."

"And what can they be?" cried the princess. "Only tell me, and I will lose no time in getting them."

"The three things, madam," replied the old woman, "are first, the Talking Bird whose voice draws all other singing birds to it to join in chorus; second, the Singing Tree whose every leaf is a song that is never silent; and lastly, the Golden Water, of which it is only needful to pour a single drop into a basin for it to shoot up into a fountain which will never be exhausted, nor will the basin ever overflow."

"Oh, how can I thank you," cried the princess, "for telling me of such treasures! But add, I pray you, to your goodness by further informing me where I can find them."

"Madam," replied the pilgrim, "I should ill repay the hospitality you have shown me if I refused to answer your question. The three things of which I have spoken are all to be found in one place, on the borders of this kingdom, toward India. Your messenger has only to follow for twenty days the road that passes by your house, and at the end of that

271

time he is to ask the first person he meets for the Talking Bird, the Singing Tree, and the Golden Water." She then rose and, bidding farewell to the princess, went her way.

The old woman had taken her departure so abruptly that Princess Parizade did not perceive till she was really gone that the directions were hardly clear enough to enable the search to be successful. And she was still thinking of the subject and how delightful it would be to possess such rarities, when the princes, her brothers, returned from the chase.

"What is the matter, my sister?" asked Prince Bahman. "Why are you so grave? Are you ill, or has anything happened?"

Princess Parizade did not answer directly, but at length she raised her eyes and replied there was nothing wrong.

"But there must be something," persisted Prince Bahman, "for you to have changed so much during the short time we have been absent. Hide nothing from us, I beseech you, unless you wish us to believe that the confidence we have always had in one another is now to cease."

"When I said it was nothing," said the princess, moved by his words, "I meant it was nothing that affected you, although I admit it is certainly of some importance to me. Like myself, you have always thought this house our father built for us was perfect in every respect, but only today I have learned that three things are still lacking to complete it. These are the Talking Bird, the Singing Tree and the Golden Water."

After explaining the peculiar qualities of each, the princess continued, "It was a Mussulman devotee who told me all this and where they might all be found. Perhaps you will think that the house is beautiful enough as it is and that we can do quite well without them; but in this I cannot agree with you, and I shall never be content until I have got them. So counsel me, I pray, whom to send on the undertaking."

"My dear sister," replied Prince Bahman, "that you should care about the matter is quite enough, even if we took no interest in it ourselves. But we both feel with you, and I claim, as the elder, the right to make the first attempt, if you will tell me where I am to go and what steps I am to take."

Prince Perviz at first objected that, being the head of the family, his brother ought not to be allowed to expose himself to danger, but Prince Bahman would hear nothing and retired to make the needful preparations for his journey.

The next morning Prince Bahman rose very early and, after bidding farewell to his brother and sister, mounted his horse. But just as he was about to touch it with his whip, he was stopped by a cry from the princess.

"Oh, perhaps, after all, you may never come back; one never can tell what accidents may happen. Give it up, I implore you, for I would a thousand times rather lose the Talking Bird, the Singing Tree and the Golden Water than that you should run into danger."

"My dear sister," answered the prince, "accidents only happen to unlucky people, and I hope I am not one of them. But as everything is uncertain, I promise you to be very careful. Take this knife," he continued, handing her one that hung sheathed from his belt, "and every now and then draw it out and look at it. As long as it keeps bright and clean as it is today, you will know that I am living; but if the blade is spotted with blood it will be a sign that I am dead and you shall weep for me."

So saying, Prince Bahman bade them farewell once more and started on the high road, well mounted and fully armed. For twenty days he rode straight on, turning neither to the right hand nor to the left, till he found himself drawing near the frontiers of Persia. Seated under a tree by the wayside, he noticed a hideous old man with a long white moustache and beard that fell almost to his feet. His nails had grown to an enormous length, and on his head he wore a huge hat, which served him for an umbrella.

Prince Bahman who, remembering the directions of the old woman, had been since sunrise on the lookout for someone, recognized the old man at once to be a dervish. He dismounted from his horse and bowed low before the holy man, saying by way of greeting, "My father, may your days be long in the land and may all your wishes be fulfilled!"

The dervish did his best to reply, but his moustache was so thick his words were hardly intelligible, and the prince, perceiving what was the matter, took a pair of scissors from his saddle pockets and requested permission to cut off some of the moustache as he had a question of great importance to ask the dervish. The dervish made a sign that he might do as he liked, and when a few inches of his hair and beard had been pruned all round, the prince assured the holy man that he would hardly believe how much younger he looked. The dervish smiled at his compliments and thanked him for what he had done.

"Let me," he said, "show you my gratitude for making me more comfortable by hearing what I can do for you."

"Gentle dervish," replied Prince Bahman, "I come from far and I seek the Talking Bird, the Singing Tree and the Golden Water. I know they are to be found somewhere in these parts, but I am ignorant of the exact spot. Tell me, I pray you, if you can, so I may not have traveled on a useless quest." While he was speaking the prince observed a change in the countenance of the dervish, who waited for some time before he made reply.

"My lord," he said at last, "I do know the road for which you ask, but your kindness and the friendship I have conceived for you make me loath to point it out."

"But why not?" inquired the prince. "What danger can there be?"

"The very greatest danger," answered the dervish. "Other men, as brave as you, have ridden down this road, and have put me that question. I did my best to turn them also from their purpose, but it was of no use. Not one of them would listen to my words, and not one of them came back. Be warned in time and seek to go no farther."

"I am grateful to you for your interest in me," said Prince Bahman, "and for the advice you have given, though I cannot follow it. But what

Prince Bahman pruned the dervish's overgrown beard.

dangers can there be in the adventure, which courage and a good sword cannot meet?"

"And suppose," answered the dervish, "that your enemies are invisible, what then?"

"Nothing will make me give it up," replied the prince, "and for the last time I ask you to tell me where I am to go."

When the dervish saw that the prince's mind was made up, he drew a ball from a bag that lay near him and held it out. "If it must be so," he said, with a sigh, "take this, and when you have mounted your horse throw the ball in front of you. It will roll on till it reaches the foot of a mountain and when it stops you will stop also. You will then throw the bridle on your horse's neck without any fear of his straying and will dismount.

"On each side you will see vast heaps of big black stones and will hear a multitude of insulting voices, but pay no heed to them and, above all, beware of ever turning your head. If you do, you will instantly become a black stone like the rest. For those stones are in reality men like yourself, who have been on the same quest and have failed, as I fear that you may fail also. If you manage to avoid this pitfall and reach the top of the mountain, you will find there the Talking Bird in a splendid cage, and you can ask of him where you are to seek the Singing Tree and the Golden Water. That is all I have to say. You know what you have to do and what to avoid, but if you are wise you will think of it no more, but return whence you have come."

The prince smilingly shook his head and, thanking the dervish once more, sprang on his horse and threw the ball before him.

The ball rolled along the road so fast that Prince Bahman had difficulty in keeping up with it, and it never relaxed its speed till the foot of the mountain was reached. Then it came to a sudden halt, and the prince at once got down and flung the bridle on his horse's neck. He paused for a moment and looked round him at the masses of black stones with which the sides of the mountain were covered and then began resolutely to ascend. He had hardly gone four steps when he heard the sound of voices around him, although not another creature was in sight.

"Who is this imbecile?" cried some. "Stop him at once."

"Kill him," shrieked others. "Help! Robbers! Murderers! Help! Help!"

"Oh, let him alone," sneered another, and this was the most trying of all, "he is such a beautiful young man; I am sure the bird and the cage must have been kept for him."

At first the prince took no heed of all this clamor but continued to

276

press forward on his way. Unfortunately, this conduct, instead of silencing the voices, only seemed to irritate them the more, and they arose with redoubled fury, in front as well as behind. After some time he grew bewildered, his knees began to tremble and, finding himself in the act of falling, he forgot altogether the advice of the dervish. He turned to fly down the mountain and in one moment became a black stone.

As may be imagined, Prince Perviz and his sister were all this time in the greatest anxiety, and consulted the magic knife not once but many times a day. Hitherto the blade had remained bright and spotless, but on the fatal hour when Prince Bahman and his horse were changed into black stones large drops of blood appeared on the surface.

"Ah! My beloved brother," cried the princess in horror, throwing the knife from her, "I shall never see you again and it is I who have killed you. Fool that I was to listen to the voice of that temptress who probably was not speaking the truth. What are the Talking Bird and the Singing Tree to me in comparison with you, passionately though I long for them!"

Prince Perviz' grief was not less than that of Princess Parizade, but he did not waste his time on useless lamentations. "My sister," he said, "why should you think the old woman was deceiving you about these treasures and what would have been her object in doing so? No, no, our brother must have met his death by some accident or want of precaution, and tomorrow I will start on the same quest."

Terrified at the thought that she might lose her only remaining brother, the princess entreated him to give up his project, but he remained firm.

Before setting out, however, he gave her a chaplet of a hundred pearls and said, "When I am absent tell this over daily for me. But if you should find that the beads stick, so they will not slip one after the other, you will know that my brother's fate has befallen me. Still, we must hope for better luck."

Then he departed and, on the twentieth day of his journey, fell in with the dervish on the same spot as Prince Bahman had met him and began to question him as to the place where the Talking Bird, the Singing Tree and the Golden Water were to be found. As in the case of his brother, the dervish tried to make him give up his project and even told him that only a few weeks since, a young man bearing a strong resemblance to himself had passed that way but had never come back again.

"That, holy dervish," replied Prince Perviz, "was my elder brother, who is now dead, though how he died I cannot say."

"He is changed into a black stone," answered the dervish, "like all the rest who have gone on the same errand, and you will become one likewise if you are not more careful in following my directions." Then he charged the prince, as he valued his life, to take no heed of the clamor of voices that would pursue him up the mountain and, handing him a ball from the bag, which still seemed to be half-full, he sent him on his way.

When Prince Perviz reached the foot of the mountain he jumped from his horse and paused for a moment to recall the instructions the dervish had given him. Then he strode boldly on, but had scarcely gone five or six paces when he was startled by a man's voice that seemed close to his ear, exclaiming, "Stop, rash fellow, and let me punish your audacity." This outrage entirely put the dervish's advice out of the prince's head. He drew his sword and turned to avenge himself, but almost before he realized there was nobody there, he and his horse were two black stones.

Not a morning had passed since Prince Perviz had ridden away without Princess Parizade telling her beads, and at night she even hung them round her neck, so if she woke she could assure herself at once of her brother's safety. She was in the very act of moving them through her fingers at the moment the prince fell a victim to his impatience, and her heart sank when the first pearl remained fixed in its place. However, she had long made up her mind what she would do in such case, and the following morning the princess, dressed as a man, set out for the mountain.

As she had been accustomed to riding from her childhood, she managed to travel as many miles daily as her brothers had done, and it was, as before, on the twentieth day that she arrived at the place where the dervish was sitting. "Good dervish," she said politely, "will you allow me to rest by you for a few moments, and perhaps you will be so kind as to tell me if you have ever heard of a Talking Bird, a Singing Tree and some Golden Water that are to be found somewhere near here?"

"Madam," replied the dervish, "for in spite of your manly dress your voice betrays you, I shall be proud to serve you in any way I can. But may I ask the purpose of your question?"

"Good dervish," answered the princess, "I have heard such glowing descriptions of these three things that I cannot rest till I possess them."

"Madam," said the dervish, "they are far more beautiful than any description, but you seem ignorant of all the difficulties that stand in your way, or you would hardly have undertaken such an adventure. Give it up, I pray you, and return home. Do not ask me to help you to a cruel death."

"Holy father," answered the princess, "I come from far, and I should be in despair if I turned back without having attained my object. You have spoken of difficulties; tell me, I entreat you, what they are, so I may know if I can overcome them or see if they are beyond my strength."

So the dervish repeated his tale and dwelt more firmly than before on the clamor of the voices, the horrors of the black stones which were once living men, and the difficulties of climbing the mountain, pointing out that the chief means of success was never to look behind till you had the cage in your grasp.

"As far as I can see," said the princess, "the first thing is not to mind the tumult of the voices that follow you till you reach the cage and then never to look behind. As to this, I think I have enough self-control to

279

look straight before me; but as it is quite possible I might be frightened by the voices, as even the boldest men have been, I will stop up my ears with cotton so that, let them make as much noise as they like, I shall hear nothing."

"Madam," cried the dervish, "out of all the number who have asked me the way to the mountain you are the first who has ever suggested such a means of escaping the danger! It is possible you may succeed, but all the same, the risk is great."

"Good dervish," answered the princess, "I feel in my heart that I shall succeed, and it only remains for me to ask you the way I am to go."

Then the dervish knew it was useless to say more, and he gave her the ball, which she flung before her.

The first thing the princess did on arriving at the mountain was to stop her ears with cotton and then, making up her mind which was the best way to go, she began her ascent. In spite of the cotton some echoes of the voices reached her ears, but not so as to trouble her. Indeed, though they grew louder and more insulting the higher she climbed, the princess only laughed and said to herself that she certainly would not let a few rough words stand between her and the goal. At last she perceived in the distance the cage and the bird, whose voice joined itself in tones of thunder to those of the rest, "Return, return! Never dare to come near me."

At the sight of the bird, the princess hastened her steps and without vexing herself at the noise, which by this time had grown deafening, she walked straight up to the cage.

Seizing it, she said, "Now, my bird, I have got you, and I shall take good care that you do not escape." As she spoke she took the cotton from her ears for it was needed no longer.

"Brave lady," answered the bird, "do not blame me for having joined my voice to those who did their best to preserve my freedom. Although confined in a cage I was content with my lot, but if I must become a slave I could not wish for a nobler mistress than one who has

The voices grew louder the higher she climbed.

shown so much constancy, and from this moment I swear to serve you faithfully. Someday you will put me to the proof, for I know who you are better than you do yourself. Meanwhile, tell me what I can do and I will obey you."

"Bird," replied the princess, who was filled with a joy that seemed strange to herself when she thought the bird had cost her the lives of both her brothers, "bird, let me first thank you for your goodwill, and then let me ask you where the Golden Water is to be found."

The bird described the place, which was not far distant, and the princess filled a small silver flask that she had brought with her for the purpose. She then returned to the cage and said, "Bird, there is still something else, where shall I find the Singing Tree?"

"Behind you in that wood," replied the bird, and the princess wandered through the wood till a sound of the sweetest voices told her she had found what she sought. But the tree was tall and strong, and it was hopeless to think of uprooting it.

"You need not do that," said the bird when she had returned to ask counsel. "Break off a twig and plant it in your garden; it will take root and grow into a magnificent tree."

When the Princess Parizade held in her hands the three wonders promised her by the old woman, she said to the bird, "All that is not enough. It was owing to you that my brothers became black stones. I cannot tell them from the mass of others, but you must know, so point them out to me, I beg you, for I wish to carry them away."

For some reason that the princess could not guess these words seemed to displease the bird, and he did not answer. The princess waited a moment and then continued in severe tones, "Have you forgotten that you yourself said that you are my slave to do my bidding and also that your life is in my power?"

"No, I have not forgotten," replied the bird, "but what you ask is very difficult. However, I will do my best. If you look round," he went on, "you will see a pitcher standing near. Take it and, as you go down the mountain, scatter a little of the water it contains over every black stone. You will soon find your two brothers."

Princess Parizade took the pitcher and, carrying it with the cage, the twig and the flask, returned down the mountainside. At every black stone she stopped and sprinkled it with water, and as the water touched it the stone instantly became a man. When she suddenly saw her brothers her delight was mixed with astonishment.

"Why, what are you doing here?" she cried.

"We have been asleep," they said.

"Yes," returned the princess, "but without me your sleep would probably have lasted till the Day of Judgment. Have you forgotten that you came here in search of the Talking Bird, the Singing Tree and the Golden Water and the black stones that were heaped up along the road? Look round and see if there is one left. These gentlemen, yourselves and all your horses were changed into these stones, and I have delivered you by sprinkling you with the water from this pitcher. As I could not return home without you, even though I had gained the prizes on which I had set my heart, I forced the Talking Bird to tell me how to break the spell."

On hearing these words Prince Bahman and Prince Perviz understood all they owed their sister, and the knights who stood by declared themselves her slaves and ready to carry out her wishes. But the princess, while thanking them for their politeness, explained she wished for no company but her brothers and the rest were free to go where they would.

So saying, the princess mounted her horse and, declining to allow even Prince Bahman to carry the cage with the Talking Bird, she entrusted him with the branch of the Singing Tree while Prince Perviz took care of the flask containing the Golden Water.

Then they rode away, followed by the knights and gentlemen, who begged to be permitted to escort them.

It had been the intention of the party to stop and tell their adventures to the dervish, but they found to their sorrow that he was dead, whether from old age or from feeling that his task was done they never knew.

As they continued their road their numbers grew daily smaller, for the knights turned off one by one to their own homes, and only the brothers and sister finally drew up at the gate of the palace.

The princess carried the cage straight into the garden. As soon as the bird began to sing, nightingales, larks, thrushes, finches and all sorts of other birds mingled their voices in chorus. The branch she planted in a corner near the house, and in a few days it had grown into a great tree. As for the Golden Water, it was poured into a great marble basin specially prepared for it, and it swelled and bubbled and then shot up into the air in a fountain twenty feet high.

The fame of these wonders soon spread abroad, and people came from far and near to see and admire.

After a few days, Prince Bahman and Prince Perviz fell back into their ordinary way of life and passed most of their time hunting. One day it happened that the Sultan of Persia was also hunting in the same direction, and not wishing to interfere with his sport, the young men, on hearing the noise of the hunt approaching, prepared to retire. But, as luck would have it, they turned into the very path down which the sultan was coming. They threw themselves from their horses and prostrated themselves to the earth, but the sultan was curious to see their faces and commanded them to rise.

The princes stood up respectfully but quite at their ease, and the sultan looked at them for a few moments without speaking. Then he asked who they were and where they lived.

"Sire," replied Prince Bahman, "we are sons of Your Highness' late intendant of the gardens, and we live in a house that he built a short time before his death, waiting till an occasion should offer itself to serve Your Highness."

"You seem fond of hunting," answered the sultan.

"Sire," replied Prince Bahman, "it is our usual exercise, and one that should be neglected by no man who expects to comply with the ancient customs of the kingdom and bear arms."

The sultan was delighted with this remark and said at once, "In that case I shall take great pleasure in watching you. Come, choose what sort of beasts you would like to hunt."

The princes jumped on their horses and followed the sultan at a little distance. They had not gone very far before they saw a number of wild animals appear at once, and Prince Bahman gave chase to a lion and Prince Perviz to a bear. Both used their javelins with such skill that, directly they arrived within striking range, the lion and the bear fell, pierced through and through. Then Prince Perviz pursued a lion and Prince Bahman a bear, and in a very few minutes they, too, lay dead. As they were making ready for a third assault the sultan interfered and, sending one of his officials to summon them, said, smiling, "If I let you go on, there will soon be no beasts left to hunt. Besides, your courage and manners have so won my heart that I will not have you expose yourselves to further danger. I am convinced that some day or other I shall find you useful as well as agreeable."

He then gave them a warm invitation to stay with him altogether, but with many thanks for the honor done them they begged to be excused and to be suffered to remain at home. The sultan, who was not accustomed to see his offers rejected, inquired their reasons and Prince Bahman explained that they did not wish to leave their sister and were accustomed to do nothing without consulting all three together.

"Ask her advice, then," replied the sultan. "Tomorrow come and hunt with me and give me your answer."

The two princes returned home, but their adventure made so little impression on them that they quite forgot to speak to their sister on the subject. The next morning when they went to hunt they met the sultan in the same place, and he inquired what advice their sister had given. The young men looked at each other and blushed. At last Prince Bahman said, "Sire, we must throw ourselves on Your Highness' mercy. Neither my brother nor myself remembered anything about it."

"Then be sure you do not forget today," answered the sultan, "and bring me your reply tomorrow."

When, however, the same thing happened a second time, they feared that the sultan might be angry with them for their carelessness. But he took it in good part and, drawing three little golden balls from his purse, he held them out to Prince Bahman, saying, "Put these in your bosom and you will not forget a third time, for when you remove your girdle tonight the noise they make in falling will remind you of my wishes."

It all happened as the sultan had foreseen, and the two brothers appeared in their sister's apartments just as she was in the act of stepping into bed and told their tale.

The Princess Parizade was much disturbed at the news and did not conceal her feelings. "Your meeting with the sultan is very honorable to you," she said, "and will, I daresay, be of service to you, but it places me in a very awkward position. It is on my account, I know, that you have resisted the sultan's wishes and I am very grateful to you for it. But kings do not like to have their offers refused, and in time he would bear a grudge against you, which would render me very unhappy. Consult the Talking Bird, who is wise and farseeing, and let me hear what he says."

So the bird was sent for and the case laid before him.

"The princes must on no account refuse the sultan's proposal," said he, "and they must even invite him to come and see your house."

"But, bird," objected the princess, "you know how dearly we love each other. Will not all this spoil our friendship?"

"Not at all," replied the bird, "it will make it all the closer."

"Then the sultan will have to see me," said the princess.

The bird answered that it was necessary that he should see her, and everything would turn out for the best.

The following morning, when the sultan inquired if they had spoken to their sister and what advice she had given them, Prince Bahman replied that they were ready to agree to His Highness' wishes and their sister had reproved them for their hesitation about the matter. The sultan received their excuses with great kindness and told them he was sure they would be equally faithful to him and kept them by his side for the rest of the day, to the vexation of the grand vizir and the rest of the court.

When the procession entered the gates of the capital, the eyes of the people who crowded the streets were fixed on the two young men, strangers to everyone. "Oh, if only the sultan had had sons like that!" they murmured. "They look so distinguished and are about the same age his sons would have been!"

The sultan commanded that splendid apartments should be prepared for the two brothers and insisted they should sit at table with him. During dinner he led the conversation to various scientific subjects and also to history, of which he was especially fond; but whatever topic they might be discussing he found the views of the young men were always worth listening to.

"If they were my own sons," he said to himself, "they could not be better educated!" Aloud he complimented them on their learning and taste for knowledge.

At the end of the evening the princes once more prostrated themselves before the throne and asked leave to return home; and then, encouraged by the gracious words of farewell uttered by the sultan, Prince Bahman said, "Sire, may we dare take the liberty of asking whether you would do us and our sister the honor of resting for a few minutes at our house the first time the hunt passes that way?"

"With the utmost pleasure," replied the sultan, "and as I am all impatience to see the sister of such accomplished young men you may expect me the day after tomorrow."

The princess was of course most anxious to entertain the sultan in a fitting way, but as she had no experience in court customs she ran to the Talking Bird and begged he would advise her as to what dishes should be served.

"My dear mistress," replied the bird, "your cooks are very good and you can safely leave all to them, except you must be careful to have a dish of cucumbers stuffed with pearl sauce served with the first course."

"Cucumbers stuffed with pearls!" exclaimed the princess. "Why, bird, who ever heard of such a dish? The sultan will expect a dinner he can eat, not one he can only admire! Besides, if I were to use all the pearls I possess, they would not be half enough."

"Mistress," replied the bird, "do what I tell you and nothing but good will come of it. And as to the pearls, if you go at dawn tomorrow and dig at the foot of the first tree in the park, on the right hand, you will find as many as you want."

The princess had faith in the bird, who generally proved to be right, and taking the gardener with her early next morning followed out his directions carefully. After digging for some time they came upon a golden box fastened with little clasps.

These were easily undone, and the box was found to be full of pearls, not very large ones but well shaped and of a good color. So leaving the gardener to fill up the hole he had made under the tree, the princess took up the box and returned to the house.

The two princes had seen her go out and had wondered what could have made her rise so early. Full of curiosity they got up and dressed, and met their sister as she was returning with the box under her arm.

"What have you been doing?" they asked. "Did the gardener come to tell you he had found a treasure?"

"On the contrary," replied the princess, "it is I who have found one," and opening the box she showed her astonished brothers the pearls inside. Then, on the way back to the palace, she told them of her consultation with the bird and the advice it had given her. All three tried to guess the meaning of the singular counsel, but they were forced at last to admit the explanation was beyond them and they must be content blindly to obey.

The first thing the princess did on entering the palace was to send for the head cook and order the repast for the sultan. When she had finished she suddenly added, "Besides the dishes I have mentioned there is one that you must prepare expressly for his majesty and no one must touch but yourself. It consists of a stuffed cucumber, and the stuffing is to be made of these pearls."

The head cook, who had never in all his experience heard of such a dish, stepped back in amazement.

"You think I am mad," answered the princess, who perceived what was in his mind. "But I know quite well what I am doing. Go, do your best, and take the pearls with you."

The next morning the princes started for the forest and were soon joined by the sultan. The hunt began and continued till midday when the heat became so great that they were obliged to leave off. Then, as arranged, they turned their horses' heads toward the palace, and while Prince Bahman remained by the side of the sultan, Prince Perviz rode on to warn his sister of their approach.

The moment his highness entered the courtyard the princess flung herself at his feet, but he bent and raised her and gazed at her for some time, struck with her grace and beauty, and also with the indefinable air of courts that seemed to hang round this country girl. "They are all worthy one of the other," he said to himself, "and I am not surprised that they think so much of her opinions. I must know more of them."

By this time the princess had recovered from the first embarrassment of the meeting and proceeded to make her speech of welcome. "This is only a simple country house, sire," she said, "suitable to people like ourselves who live a quiet life. It cannot compare with the great city mansions, much less, of course, with the smallest of the sultan's palaces."

"I cannot quite agree with you," he replied, "even the little I have seen I admire greatly, and I will reserve my judgment until you have shown me the whole."

The princess then led the way from room to room, and the sultan examined everything carefully. "Do you call this a simple country house?" he said at last. "Why, if every country house was like this the towns would soon be deserted. I am no longer astonished that you do not wish to leave it. Let us go into the gardens which I am sure are no less beautiful than the rooms."

A small door opened straight into the garden, and the first object that met the sultan's eyes was the Golden Water.

"What lovely colored water!" he exclaimed. "Where is the spring and how do you make the fountain rise so high? I do not believe there is anything like it in the world." He went forward to examine it and when he had satisfied his curiosity the princess conducted him toward the Singing Tree.

As they drew near, the sultan was startled by the sound of strange voices but could see nothing. "Where have you hidden your musicians?" he asked the princess. "Are they up in the air or under the earth? Surely the owners of such charming voices ought not to conceal themselves!"

"Sire," answered the princess, "the voices all come from the tree which is straight in front of us; if you will deign to advance a few steps you will see that they become clearer."

The sultan did as he was told and was so rapt in delight at what he heard that he stood some time in silence.

"Tell me, madam, I pray you," he said at last, "how this marvelous tree came into your garden. It must have been brought from a great distance or else, fond as I am of all curiosities, I could not have missed hearing of it. What is its name?"

"The only name it has, sire," replied she, "is the Singing Tree, and it is not a native of this country. Its history is mixed up with those of the Golden Water and the Talking Bird, which you have not yet seen. If Your Highness wishes I will tell you the whole story when you have recovered from your fatigue."

"Indeed, madam," returned he, "you show me so many wonders that it is impossible to feel any fatigue. Let us go once more and look at the Golden Water, and I am dying to see the Talking Bird."

"The only name it has, sire, is the Singing Tree."

The sultan could hardly tear himself away from the Golden Water, which puzzled him more and more. "You say," he observed to the princess, "that this water does not come from any spring, neither is it brought by pipes. All I understand is that neither it nor the Singing Tree is a native of this country."

"It is as you say, sire," answered the princess, "and if you examine the basin, you will see that it is all in one piece, therefore the water could not have been brought through it. What is more astonishing is that I emptied only a small flaskful into the basin, and it increased to the quantity you now see."

"Well, I will look at it no more today," said the sultan. "Take me to the Talking Bird."

On approaching the house the sultan noticed a vast quantity of birds, whose voices filled the air, and he inquired why they were so much more numerous here than in any other part of the garden.

"Sire," answered the princess, "do you see that cage hanging in one of the windows of the salon? That is the Talking Bird whose voice you can hear above them all, even above that of the nightingale. And the birds crowd to this spot to add their songs to his."

The sultan stepped through the window, but the bird took no notice, continuing his song as before.

"My slave," said the princess, "this is the sultan; make him a pretty speech."

The bird stopped singing at once, and all the other birds stopped too. "The sultan is welcome," he said. "I wish him long life and all prosperity."

"I thank you, good bird," answered the sultan, seating himself before the repast which was spread at a table near the window, "and I am enchanted to see in you the sultan and King of the Birds."

The sultan, noticing that his favorite dish of cucumber was placed before him, proceeded to help himself to it and was amazed to find that the stuffing was of pearls. "A novelty, indeed!" cried he. "But I do not understand the reason of it; one cannot eat pearls!"

"Sire," replied the bird, before either the princes or the princess could speak, "surely Your Highness cannot be so surprised at beholding a cucumber stuffed with pearls, when you believed without any difficulty that the sultana had presented you with a dog, a cat, and a log of wood instead of children."

"I believed it," answered the sultan, "because the women attending on her told me so."

"The women, sire," said the bird, "were the sisters of the sultana who were devoured with jealousy at the honor you had done her and in order to revenge themselves invented this story. Have them examined, and they will confess their crime. These are your children, who were saved from death by the intendant of your gardens and brought up by him as if they were his own."

Like a flash the truth came to the mind of the sultan. "Bird," he cried, "my heart tells me that what you say is true. My children," he added, "let me embrace you, and embrace each other, not only as brothers and sister but as having in you the blood royal of Persia, which could flow in no nobler veins."

When the first moments of emotion were over, the sultan hastened to finish his repast, and then turning to his children, he exclaimed, "Today you have made acquaintance with your father. Tomorrow I will bring you the sultana, your mother. Be ready to receive her."

The sultan then mounted his horse and rode quickly back to the capital. Without an instant's delay he sent for the grand vizir and ordered him to seize and question the sultana's sisters that very day. This was done. They were confronted with each other and proved guilty, and were executed in less than an hour.

But the sultan did not wait to hear that his orders had been carried out before going on foot, followed by his whole court, to the door of the great mosque, and with his own hand drew the sultana out of the narrow prison where she had spent so many years.

"Madam," he cried, embracing her, with tears in his eyes, "I have come to ask your pardon for the injustice I have done you and to repair it as far as I may. I have already begun by punishing the authors of this abominable crime, and I hope you will forgive me when I introduce you to our children, who are the most charming and accomplished creatures in the whole world. Come with me and take back your position and all the honor that is due to you."

This speech was delivered in the presence of a vast multitude of people, who had gathered from all parts on the first hint of what was happening, and the news was passed from mouth to mouth in a few seconds.

Early next day the sultan and sultana, dressed in robes of state and followed by all the court, set out for the country house of their children. Here the sultan presented them to the sultana one by one, and for some time there was nothing but embraces and tears and tender words. Then they ate of the magnificent dinner which had been prepared for them, and after they were all refreshed they went into the garden, where the sultan pointed out to his wife the Golden Water and the Singing Tree. As to the Talking Bird, she had already made acquaintance with him.

In the evening they rode together back to the capital, the princes on each side of their father and the princess with her mother. Long before they reached the gates the way was lined with people, and the air filled with shouts of welcome with which were mingled the songs of the Talking Bird, sitting in its cage on the lap of the princess, and of the birds who followed it.

And in this manner they came back to their father's palace.

Scheherazade at this point, seeing that it was day and knowing that the sultan always rose very early to attend the council, stopped speaking.

The morning came when the sultan did not join his council at once.

"Scheherazade," he said, "let it be understood that you shall reign as sultana, for now you are my beloved. It may be that in times to come men will say, "Then lived Scheherazade who was as wise as she was beautiful."

AFTERWORD

$\mathcal{A}$FTERWORD

By Pete Hamill

One of America's foremost journalists, Pete Hamill is a contributing editor of Esquire *and* New York *magazines and a columnist for the* New York Post, *the country's oldest daily newspaper. He is also the author of numerous scripts for television and film, as well as several novels.*

In those ancient days before television scrambled and coarsened the imagination of American children, the public library was the great treasure cave of our neighborhood. It was not the only one, of course; once a week, after scraping together pennies and nickels, we went to the movies. But the library was always there, its shelves jammed with stories and secrets, and there was no charge for admission. One drizzly spring afternoon, in a badly lit aisle of that library, I discovered this book. I was 11 years old. The library's copy was on the top shelf, where I always imagined the librarians hid the most forbidden fruit. Almost furtively, with the help of a small stepladder, I took the volume down, held it in my hands, and ran my fingers over the gorgeous inlaid cover, which in memory was blue and gold. No book—as an object—has ever felt more sensuous.

Somehow, through carelessness or exhaustion or perhaps some secret sense of delight, the stout female librarian allowed me to borrow this exquisite and subversive volume. Covering it with my jacket, I hurried home to the Brooklyn tenement where I lived, and late that afternoon, as the rain fell steadily, I entered for the first time the astonishing world of *The Arabian Nights.* Hour after hour the woman named Scheherazade told her tales, not simply to the caliph Schahriar, but to me. She was some woman. There was an elegant drawing of her,

297

all swirling lines and great undulating bunches of hair, her lips pouting in a sloe-eyed oval face; and as I devoured the tales, I kept turning back to look at her. To my relatively innocent eye, she looked like the actress Yvonne De Carlo, who looked like nobody at all in our neighborhood, and the resemblance was emphasized by her clothing. In that rococo and sensual drawing, she was wearing the diaphanous garments that I'd seen only in movies, all earrings and breastplates and silky trousers, the curves of her long body hinted at but not fully stated. And staring at her, then reading the tales, I could hear her voice: whispering, full of sudden emphases, dramatic pauses, her tone shifting as she moved from one character to another, the whole performance designed to keep the caliph entranced, so that she herself might live.

In the process, she did what every artist only hopes to do: she told tales that traveled across vast continents and into distant centuries, and even found landfall in a place called Brooklyn. For weeks my imagination was peopled with genii and ghouls, dervishes and vizirs. I retreated before ferocious men wielding bloody scimitars. Occasionally, I even glanced at the sky, fearful of the giant roc. Most of all, I sailed with Sinbad, out upon uncharted seas, those great vast oceans that still lie out beyond the New York harbor, seas where my grandfather had sailed at the end of the 19th century, along with so many thousands of other former boys. Shipping with Sinbad, I survived the most terrible storms. I lay shipwrecked with him on the dangerous beaches of nameless desert islands. I helped him in his desperate struggles before returning home with him to Baghdad on slender ships groaning with cargoes of rubies and emeralds and gold. And then, sickening of the suety life of cities, I went out with him again to sail into the vast unknown.

Those tales filled me with the kind of wonder that I've seldom felt again from stories printed on paper. They made me long for other worlds, strange places, the sound of exotic languages. It was inevitable, I suppose, that as I grew into adolescence, I would join the navy and later spend so much of my adult life traveling in foreign lands and writing about their wonder or menace. But there was more to *The Arabian Nights* than a string of glorious adventures, foreign and domestic. From the apparently artless tales of Scheherazade, I was also learning for the first time the lesson that almost every great writer teaches: Things Aren't What They Seem To Be.

Here, in the most casual way, men were transformed magically into dogs, slaves into cows. Here, a man discovered that his beloved wife was actually a fairy. Here, brine-encrusted jars were fished from the sea and contained vengeful genii. Or an Indian princess was really an ogress who ate young men. Or an enchantress could transform a handsome prince into black marble and a city into a giant lake. In tale after tale, the storyteller stripped away every mask, creating permanent doubt about appearances and spoken promises. These were useful lessons for an 11-year-old to learn; doubt, after all, is the beginning of wisdom.

From its first pages, it was clear that *The Arabian Nights* was not the sort of prose pablum that passed for children's literature in those days, collections of tame incidents buttered together with platitudes. The world Scheherazade described was often violent, arbitrary, and unjust; that is, it resembled the world into which I was born. In her world, kings and caliphs had the power to murder any subject, without reason or challenge. In my world, all those centuries later, Hitler could do the same. So, on a different scale, could the agate-eyed Mafia hoodlums who cruised our neighborhood in Cadillacs and Packards, their pinkie rings glinting in the sun. For all its opulent vision, for all its *different-ness, The Arabian Nights* had an underlying social structure that was believable even to kids from the hard streets of American cities.

In a different way, it also made clear that life was complicated, and so was the telling of its stories. There were stories within stories, Scheherazade telling tales of merchants who told tales of viziers who told tales of scheming wives. They were woven together seamlessly, the individual narratives carrying me along, with Scheherazade controlling the grand design of the tapestry. She didn't preach or moralize;

instead, she kept her characters moving, illustrating a literary principle stated many centuries later by F. Scott Fitzgerald: "Action is character." As a nascent writer, I was learning much here about craft, including the two most fundamental words of any narrative: *and then.*

To be sure, some tales were mere sketches or parables, quickly read and instantly forgotten. In the original collection, introduced to Europe in a French translation in the early 18th century, there were 264 tales. Most of the trivial stories have fallen away over the years; the overtly sexual tales have also been bowdlerized and sanitized (although even in the tame edition I read as a boy the sensuality of the world of Scheherazade came through). What is extraordinary is how many stories have endured, in spite of bad translations, clumsy censorship, and the remorseless erosions of Hollywood. Like all great stories, they seem always to have been part of what we know. I knew the name Ali Baba, for example, before I ever read the story. There had been a movie, perhaps two or three, and though I hadn't seen the movie version, the characters were part of our own folklore. The older people in our neighborhood referred to the mayor and his cronies as Ali Baba and the Forty Thieves. When zoot suits were in fashion at the end of World War II, the billowing trousers with wide knees and tight cuffs were called Ali Baba pants. Then I read the story. And I wished somehow that I, too, could secretly watch a gang of thieves say "Open, Sesame" and stroll into a treasure cave. I wished that I, too, possessed such magic words. Every aspiring writer does.

But from that story I also learned that unearned treasure could be a curse. For Ali Baba waited for the thieves to depart and then used the magic phrase to enter the cave. As easy as it was to say "Open, Sesame," he carried away gold and silk, brocades and silver, and took this hoard home on the backs of his donkeys. I was thrilled. To rob the robbers: surely *that* was moral. But then, as in any good story, there were complications. A rich relative discovered the sudden riches of poor good-hearted Ali Baba, decided to cut himself in and become even richer, and this boundless envy and greed led to one horrendous problem after another. In a way, nothing much changes in human behavior; ask those tormented human beings who have won lotteries.

In the story of Ali Baba, of course, there is a happy ending, but not because of the courage or intelligence of the naive protagonist. Again and again, Ali Baba is saved by a female slave named Morgiana. She first changes the chalk marks placed on his door, marks intended to set him up for an assassination. She then pours boiling oil upon the thieves concealed in leather jars in Ali Baba's garden, killing them all. Finally, after doing an exotic dance at an elegant dinner party, she plunges a dagger into the heart of the treacherous leader of the 40 thieves. I didn't know it then, but Scheherazade was clearly a feminist of great subtlety.

That's among the many things I see now that I didn't see when I first read these tales as a boy. The stories of *The Arabian Nights* comprise the first great book written—or told—from the point of view of a woman. (Perhaps they *were* written by a woman, although scholars believe they were centuries-old tales with Indian, Persian, and Arabian antecedents, told and retold in the bazaars of the East until finally written down by some forgotten scribe around the time Columbus sailed into the Western Hemisphere.) Certainly, Scheherazade was making an indirect point to the caliph, telling him that women, too, were courageous, intelligent, and loyal. They were also dangerous. But in the end, they were indispensable.

There are other themes in the book. Without making any ideological points or discoursing on economics, the narrator made a glorious adventure out of the first stirrings of world trade. In most of these tales, travel leads to immense fortune, if only the traveler has the courage to risk death in the unknown parts of the earth. For a boy the lesson was a simpler one: adventure begins with running away from home. There are also glancing references to religion, lip service paid to the forms and rituals and austere precepts of Islam. But the truest religion is wealth. In one story a man loses a fortune *because* he makes his ritual pilgrimage to Mecca (he regains it, of course—Allah be praised—but not without pain, grief, and amazing difficulties). Often, as in the saga of Ali Baba, the plots turn on the irrational greed of people who no doubt considered themselves good Moslems. This is now a familiar revelation of human character; among all believers, of whatever faith, there is too often a disjunction between creed and practice. Scheherazade, however, almost never moralizes. In matters of faith and morals, she is simply a reporter.

The form of her stories, however, is not reportage. The modern reader might smile (or groan) at the coincidences, accidents, and implausibilities of many of the plots. A bird flies off with a magic talisman, sending the hero on an arduous, dispiriting, and dangerous search. Years pass, hazards and humiliations are endured, exile hurts the heart. And then some birds fight in the garden of exile; one is slain, and in his belly our hero finds . . . the lost talisman. *Of course!* Our literal minds say: Come on, this is too neat, too simple, too convenient. But these are *tales*. They are not intended to be read in a literal way, nor subjected to the icy algebra of plausibility. They are triumphs of the imagination, and the reader must simply surrender to them or lay the book aside forever.

Millions have surrendered over the centuries, including writers as various as Marcel Proust, Thomas Hardy, George Eliot, G. K. Chesterton, and Ben Hecht. Thomas Carlyle and Robert Louis Stevenson, Daniel Defoe and Jonathan Swift were also swept into the perfumed gardens of *The Arabian Nights*. And the Russian composer Nicolai Rimsky-Korsakov celebrated its mood, sensuousness, and exuberance in his symphonic work, *Scheherazade*. None of this is surprising. Long after all of us are gone, for as long as there are men and women who read, these tales will inspire, instruct, or delight.

I believe these stories have survived through the centuries because they contain that human emotion that has been most damaged by the remorseless force of mass communications: *wonder*. They are literally wonderful. I envy those who enter this magical world for the first time, and pity those who are so prematurely jaded that they can't be swept away. Here, birds talk and trees sing, and even human beings, the most inconstant of the world's creatures, are capable of selflessness and courage. Surrender to their spell, and you can join Prince Houssain on his magic carpet, hold Aladdin's wonderful lamp, sit under the magic tent of Ahmed, a tent that expands to hold entire armies and yet can be folded into the palm of a human hand. Come to the Spice Islands or to Serendib, where rubies appear like plums. Pause, stretch out upon this silken cushion and listen. The woman is telling a story.

In the end, of course, Scheherazade pulls off the most important of all feats of magic: she lives. Perhaps that was the most valuable of the many lessons I learned on those enchanted afternoons during a cold spring long ago. In different ways, that lesson has been learned by millions of others across the centuries of this book's existence. It's very simple. Human beings write stories, and read them, for the same good reason: to live.

July 1990
New York City